FACIAL Recognition

A Serenity Spa Novel

JENNIFER PEEL

Dedication

To Jeremy: Thank you for always seeing me.

Chapter One

"How was your lunch date, Gracie?" Lorelai sang two octaves above her normal sultry voice.

I leaned against our welcome desk at the spa and sighed. "Well, it was going good until he took his socks and shoes off and put his foot on the table. He wanted to make sure I got a good visual of how freakishly high his arches were. Apparently, he was written up in some medical journal. Not only were his arches higher than the Saint Louis Arch, but I had no idea a man could grow so much hair on his feet. It was worse than a hobbit." I shuddered, trying to shake the thought of it out of my head. I knew I was going to have nightmares about the bushes of hair on his feet.

Lorelai laughed hysterically. "No wonder he became a podiatrist." She grabbed her phone and started scrolling. "Let me see who else I know that I can set you up with. I'm running out of options. How many blind dates have you been on now?"

I bit my lip and started throwing up my fingers to help me count. "I think the podiatrist made it thirty-five." I blew out a deep breath, making my bangs take flight. "I'm doomed to go to my twenty-year high school reunion alone. What's worse is I'm in charge."

"Don't give up hope yet. You still have two months."

1

"Yeah, but Mr. Right—or even Mr. Right Now—and I need time together so it's not awkward. You know how epic I hope the night will be. There's no leaving it to chance."

"Don't you worry, darlin', we'll find someone."

Yeah, I'd been telling myself that for the last eight years. Being single never bothered me until I turned thirty and began to seriously question if I would ever get married and have children. The last few years, I had started taking ovulation tests just to make sure my ovaries were still spitting out eggs. The good news was that I was still fertile; the bad news was there was no fertilizer in the foreseeable future, and I was afraid my uterus might become a desolate wasteland soon.

"Keep scrolling," I begged her. "Maybe number thirty-six is the charm." I refused to show up alone to the reunion. It would be like prom all over again. I was the only prom queen in the history of Pecan Orchard High to ever get stood up. I had to push the horror out of my mind.

Beautiful Lorelai, who looked so angelic with her platinum-blonde hair and big, blue-as-the-sky eyes, smiled at me. "Don't worry, I'll call my momma if I have to. She's the biggest meddler in all of Texas."

Poor Lorelai was always dodging the men her mother threw her way after Lorelai's husband had died a few years ago. God rest William's soul. He was a dear, sweet man. But there was no time for reminiscing as Zoe, one of our attendants, popped her head out of the door that led to our treatment rooms. "Gracie, your two o'clock is here. A facial massage in treatment room one."

"Oh, yes." Lorelai began to fan herself. "I checked him in and ooh la la. I wouldn't kick him out of my bed for eating crackers, I'll tell you that."

I giggled.

"Although I have to say he had a brooding energy about him," Lorelai added. She was our resident energy healer and yoga instructor. "Perhaps you could help lift his spirits. Maybe he could be number thirty-six."

"I thought we agreed when we opened this place, we wouldn't date the clients or our coworkers."

She wagged her brows. "Wait until you see this man—you'll be calling an executive meeting and begging us to bend the rules." Lorelai, Colette, and I had deemed ourselves the executives when we opened Serenity Spa two years ago. We were three best friends who were tired of working for other people, and we'd finally saved up enough money to open our own place here in the fabulous city of Fort Worth.

I flipped my curled strawberry blonde hair. "Well in that case, if you hear loud gasping, don't come in. It will only be me checking to make sure he knows how to properly administer a good night kiss," I teased. We weren't that kind of a place. No kinky stuff on the premises.

"Do what you gotta do, girl." She winked.

"I better hustle and change back into my scrubs. You, please keep scrolling." I was getting desperate.

She saluted me. "I'm on it. Have fun."

I darted off toward the "executive" bathroom in the back. We had to have some perks as the owners. Basically, it was a multipurpose room. We held most of our so-called meetings in there, sitting on the oversize sage ottoman, mostly laughing between discussing our business. It was also our dressing room, crying room, and on occasion, we used the toilet in there.

I never tired of taking in our surroundings; it was as serene as our name indicated. White walls with whitewashed wood floors, accented with natural wood furniture and plants of every kind. In the background there was always some sort of meditative instrumental music playing. And it smelled like eucalyptus and peppermint. It was a place I was proud to be a part of.

Once in the bathroom, I shimmied out of the peach sundress I had worn for my date. I liked this dress because it showed off my toned legs, as white as they were. But when you had skin as fair as mine, tanning wasn't an option. I had to wear SPF 150 just to go outside and withstand the Texas sun. I got back into my green scrubs and threw my hair up into a messy bun. Heavy on the messy—my long hair had some serious curls. I did a quick brush of my teeth while looking in the mirror and begging God to hold off on the crow's-feet a little longer. I dabbed some pink lip gloss on and popped in a mint, just in case my next client really was the one.

I was beginning to wonder if I was being too picky. Should I just take hobbit, high-arch man? I mean, he at least chewed with his mouth closed. Except he had put his foot on the table. Still, he was polite, and he had gorgeous azure eyes. Unfortunately, I didn't hear the *voice*. Not sure why I kept putting stock into the voice. It was obviously so wrong. Plus, I was only fourteen when it first spoke to me. Who gets told at fourteen who they should marry? Yet I couldn't forget that feeling I'd had the first time I saw Brooks Hamilton. I was sitting in my new backyard, picking grass and feeling sorry for myself. We had just moved to Pecan Orchard from Oklahoma so my momma could be closer to the hospital in Fort Worth that dealt with her special heart condition. Not only had I been missing my friends, but I was afraid to lose Momma. That's when Brooks had popped his head over the fence and asked if I was okay. I remember locking eyes with his deep chocolate ones, and then I'd heard a piercing voice say: *You're going to marry that boy someday.* Too bad Brooks only ever saw me as his and his twin sister's friend. And it was more than unfortunate that he'd ended up being the jerk who left me crying on our senior prom night when he stood me up. I'd finally thought he had feelings for me, like the overwhelming ones I had for him. That was wishful thinking. Not only did he stand me up, but he then ignored me all the way until we graduated. Then he had left Pecan Orchard forever. I couldn't exactly blame him for the reason he'd never returned, but that was another story.

I hadn't seen him in twenty years. It's not like I had been pining for him all this time. I just needed the voice to come to me again and tell me who the right man was. I prayed that whoever he was, he had normal feet.

I scooted over to the treatment room, smiling at each guest clothed in one of our white robes, walking between treatments. The look of pure contentment on their faces had me feeling renewed and hopeful. I was going to find the right man to take me to my reunion and hopefully share my life with. With a relaxing exhale, I grabbed my client's paperwork hanging outside of the door, and without looking at it like I should have, I knocked on the door. "May I enter?"

"Yes," a deep masculine voice responded.

I opened the door to find a very familiar, half-naked man staring at me. The sight of him made me swallow my mint whole, which made me cough and splutter it back up so I didn't choke to death. Though dying might have been better for me in the moment.

Brooks—who should have been lying down on the treatment table under the blanket that had been provided for him—was sitting up, bare chested, his long legs dangling and covered in charcoal dress pants. He was totally ripped, I might add. Sun kissed and as perfect as he had always been, with tousled golden-brown hair that had the right amount of curl to it. The last twenty years had been more than kind to him.

He looked at his pricey watch. "You're late." No, *Hi, how are you? Sorry I stood you up and ruined the day you had dreamed of all your adolescent life.*

"I think your watch is fast." I knew for a fact I was right on time, as I had checked my phone before I left the bathroom and it was 1:59. It didn't take me a minute to walk over here.

He grimaced at me, yet said nothing.

He might not have been talking, but the voice was back and piercing as ever. *You're going to marry that beautiful man someday.*

FACIAL RECOGNITION

The voice startled me and made me drop the clipboard I was holding with Brooks's paperwork on it. Holy crow. Could I be any more ridiculous? I picked up the clipboard and silently told the voice it was full of crap.

Brooks was staring at me with his head tilted. "Are you all right?"

"Fine, just fine. It's been a long time since we've seen each other." I tried to keep the bitterness out of my tone, all while kicking myself for not checking his stupid chart before I came in here. If I had, I could have asked Anastasia to take him or faked an illness. That's what I got for being all hopeful earlier.

Brooks narrowed his eyes. "I've never been in here before."

It took me a moment to comprehend what that meant. When I finally realized what his words implied, I swore lots of big four-letter words in my head. How was it that he didn't recognize me? I knew it had been a long time, but it's not like I had shriveled up and succumbed to old age. Hello, I was still ovulating. And I still wore the same jeans size I had back in high school, thank you very much. I came close to chucking the clipboard at his head. Instead, I professionally scanned it to see if he was allergic to anything I had in my arsenal of cleansers and essential oils. I wasn't above giving him a rash or some minor breathing difficulties. Unfortunately, I was the one who got the breath knocked out me.

While reading his paperwork, I almost choked on my mint again when I noticed that he was referred to us by Morgan Bronson, my nemesis, the girl I used to love to hate in high school. The girl who had owned Brooks's heart even though she was awful. Miss Valedictorian had toyed with Brooks all during high school. If she'd told Brooks to jump, not only had he brought out the trampoline, but he'd done tricks in the air just to keep her attention. The girl used to wear pencil skirts to school almost every day. She had thought high school was so beneath her, she'd refused Brooks's invitation to be his prom date. That's when I'd stepped in and asked him. What a fool I had been. Even so, he was a bigger one for still having anything to do with the woman.

I wondered if Carly, Brooks's twin, knew her brother was still in contact with Morgan. Sadly, Carly and I had seen each other only a few times since we'd graduated from high school. Nothing had ever been the same since then. I'd missed her and Brooks's friendships more than they would ever know. Carly and I only semi kept in touch now over social media. Though she was planning on coming to our reunion in July. I could imagine her going ballistic if she knew about Brooks and Morgan. She hated Morgan more than I did. Perhaps Morgan had changed her manipulative ways. Maybe she and Carly were even friends now. After all, twenty years was a long time.

I plastered on a fake smile and looked up at an impatiently waiting Brooks. "My mistake. Shall we begin?"

Chapter Two

I turned off the lights and flipped on the meditative instrumental music, hoping it would calm my soul. The soft sounds of piano and rain normally made me feel peaceful. Not today. I couldn't believe Brooks Hamilton was here and he didn't recognize me. What happened to the sweet boy who had brought me cookies the day he'd caught me crying on my lawn? I still remembered him saying, "My momma calls these her happy pills." We had eaten the entire plate. Then he'd introduced me to Carly. Their friendship that summer before our freshman year was a lifeline.

Now before me sat a man—albeit the most attractive man I'd ever laid eyes on—who looked cold and vacant. I knew he was a divorce lawyer because his daddy was still our neighbor and was like a second father to me. Tom Hamilton was a broken man, but one of the best, in my opinion. I knew Brooks would disagree with me, seeing as he hadn't seen his daddy in twenty years.

With a deep breath of courage, I faced Brooks. "Mr. Hamilton, please lie down and pull the blanket up to just under your arms."

Brooks's brow scrunched. "You look familiar."

Oh, I look familiar. *Gee, I wonder why?*

"I didn't catch your name," he interrupted my snarky internal dialogue.

Normally, I would have introduced myself, but not only had I gotten flustered, I was mesmerized by his washboard abs. Like an idiot, I responded without thinking, "You can call me Jane." Like Jane Doe, dead on arrival. *Why did I lie?*

"Jane," he repeated as if he were confused. Believe me, he wasn't the only one.

"Yep, Jane. Just Jane." I wouldn't shut up. What was wrong with me? You know, other than that I heard a voice that was an obvious liar. And I was a liar too. That was so not me. Well, I had to run with it. It wasn't like we would ever see each other after this. So what if I lived next door to his daddy and sometimes commented on his sister's Facebook posts. The odds were still extremely low. According to his daddy, Brooks had vowed never to speak to him again, and as far as I knew, Brooks lived in Dallas, which was like forty-five minutes away from Pecan Orchard. Except what if he checked our website and saw my picture and name? Honestly, did I care if he knew I was a liar? The answer was yes because, generally speaking, I was a good person. However, in this instance I was choosing the path that led straight to hellfire and damnation.

"Please lie down," I repeated.

He followed instructions this time. I had to admit I was sorry to see his pretty chest and abs go away. I wondered what kind of exercises he was doing. In high school he'd been on the track team. And although the cheerleaders didn't cheer at track meets, I still decorated his truck before each one. Because I was a lovesick fool.

I took my place at the head of the treatment table and pushed the controls to raise it, trying to get my heart rate to calm the heck down. "Are you comfortable?" I eked out. Not that I cared if he was, but I had to say it.

"Yes," he replied gruffly.

"Is there a specific reason for your visit today?"

"Other than using the gift certificate my girlfriend gave me so she'll get off my back, no."

"You have a girlfriend," I squeaked. "How nice," I lied again, because it was probably Morgan.

He cleared his throat. "Nothing official, we're just dating."

I wanted to roll my eyes. How very noncommittal. It was definitely Morgan. When had she come back to Texas? Last I heard she was at some uppity school back East and then got a bigwig corporate job. She, like Brooks, never came to Pecan Orchard, even though her parents still lived there and her older brother, Julian, lived in nearby Cherry Hills. Occasionally I saw him. Like his sister, he was gorgeous, driven, and full of himself. He was an OB-GYN and on his third marriage, I believed. However, he wasn't as uptight as his sister and always waved a friendly hello whenever he saw me.

Brooks was staring straight up at me. Wow, did he have some luscious, thick eyelashes. It was disconcerting to have him peering at me. Most clients closed their eyes.

"I can't shake the feeling that I know you."

I shrugged and reached for the bergamot oil that smelled like citrus, and then I remembered he hated anything lavender scented. He used to get on Carly for using lavender lotion. I evilly grabbed that bottle instead. I rubbed some in my hand. "Close your eyes." I cupped my hands and placed them a few inches above his mouth and nose. "Breathe deeply in and out."

His warm, minty breath tickled my hands.

"Again."

His chest rose and fell before he started to splutter. "Ugh. I can't stand lavender."

I smiled to myself. "Oh, I'm so sorry."

He wrinkled his nose. "It's fine, just use something else." His manners were so brusque. I wondered what had happened to him to make him that way. The boy I remembered had never been happy-go-lucky, but he'd had a kind spirit to him.

"Just relax," I whispered in soothing tones while squirting some almond oil in my hands, even though I felt on edge myself. I wasn't sure I wanted to touch Brooks. I had given hundreds of facial massages, yet this seemed wrong. Probably because I knew part of me would enjoy it while the other part would want to smother him with a warm, wet towel. We weren't supposed to treat our clients like sexual beings nor kill them. So, you see where this got tricky for me.

My eyes darted between my hands and Brooks's tousled hair—gorgeous hair that I had always wanted to run my hands through. I'd had dreams about it all growing up. I'd hoped on prom night I would have gotten the pleasure, and then he would have fallen madly in love with me and decided he couldn't live without me. Obviously, none of that panned out. The jerk didn't even remember me.

Brooks made it more uncomfortable because he popped his eyes open. Dawning appeared on his face. "You really do remind me of someone I used to know."

"Oh really," I said, way too high pitched. "Who? Maybe I know her."

He let out a long sigh. "Her name is Gracie Cartwright, but I called her Grace." His lips twitched, almost forming a smile.

The way he said my name so reverently made my heart pitter-patter. I had forgotten how much I liked that he called me Grace. It gave me the courage to plunge my hands into his fantastic hair. Holy crow, it was like dying and going to heaven. His hair was thick and soft. His scalp was perfectly smooth. I had to clear my throat before I had a moment. I really needed a boyfriend.

FACIAL RECOGNITION

"Why did you call her Grace?" What a ridiculous question to ask a stranger—you know, if he had been one. Yet I had always wondered and never asked him back in high school. Besides, I'd had much odder conversations in this room. Most people don't want to talk, but with some people it's all they want to do. I'd found out all sorts of things about my clients. I had one lady confess that she wore cat costumes whenever she was at home and sang "Memory" on repeat.

He closed his eyes as if he reveled in my touch. I even saw goose bumps appear on his shoulders and chest. That filled me with pride, though it was wrong. So very wrong. This was not a place where anyone should be turned on.

"The name just fit her," he finally responded. That was sweet and gave me some goose bumps.

Just for that, I made sure my fingers worked some magic on his scalp. "You must have been close to her."

"We were only neighbors."

What! Only neighbors? This was coming from the boy who had sneaked into my room the night after my mother died and held my hand as we sat on the floor while I sobbed. Not to mention we had kissed once. I had come to him crying our junior year when Danny Kershaw told me I wasn't a very good kisser. Brooks had offered to give me some pointers. The only feedback I had gotten after our dizzying kiss was that Danny Kershaw had no idea what he was talking about. I'd hoped, after the best kiss I'd ever had, that Brooks would see me differently. That the boy who had whispered my name before tenderly parting my lips and who had taken his time letting his tongue sweep the inside of my mouth would realize we were meant to be together. That had been wishful thinking. He'd acted like it never happened. The memory stung. That was it—he was getting the cleanser I'd had some burning complaints about.

His eyes fluttered open, and he took another good look at me. "Come to think of it, she would be a lot older than you."

I had to keep from snarling. I was the same age as him, and he had aged well. Did he think I had grown up to be a hag? Joke was on him, though—not only did I have good genes, I was definitely going to torture him a bit. I immediately stopped the goose bump–inducing scalp massage and grabbed a warm towel to wrap around his head. I resisted the urge to smother him with it.

I grabbed the deep cleanser from the counter behind me. Zoe had done a beautiful job of neatly organizing all my supplies. "So, has your girlfriend been here before?" If she had and it was indeed Morgan, I couldn't believe I hadn't seen her. Unlike Brooks, I would recognize my old classmate.

"I don't think so, but she heard this was the best spa in Fort Worth."

I had to smile. We had worked hard to earn that reputation. "We'd like to send her a thank-you note for the referral." That wasn't exactly a lie. We did like to send people thank-yous, but if it was Morgan, she was getting nothing. "What's her name?"

"I put her name on all the paperwork you made me fill out. Which is overkill, by the way," he growled.

I grabbed my chest. He really was seeing Morgan. And he was a jerk. I shouldn't care about either; except I had thought I would marry the man someday. And apparently some random voice did too. I should probably get that hearing-voices thing checked out. Possibly with a local priest. The voice was obviously evil.

"I'm sorry you feel that way. We're only trying to be thorough and make sure each client receives the best care," I replied more snippily than I normally would have.

He opened his mouth as if he were going to say something, but not a word came out. Fine by me. I was done talking to him. I had to say, though, I was glad he came in here. He'd proven to me that I hadn't missed out on a thing. In fact, I was lucky he had stood me up. Not only that, I could tell his daddy to quit fretting over his estranged relationship with his son. Okay, so I wouldn't do that. I wouldn't even tell Tom I'd seen Brooks. Poor Tom was still beside himself over what he had done to push Brooks away, though I believed Tom had done his penance. And Brooks's behavior today only cemented that he was a spoiled brat for not reciprocating Tom's attempts to mend their relationship.

I squeezed a generous amount of the lemon-and-sage–scented cleanser in my hand and with gentle sweeping motions applied it to his upper torso and then his angular, perfect face. So maybe he had some blackheads on his nose. I supposed that meant I should throw in an extraction for him. What a pity. He deserved a little torture.

"That stuff stings," he complained.

"It's the price you pay for beauty," I sang, not even caring that he was shifting in discomfort while I continued to apply the cleanser. To be more wicked, I added in, "You have really large pores, and I see a lot of lines on your face. I recommend getting a good moisturizer."

"I have wrinkles?" He sounded oh so vain. His eyes flew open, begging me to tell him it wasn't true.

I had to press my lips together before I smirked at him. "There are different types of wrinkles. You have some frown lines around your brow. I suggest smiling more."

He narrowed his eyes. "How do you know I don't?"

"Just a hunch."

"You're awfully presumptive, Jane."

"Am I wrong?" I challenged him. Which I would have never done with any other client. But Brooks was different. He always had been for me.

He gave me an icy stare. "I don't see why that is any of your business."

"My apologies. You're right. You are absolutely none of my business," my stupid voice cracked. I mean, it wasn't like I hadn't been in love with him for over half my life.

Chapter Three

I let out a huge sigh the moment I reached Pecan Orchard's city limits. There was something so soothing about my hometown. I wasn't sure if it was all the cute shops on Madison Street—the main thoroughfare—that were tightly knit together and made of brick with classic awnings. Or the way the shopkeepers still swept the sidewalks and dressed their business windows for each holiday. Currently they were all decked out in red, white, and blue in commemoration of Memorial Day, which would be in a couple of weeks. Life was slower in Pecan Orchard, and I loved it. When you went to the grocery store here, you learned to always get your frozen foods last because it was inevitable that you would run into someone, or several someones, you knew, and long conversations would ensue. Many cartons of ice cream had melted at Dixon's Grocery Store while people were shooting the breeze.

Tonight, I needed home more than ever. My time with Brooks today had me reeling. Which was ridiculous. I was a grown woman who had not spent the last twenty years mourning Brooks. Sure, I had thought about him more than I would like to admit. So maybe I stalked any photos Carly posted of him on Facebook. Perhaps I had even checked him out on LinkedIn. And whenever Tom had any news of him, I paid extra close attention. Could anyone blame me? I'd had a voice in my head tell me we would get married. With all that said, him not recognizing me today hurt. It felt like prom night all over again. I was the forgotten girl.

It had been one thing for Brooks not to see me romantically, but I'd thought we were friends. Like best friends. At least good enough for him to have given me a heads-up that he had been planning on ditching me. Good enough that even after twenty years he would have recognized me. Although, after two decades of no word from him, it was stupid how hurt I was by it all. Thankfully, I would never see him again. He had made sure to mention to me after his appointment that while I had done a good job, my attitude was severely lacking and he would be posting a poor Google review. I'd told him I looked forward to writing my rebuttal. He'd sneered at me before I'd walked out to allow him to get dressed.

Lorelai and Colette got a big kick out of him complaining about me to the owners. I'd had my wits about me and knew he would be one of those complainers, so before he got to them, I had made sure to tell Lorelai and Colette that he thought my name was Jane. They'd happily played along and said all the right things, including that they would discipline *Jane*. We'd all had a good laugh about it, even if inside I had been crying a bit. I missed the old Brooks. Not to mention I was having a hard time forgetting how wonderful it had been to touch his broad shoulders and taut chest. It was as if my fingers were meant to touch his skin.

I had to shake those thoughts. It was poker night with the boys, a.k.a. my daddy and Tom, and I needed to be on my A game. Plus, I had to conceal from Tom that I'd seen Brooks today. He would be ashamed of him if he found out how deplorable his son had behaved. Or worse, he would blame himself. Poor Tom.

I turned onto Poplar Street, located in the historic district of Pecan Orchard. It had been home for the last twenty-four years. Most women would be embarrassed to admit they still lived at home with their father. However, I saw myself more like Jane Austen's Emma. My daddy and I were both respected members of the community, and I didn't live at home because I had to—it was purely by choice. I had more than enough money to live on my own, but with Daddy being a widower intent on never remarrying, it seemed silly to move out.

Daddy and I had fallen into a good routine. We took turns cooking, and I paid him rent, though I knew he was saving it all to give it back to me for a down payment on my own house. He was also good about giving me my space. The entire upstairs was mine to do with as I pleased. Besides that, Daddy's face lit up every time I walked through the door. He was cuter than a Labrador retriever. Don't get me wrong, I would love to come home to a man who would take me up in his arms and kiss the daylights out of me while feeling all my curves, but I was beginning to think I would have to make do with a kiss on the cheek from the best dad around.

When I pulled into our drive, I took a moment to admire the butter-yellow colonial revival home with clapboard siding and white shutters. Momma loved pastels. Poor Daddy still lived in a pink bedroom, and we had a robin's-egg–blue kitchen because Daddy couldn't bear to change it. It looked like the Easter Bunny had thrown up in half our house. Daddy had even managed to keep the peonies alive year after year. It was the big stately pecan tree, though, that was the king of the yard. Every house on the street had one. Heck, probably every house in the town had one.

Momma had loved that tree. The first fall we lived here, Momma had tried every pecan recipe she could think of. Pecan pies, butter pecan fudge, maple pecan pork chops. The list could go on. Unfortunately, Momma couldn't eat most of those things, and she'd died the following fall. The dilated cardiomyopathy brought on by her diabetes had bested her. My world had never been the same since. Maybe it was why I still lived at home—she was still here.

I hustled into the house and was greeted by my two favorite men shouting "Gracie" from the living room. I couldn't help but dart their way to kiss their heads. Before I bestowed my kisses, I took a second to smile at my men. Each so different, yet they were the best of friends. Daddy was on the shorter side, thin, with wispy gray hair. He sipped merlot and wore khaki pants and dress shirts even when he was at home. Though he'd married a country girl, he was all city and had grown up in New York. For as long as I'd been alive, he'd worked as an electrical engineering consultant for wastewater treatment facilities. He should have retired by now, but I think work kept his mind off Momma.

Tom, on the other hand, was big and boisterous. He drank way too much beer and ate more than he should. He was one of those men who had been the cat's meow back in the day, but his unhealthy habits had gotten the best of him. He had been a brilliant corporate lawyer for an oil company until he'd recently retired. Several years ago, Tom had almost lost his job following his divorce from June. After his indiscretion, he never forgave himself, and his life had never been the same. Yet he still had a big smile for me and always made sure to have a fizzing glass of Diet Pepsi with a twist of lime waiting for me during poker night. And he was always the first person to compliment me. Well, besides my daddy. But Daddy was always quiet about it. Tom boomed.

First, I kissed Daddy's head. "How was your day?"

"Fine, sweetheart." He patted the hand I had rested on his shoulder. He still wore his wedding ring. I loved it so much, yet it broke my heart.

Tom was next. I kissed his salt-and-pepper mop. For his age, he had a lot of hair. It reminded me of Brooks. After running my hands through Brooks's hair today, I knew he would be lucky like his daddy and keep it for a long while. "Looks like I need to get my shears out." When I'd graduated from cosmetology school many moons ago, I had started out as a hairstylist. I didn't do it very long before I went back to aesthetician school. Now I only cut hair for Tom and Daddy.

FACIAL RECOGNITION

Tom took a swig of his Bud Light. "Not tonight, darlin', we have some serious business to take care of."

"Give me a minute, and I'll be back to kick your booties."

Both men chuckled. They knew I was headed to change into my Lucky Charms shirt that stated I was magically delicious. I only ever wore it in the house during poker night. Maybe I should wear it around town to advertise. Although I preferred blind dates. I thought maybe the voice would appear if I dated men I'd never seen before. Just like when Brooks had popped his head over the fence. Or shown up out of the blue today. I had to stop thinking about it. Perhaps I should forget the voice and just choose someone myself. Not the podiatrist, though.

When I walked away, I heard Tom tell Daddy, "Steve, you're a lucky man. That girl of yours is pure gold. I can't believe some fella hasn't snatched her up yet."

"All in good time," Daddy responded, as if he were okay with the fact that I was going to be a spinster. I truly was living the life of Emma Woodhouse. I had a doting father who didn't want me to leave the nest, my mother was dead, and I lived in a beautiful house, albeit a little too pastel. Perhaps, though, it meant I would get my Mr. Knightley. A handsome, distinguished man I'd known forever but hadn't considered to be husband material. Maybe I should start flipping through my own contacts. Brooks popped into my head. Absolutely not. I didn't care that he had challenged me today, just like Mr. Knightley did with Emma. Or that he was handsome and distinguished. The man didn't even recognize me.

With those lovely thoughts, I raced up the stairs and into my room, which was really two rooms. Daddy had knocked down the wall between my bedroom and the old guest bedroom, so it was more like a suite with a private bathroom. Totally Emma Woodhouse worthy. Except my room was more like a homage to Dr. Noah Drake, a.k.a. Rick Springfield of *General Hospital.* My momma had been obsessed with the show and him.

Momma had said I would be a blessed child since I was born on March 25, 1981. The same day Dr. Noah Drake made his debut. Her water broke with me right after the episode was over. She'd told me she had cried for a week straight when he left the show in 1983 to focus on his music career. I only wished she had been around when he came back to the show in 2005. She would have squealed.

Momma had loved the show so much she used to tape episodes on our old VCR. I remember watching them with her when she would get really sick and have to stay in bed. I would curl up next to her and drool over the handsome doctor. I had vowed to Momma that if I ever had a son, I would name him Noah. It was the last thing she had whispered to me. "Don't forget your promise, Gracie. I want a grandson named Noah." I'd cried and laughed. Leave it to Momma to say something so silly as her last words. I'd kept all her old tapes and bought the last model of the VCR they ever made in 2016, just to make sure I could keep on watching them. Dr. Noah honestly was quite the rake, but there was something about him. Regardless of what a hot cad he was, watching those old tapes kept me connected to Momma.

I walked through my room and brushed my hand over one of my many Rick Springfield posters hanging on the walls. It was a fresh-faced one of him in scrubs. Wow, was he a looker. I stopped and sighed, gazing into Rick's hazel eyes. Momma had been so thrilled when my eyes turned out to be hazel too.

"Don't tell the guys downstairs, but oh, did I have a day today. You remember Brooks. He used to make fun of you, and of me for liking you. Yeah, I should have known then he wasn't the one. Well, I saw him today. And I heard the voice again. I know, I'm as surprised as you. Obviously I need therapy. For goodness' sake, I'm talking to a poster. Still, what's your opinion? And how hairy are your feet?"

Rick stared back, just smiling, not saying a dang word.

FACIAL RECOGNITION

"Fine. Be the strong, silent type." I sighed and leaned my head against Rick as if he could really hug me. "Tell me, when is it going to be my turn?"

Chapter Four

I rubbed my hands together and stared down my opponents. I was equipped to win in my lucky shirt and cutoff shorts. "Who's ready to lose?"

Tom laughed, making his belly and man boobs jiggle.

My almost flat chest was jealous.

"Not tonight, girly." Tom took a swig of beer.

I really wished he wouldn't. He worried me. I don't know if I would call him an alcoholic, but he teetered on the edge. At least he was a happy drunk. Though sometimes he waxed very sentimental. He missed his kids and ex-wife something fierce. Carly had opened the door for reconciliation and had even visited him briefly a couple of times so Tom could meet his grandsons. I wasn't sure, though, that their relationship would ever be the same as it had been before he'd cheated on Mrs. Hamilton while on a business trip during our senior year. When it had come to light, it had rocked everyone's world and created a seemingly uncrossable rift between Tom and his family. Carly had had a family-only destination wedding twelve years ago. Tom hadn't been invited. Brooks wouldn't allow it, according to Carly. It was either Brooks or Tom, and Carly had chosen her brother.

The breakup of the Hamiltons' marriage had even upended my world. When June and her children had moved out, not only had I suffered the loss of my two best friends, but June Hamilton had been like a mother to me. After I lost Momma, she had taken me under her wing like a little chick, helping me pick out prom dresses and even buying me tampons. When she left to move back to her hometown in Arkansas to be closer to her parents, I thought she would keep in touch, but I guess anything related to Pecan Orchard was too painful, even me.

I smiled at Tom. "Bring it on."

"Watch and learn." Tom shuffled the cards before dealing us each two, facedown. He loved playing Texas Hold'em.

"How was work today, sweetie?" Dad asked me while peeking at his cards.

I thought about how to answer that truthfully, without revealing that Brooks had been there. I'd already used up my lying quota for the day. "Um . . . it was interesting. I had a really rude client, but I gave him the what for, and I won't be seeing him again." I peeked at my cards, trying to keep a straight face. They were excellent—two queens.

"Good for you, honey." Dad held his cards close to his chest.

"He didn't come on to you, did he?" Tom growled.

I wish. Wait. No I didn't. At least I hadn't for a while. So maybe that was a lie too. "No, he didn't."

Tom set the deck down. "Good. Or I'd have to find him and beat the hell out of him."

Oh, that probably wouldn't go over well. Though Brooks probably needed a good talking-to. However, Brooks would easily best his dad if a physical altercation ever occurred. The man was pure muscle. I was trying not to think about it. But holy crow, it was hard not to think about his body.

"Let's move on to more serious matters," Tom interrupted my sizzling memories. "Have you caught up on *The Nanny*?"

Tom and I had a thing where we binged on old TV shows and then discussed them. We'd watched everything from *I Love Lucy* to *The Golden Girls*. I still couldn't convince him to get into *General Hospital*. I had to settle for the fact that I'd made Carly a fan for life of the greatest soap opera ever.

"I watched a few episodes last night."

"I can't believe Maxwell doesn't want C. C." Tom threw some poker chips into the pot to get the betting going.

"What? C. C. is awful. He's supposed to fall for Fran." I shouldn't be surprised that Tom had a thing for C. C. He'd fallen in love with Bea Arthur's character from *The Golden Girls* too. Something about tall, strong women, I guess. It made sense since June, though a beautiful woman, was more on the masculine side. When I knew her, I swear she could have beaten the crap out of almost any guy. She was six feet tall and had broad shoulders like a linebacker. She had also rocked some stilettos, and she had some serious curves. Carly had gotten her momma's height and had towered over all of us on the cheerleading squad. Poor thing was always on the bottom of the pyramid. But, boy, could she shake it.

"Fran?" Tom scoffed. "She talks with her nose. I would have to shoot myself if I had to listen to her voice every day."

"But she's good with the children." Daddy surprised us both and jumped in.

My head whipped in Daddy's direction. "You're watching *The Nanny*, Daddy?"

His ears pinked a bit. "I thought I should check it out since you said you loved it."

Aww. This was why I would forever be a daddy's girl and believe that there were good men out there. I had to believe there was one for me. "What do you think of it?"

FACIAL RECOGNITION

Dad pressed his lips together. "It's no *Star Trek*, but it's fun." Dad was a devoted Trekkie and had even gone on one of their cruises. I had never gotten into it until the reboots where they cast Chris Pine as Captain Kirk. That was an excellent choice. You know, I think I could feel some things for Chris Pine. I wondered if he was single and looking to get married and have some kids. I bet he didn't have overly hairy feet.

"You're telling me that you'd rather be with the nanny than C. C.?" Tom found it incredulous. "That C. C. is one hunk of woman. She has some meat to her." Tom grinned over at me. "Not to say that you aren't beautiful, even though a light breeze could blow you away. However, I need a woman I can dig my hands into." His chocolate-brown eyes that reminded me so much of Brooks's got misty. They did that whenever he was thinking of June.

Daddy cleared his throat, knowing Tom might start blubbering. "Why don't we get back to the game? I'll see your two and raise you five." Dad threw his chips into the pot. He must have had some good cards too.

"I'll see that bet." I tossed in my own chips.

Tom scrunched his faced and rubbed his burgeoning belly. "I'm going for it." He pushed forward his chips. He then dealt the three community cards. Tom was the worst poker player ever. It was surprising, considering he was a lawyer. He groaned, giving away that the cards weren't to his liking. Downing the rest of his beer was also a dead giveaway.

Daddy was ever stoic and gave not a thing away. He gently sipped his wine and tossed in his bet.

I mirrored his unemotive face, but inside I was dancing. I casually matched his bet.

Tom folded and grabbed another beer from the cooler he'd brought with him. Once he'd popped the top off his bottle, he dealt the last two cards.

Dad and I studied the cards and each other before placing our last bests. We eyed one another, grinning before turning over our cards.

"Four of a kind," I said at the same time Daddy said, "Flush."

"Yes!" I scooped up my winnings.

Tom patted my knee. "You've always been a lucky one, Gracie, darlin'."

Daddy gave me a wink. "I would say she's always been smart."

"Right you are," Tom agreed with Dad.

I wasn't sure how smart I was. I mean, I heard strange voices. And as far as lucky went, I was definitely not lucky in love, but . . . I stared at my men. I supposed I was pretty darn lucky. I stood. "Now that we've gotten the first butt kicking out of the way, I'm going to grab a snack. Any takers?" I always tried to make it something healthy, as I knew it was probably the only fruits and vegetables Tom would get all week.

Daddy nodded, but Tom stared blankly and dropped his beer. It splattered all over the wood floor. Before I knew it, Tom was falling out of his chair and making an awful gasping sound. A noise I was all too familiar with. My mother had made the same sounds when she was dying. Both Daddy and I rushed to his side.

"Tom, can you hear me?" I cried.

His eyes rolled back, and he stopped making any noise.

"Daddy, call 911." I checked Tom's pulse but couldn't find one, and he had stopped breathing. "No, no, no." I wouldn't lose someone else I loved. I began CPR while Daddy talked to the emergency dispatcher. Time seemed to stand still as I did chest compressions while silently begging God not to take Tom. "Please, Tom, fight. Fight hard. Ryker and Axel need their granddaddy. Daddy and I need you," I cried. This went on for ten minutes until the EMTs arrived and took over. They immediately brought out a defibrillator and shocked him. I stood in horror, watching from Daddy's arms.

FACIAL RECOGNITION

After shocking him twice, I heard some of the best words ever: "He has a pulse."

I turned into Daddy, and emotion poured out of me and onto his shirt. They worked on Tom for what seemed like hours, but it was really minutes before they were transporting him out of the house.

"Which hospital are you taking him to?" Daddy asked.

"Regional Medical Center," the EMT responded.

I guess I knew where I would be spending the night, and praying that Tom was luckier than me tonight.

Daddy and I sat in the ICU waiting room while they sedated Tom and placed him in therapeutic hypothermia. Tom had gone into what they called sudden cardiac arrest. They believed lowering his body temperature would reduce his risk of brain damage. That was, if he survived. The odds weren't in his favor, but the doctor told us we shouldn't lose hope. He had seen patients recover. He said I had increased his chances by administering CPR right away.

I'd messaged Carly through Facebook, as I didn't have her number. I hated to tell her in such a way. I gave her my number, and she'd called immediately. Poor thing was beside herself. She was beating herself up over missed opportunities and not seeing Tom more over the years. She was even remorseful about letting our relationship slide. She and her family were flying in tomorrow from California. Thankfully, Daddy and I had been Tom's emergency contacts for a long time, so the doctors were able to communicate with us.

I rested my head on Daddy's bony shoulder, exhausted but not able to close my eyes. I kept seeing flashes of Tom's lifeless body. If he survived this, I was going to start cooking for him every day and making him exercise. No more beer and bratwurst. He was going to become the vibrant man I used to know.

Daddy and I sat in silence for several minutes. I knew how much he hated hospitals. Momma had spent way too much time in them and had died in one. I was just about to tell him to go home, even though I knew he would protest, when my fourth-worst nightmare walked in. Ahead of this one was Daddy dying, Tom dying, and Rick Springfield canceling his summer tour, three concerts of which I had tickets for.

My head popped up when Brooks and his momma came walking in through the waiting room doors. Brooks had his arm around his momma, who had obviously been crying. Her eyes were as puffy as pastries. Though she was tall—only four inches shorter than Brooks—for some reason she looked so diminutive next to Brooks's take-charge attitude. He was dressed to the nines in a designer black suit, looking like he had come from a fancy dinner or something, and his entire demeanor screamed that he wasn't happy to be there. Except I detected a hint of sadness in his eyes. I only recognized it because I'd seen it my own when Momma had died.

Unfortunately, there was only one way in and one way out of the waiting room. And I'd been so stunned to see him walk in, I didn't have enough wits about me to run and hide in the bathroom. This was what I got for lying today. Yep, the good Lord was punishing me.

June and Brooks locked eyes on me as my eyes nervously darted back and forth between them. June's eyes flooded with tears while she called out my name, "Gracie." At the same time, Brooks's brow creased exponentially when he growled, "Jane."

Oops.

"Jane?" June smacked Brooks's chest. "What's wrong with you? Don't you recognize *our* Gracie?" She flew toward me with open arms

FACIAL RECOGNITION

I had no choice but to stand and face the music. First, though, I received June, who about bowled me over. For a woman in her midsixties, she still packed a punch. She was definitely a woman who had some meat to her, just like Tom preferred. And by the looks of her skin, she was still into spray tans.

"Oh, Gracie, my darling girl," she bawled.

Since I was about six inches shorter than her, my head landed in her big bosom. I didn't mind—it kept me from having to face Brooks. And, man, had I missed her. I snuggled in close, shaking from the fear of knowing I would have to pay the piper any minute now because of my lie and crying because June felt like home and a momma. Did I ever need a momma now.

I heard Daddy stand up and greet Brooks. "It's been a long time. It's good to see you," Daddy said.

"Yes, sir, it has." Brooks still had some manners to him. Which surprised me after our encounter earlier today. I was even more flabbergasted that he was here. I'd thought he'd sworn to never see his daddy again. In fact, I had counted on it. Hence my lie.

June clung to me for dear life, blubbering.

"I didn't know you were in town," I said, muffled against her chest.

"I've been visiting Brooks," she stuttered between sobs. "Carly called us. She said you saved Tom's life."

"I wouldn't say that. He's not out of the woods." I could hardly say it.

June leaned back. "He can't die. There's so much I need to say to him." Her blue, watery eyes bore a pain so deep it pierced my heart. The Hamiltons' divorce was one of the biggest shocks of my life. To me, they had been the ideal couple. They were flirty and fun. Sure, they could toss some zingers at each other, but they had always been affectionate. Not only to each other but to their children and their children's friends. Especially to me.

"There's so much I want to say to you." She patted my wet cheeks. "I've missed you, dear Gracie."

"I've missed you too," my voice croaked.

She took my hand, and it was time to face Brooks. Crap. It was made more *pleasant* by the fact that I was still wearing my *I'm Magically Delicious* shirt and cutoffs. My only saving grace was that my legs were toned and shaved.

Together, June and I faced Daddy and Brooks.

Brooks stood with his arms folded, looking me over. His lips were curled up into a snarl.

I rose to the occasion. "Brooks, you're looking so fresh faced. You have that *facial* glow."

June spat out a weak laugh. "How funny. He did have a facial today. Apparently, the aesthetician was something else. She really got under his skin. Brooks ranted about her for over an hour after he got home."

I had to press my lips together to keep from smirking. "That's so awful."

"Carly said you own a spa now, is that right?" June asked me.

I was surprised Carly knew that; she had probably seen me post about it on Facebook. I was constantly touting Serenity Spa on there. I nodded while watching Brooks's eyes widen at the news.

"Perhaps you can give Brooks some advice on how he should handle his poor treatment."

I gave Brooks a brilliant smile. "You should definitely write a scathing review online."

"I plan on it," Brooks growled.

"I can't wait to read it."

31

Chapter Five

There were few things more uncomfortable in my life than sitting in the waiting room with Brooks staring at me while his momma took a moment to be alone with Tom. Things like having your date put his hairy, overarched foot on the table, getting a cavity filled, gynecology appointments, and being stood up for prom. However, I would have taken any of them rather than be alone with Brooks right now. Daddy had left to get some rest. Unfortunately, I couldn't, even if it meant facing Brooks. Tom needed someone by his side who loved him and stuck it out with him, just in case the unthinkable happened. Not that I blamed June for leaving Tom; I couldn't imagine that kind of betrayal. Brooks, on the other hand, should have at least reciprocated some of his father's attempts to reconcile, in my opinion. Even a card on his birthday would have been nice.

Brooks sat one seat away from me on the stiff waiting room chairs. We were the only souls around in the ICU waiting room, as it was around midnight. The only sound that could be heard was the low hum of the TV playing in the background.

My peripheral vision told me Brooks was glaring at me, and my senses could feel the iciness of his gaze. All I could do was stare aimlessly at my phone.

"Why did you lie to me today?" Brooks's deep voiced shattered the silence.

I set my phone in my lap and turned toward him. Dang, the five-o'clock shadow played well on his face. His facial hair was much darker than his golden-brown locks, and it really added to his broody persona. Not that it mattered how attractive he was. He was a jerk and dating Morgan.

I tapped my lips. "Could have something to do with the fact that you didn't recognize me. Or perhaps I'm still a little salty that you stood me up on prom night. Or maybe it's because I'd thought I was one of your best friends, and you treated me as if I never existed." I had to work hard to keep the emotion out of my voice.

His lips parted, but he said nothing.

Figures. I went back to staring at my phone.

"If you had been truthful today, I would have put two and two together. I told you, you looked familiar. And the setting we were in was out of context," he defended himself.

I couldn't believe that was all he had to say to me after twenty years. After the history we shared. "Congratulations, Mr. Hamilton, you've won your case." I didn't even bother looking at him. In fact, I turned more away from him and decided watching late-night TV was the ticket. Who didn't need more talk shows in their life? Not that I could really pay attention. I was more than worried about Tom, and being near Brooks was disconcerting. The tension between us was strung tighter than my string bikini.

After several minutes, Brooks moved to the seat next to me. "Grace."

A shiver went down me. How ridiculous. It's just there was something in the way he always said my name. My God-given Christian name that only he used.

FACIAL RECOGNITION

"I am sorry," he cleared his throat as if he hadn't said those words in a long time, "for not being more perceptive today. I've done my best to forget everything about Pecan Orchard that I could."

My head whipped toward him. Did he have any idea what a punch to the gut that was? I obviously had meant nothing to him. I took a moment to search his eyes, desperate to see anything of the boy I'd known, or thought I'd known. The boy I had loved. I sighed when all I saw was a steely determination. "You've done an excellent job." I stood and walked over to the other side of the empty room just before the tears started to fall.

I put my arms around myself, cold from the air conditioner and Brooks's response. I don't know why I was so surprised. His behavior twenty years ago and today were pretty pathetic. I stared blankly out the glass door that led to the rest of the hospital. There wasn't much to look at other than a drinking fountain and a picture of some old guy. I rubbed my arms, shifting my thoughts to Tom and praying he would make it. The doctor said he was stable for now, and his temperature was coming down. I wanted nothing more in that moment than to be sitting next to Tom and holding his hand. It would be an added bonus to be away from Brooks's gaze. I don't even know why he came here in the first place. He'd refused to go back and see his daddy when given the chance earlier.

Amid my silent contemplation a suit coat that smelled of orange tree blossoms with a hint of spice was being draped over my shoulders, engulfing me. I instantly felt warmer.

"You look cold," Brooks crooned from behind me.

I was cold, but I didn't need his kindness. "I'm fine. You can keep your suit coat." I tried shrugging it off.

Brooks placed his hands on my shoulders. "Please take it."

34

I begged myself not to revel in his touch or the way he smelled. The voice that kept telling me Brooks was meant to be mine was wrong about him, and I had been too. "Really, I'm okay."

"Don't be stubborn. Your magically delicious shirt is paper thin." I heard the smile in his voice.

"Are you making fun of my shirt? I'll have you know, because of this baby, I beat your daddy," my voice cracked, "and mine every week in poker."

Brooks dropped his hands. "You play poker with *Tom?*"

I turned with a scrunched brow. "He's your *daddy,* and yes I do. We also have a monthly book club, manicure Mondays, salsa Sundays, and occasionally fried food Fridays, which, under the circumstances, are now canceled." I felt sick thinking I had contributed to Tom's condition. I should have been firmer with him about his eating habits, but his favorite saying was, "I'm a Texan, and it's our God-given right to eat badly." His other favorite was, "Go big or go home."

Brooks ran his hands through his tousled hair. "I didn't realize you two were still so close."

"I think there's a lot you don't realize." I took off his suit coat and handed it back to him. I'd rather freeze than be tortured by his yummy scent.

He stared down at his jacket. "You have no idea what he did to our family." Brooks seethed.

"That's where you're wrong. And if you don't think your daddy has felt the repercussions of what he did every day of his life, you're sorely mistaken. That man loves you so much. He's so proud that you followed in his footsteps and became a lawyer."

Brooks's head jerked up. "I'll never be like him."

"Sadly, that's probably true."

Brooks's icy glare made me shiver, but I held his gaze. He tilted his head. "You're different than I remembered."

"How so?"

"You used to be a lot nicer."

My hand flew to my heart. I was a nice person. At least until Brooks had appeared today. "I could say the same for you." I headed back for the chairs and took a seat, shaking.

Brooks paced and paced, rubbing his neck as he went.

I tried to ignore him and pulled out my phone to read our book club choice for the month—*Twilight*. I smiled to myself thinking of Tom's pick. He had chosen it because Carly loved that series and he was desperate to connect with his kids in any way. I hadn't read the book in years, so I was brushing up. Unfortunately, lusty teen angst couldn't keep me distracted.

Brooks eventually threw himself into the chair next to me. He leaned forward, resting his elbows on his knees, his face in his hands. He inhaled and exhaled loudly. "Grace, I don't want to fight with you. My father could die," he choked out.

My heart instantly softened toward him, and before I could stop myself, I rested my hand on his back. "I know. And I'm sorry." Sorry for what could happen and sorry I hadn't been kinder. Tears welled in my eyes.

He turned his head toward me, the corners of his mouth slightly ticked up. "I should apologize to you."

"Probably." I smiled.

That elicited a full grin from him. In his smile, I saw the boy I used to know and love. It had me removing my hand from his strong back. My heart couldn't afford to waste its time on a lost cause.

He leaned back and rubbed his eyes. "Has he been sick?"

"No. I mean, he hasn't exactly taken care of himself for the better part of the last two decades, but he hasn't had any major illnesses."

"Do you still live in Pecan Orchard?"

"I still live with Daddy. I do my best to keep both men out of trouble."

"You still live at home?" His tone teetered between surprise and judgment.

"Yes, I do, and I'm not ashamed of it. It's completely respectable. I make a good living, so it's all by choice."

"Yes, I got a taste of your livelihood today."

"You're welcome, by the way. Your skin looks great."

He chuckled. "I'll give you that. Your bedside manner, though, was lacking."

"You're the only person who would say so. Despite what you think about me, I'm generally adored," I teased.

He turned, making sure we locked eyes. "I do remember that about you."

I swallowed hard. *Holy crow.*

He reached over and took my hand. "I'm sorry for not recognizing you today."

I stared down at our hands. They looked good together. His were all masculine, and mine were feminine and slender. We both had well-kept nails, except mine were painted the perfect shade of taupe. Not only did they look good together—they felt as if they belonged, like the last two puzzle pieces that came together, allowing you to see the completed picture.

I bit my lip, wanting to hold on to him for as long as I could, forgetting he was a lost cause and that he'd hurt me. "I guess I can forgive you. I'm sure it was because I still look so young," I joked.

He leaned in closer. His cinnamon breath lingered between us. His lips parted to speak right as his phone buzzed loudly. He dropped my hand like a hot biscuit. "I need to take this. It's Morgan. Do you remember Morgan Bronson?"

Ugh. Unfortunately, yes. She was still interrupting me. "Looks like you didn't forget everything about Pecan Orchard." I stood. "I'm going to go check on your daddy." And check my brain while I was at it.

Chapter Six

I wasn't sure what broke my heart more: looking through the glass door and seeing Tom hooked up to so many machines in an effort to keep him alive, or watching June silently cry by his bedside. She kept attempting to hold his hand, yet each time she wouldn't allow herself to. I hated to interrupt, but I needed to see Tom and get away from his son. I stepped closer so the automatic doors would open.

June's head snapped up, and she wiped her eyes.

"I'm sorry to intrude."

She waved her hand. "Darlin', you aren't intruding. You've been more his family than anyone. The doctor told me he's only authorized to speak to you, since you are his primary caregiver. Tom probably didn't trust any of the rest of us not to pull the plug on him." She half laughed, half cried.

I pulled up a chair next to her and took her hand.

Her unusually large hand squeezed the life out of mine. "You're a good girl. Always were."

"I don't think Brooks would agree."

She chuckled. "I gather from your exchange that you were the aesthetician he saw today."

"Guilty."

"Whatever you did to him, he deserved it for not recognizing you. You haven't changed a bit, other than being more beautiful."

"I think the tears in your eyes are clouding your vision."

She patted my hand. "I've been blind about a lot of things but not that." She looked wistfully at Tom. "You know," her voice cracked, "we'd always hoped you and Brooks would end up together. Tom used to say, 'If Brooks is smart, he'll realize Gracie is the catch of a lifetime.'"

"We were just friends," I stuttered. Though inside I was flattered Tom and June wished the same thing I had.

"Uh-huh. We saw the way you two used to look at each other."

I tucked some tendrils behind my ears. "We were like siblings, and Brooks always loved Morgan," I hissed her name. Brooks had never looked at me the way he used to look at Morgan. With her it was always with wide-eyed wonder. As if she were this magical, exotic creature. When he used to look at me, it usually bordered on amusement and annoyance. Carly and I were always trying to talk him into something. Whether it was being a participant in the school carnival's kissing booth or making him help us with the homecoming parade float. He would eventually give in but not without giving me a look that said he'd rather wring my neck.

June grimaced. "Morgan," she spewed. "I have no idea what my son sees in her. They're dating again."

"So I heard. He's talking to her now."

"She's probably complaining that Brooks ruined her night by having to leave her company's dinner party early. Any girlfriend worth her salt would have left with him and come to the hospital. His daddy is dying, for goodness' sake," she croaked. "But not that one. She's as selfish as she's always been," she ranted. She took a deep breath in and out. "Enough about her; tell me how you've been, honey."

I reached out and smoothed the cooling blanket draping Tom. Tears silently streaming down my face. He looked so devoid of life. The only thing that told me he was alive was the beeping of the machines monitoring his heart and blood pressure.

"I've been great until tonight. I should have tried harder to make him eat healthier and stop drinking. I could have made him listen."

June wrapped an arm around me, forcing my head onto her shoulder. "Don't you dare blame yourself for this. If anyone's to blame, it's me. I hated him so much for what he had done to me, I turned our children against him. Took away everything he loved most in this world, except you and your daddy."

"He only ever blamed himself."

"A few years ago," she sighed, "I would have been happy to hear that. But lately, I've realized how bitter I've become. How I let it turn me into someone I'm not proud of. It's even made me question leaving Tom. He begged me to work it out." She sobbed. "I was too proud to even consider it, even though he was the love of my life." She rubbed my arm. "To spite him, I gave up so many of the people and things I loved too. Including you, darlin'. I'm so sorry. I was too weak and humiliated to face anyone or anything associated with Pecan Orchard." She hiccupped. "And I'm afraid my hard heart has ruined my son."

My head popped up. "How?"

She rested her hand on my water-logged cheek. "He's so cynical. He thinks marriage is a hoax."

I rubbed my heart. That was unfortunate news, considering I had a weird voice telling me we would get married. Of course, I wasn't stupid enough to believe it. Okay, so maybe I did a long time ago, but I had gotten wiser. Sort of. "Well, he is a divorce lawyer. He probably sees a lot of crazy things." I tried to make her feel better, even though I believed the real reason was because he was self-centered. He and Morgan were two peas in a pod. Except they were probably too selfish to share a pod.

"You're sweet to say that, but my boy has never been the same since I left his daddy." She dropped her hand and gazed at Tom. "We had so many dreams. We should be traveling the world together now and covered in grandbabies."

"Tom would have liked that very much. He loves to tell me stories about how you met in college and you wouldn't give him the time of day." I laughed softly.

She half smiled. "Oh, he was a charmer. Too charming—I couldn't believe it was real. But he was the real deal. He talked my roommates into letting him in our apartment while I was in class. He hung up pictures of himself everywhere. He wrote on every single one, 'Call me for a good time.'"

"No way," I giggled.

"Oh yes."

"What did you do?"

"I eventually called him after a week. It took everything I had in me not to call him the second I got home. I thought I needed to play a little hard to get. I wish I wouldn't have waited. I've always been too stubborn for my own good."

"I think everyone is, to some degree. I mean, I had ample opportunity to tell Brooks who I was today. Instead I painfully extracted his blackheads and subjected him to my mag light. Then I may have fudged the truth about how many wrinkles he has." I felt better after confessing my sins and for making June laugh uncontrollably.

When she got her giggles under control, she said, "Darlin', I always loved your feisty spirit. And I have no doubt my son deserved whatever you threw at him."

"I probably let my pride get in the way. I was hurt he didn't recognize me."

"As you should have been."

"And I may or may not still hold a grudge that he stood me up on prom night."

June swallowed hard and shifted in her seat. "Please don't blame him."

I tilted my head while she hung hers.

"Honey," she whispered. "That was the day I found out about Tom's affair. Tom and I agreed not to tell Carly and Brooks until after graduation, but Brooks caught me crying in my room. He had come in to ask me how to pin on your corsage." She sniffled. "I tried to brush off the tears, but Brooks knew something was wrong. To this day I feel so awful telling him the way I did. For ruining your night."

Ugh. Now I felt terrible too. Here I'd been cursing him for over half my life. Thinking back, June and Tom had seemed off that night when all the parents were taking pictures of us. And it was odd that they hadn't been more frantic about not knowing where their son was. I had been too wrapped up in my own disappointment to question any of it. Or to think there was more to the story. I had figured Brooks didn't want to go if Morgan couldn't be his date. I'd pictured all sorts of torrid things they were doing while I was trying to hold back the tears at prom during all the slow dances or when the photographer wanted to take a picture of the prom king and me with our dates. Looking back, nothing was ever the same after that day. The Hamiltons, in a way, ceased to exist. "I didn't know."

"How could you have? I made Brooks swear not to tell his sister. She'd always had more delicate feelings, and we wanted her to enjoy the last bit of her senior year. It was a huge burden for Brooks to carry. One I still feel guilty about. And you . . ." She brushed my cheek. "You must have been so hurt. I knew how excited you were. I knew how much you liked my son." She gave me a knowing look.

I bit my lip. "It was only a silly high school crush," I lied. It was a good lie, though. I wanted to spare June some guilt, but she was smart.

"I don't think so. You treated Brooks as if you expected a future with him."

Heat flooded my cheeks.

"Don't be embarrassed."

This was way more than embarrassment. I wasn't even sure there was a word for how embarrassed I was. "It was a long time ago. I was young. Too young. I moved on forever ago. So far back I don't even remember how long. And I date a lot. Like a lot, a lot," I rambled like an idiot.

She gave me a sad smile. "I'm sure you do. You're a gorgeous woman inside and out."

"I wish Brooks would have told me. You know, after we graduated."

"Darlin', we were all hurting so much. Sometimes when you're in that kind of pain, it's the ones you're closest to who you fear being around the most."

"Why?"

She thought for a moment. "That kind of pain brings a vulnerability that will scare the living daylights out of you. And I don't think Brooks, even on a good day, was ever good with owning his feelings. I think that's why he keeps going back to that woman. Morgan's so emotionally closed off, Brooks feels safe around her."

"See, I always thought it was her voluptuous chest." I stared down at my mostly flat one.

June chuckled and swatted my arm. "Darlin', I do love you. I hope you can forgive me. I hope Brooks will too. I have a feeling when he finally wises up, he's going to realize what I made him miss out on." She tapped my nose. "Yes, I'm talking about you."

I shook my head. "No. No. Like I said, we were only friends. And he and Morgan, well . . . I don't know what they are, but apparently they are

44

meant to be." Those words tasted bitter, like a mouthful of coffee grounds.

"You think so?"

I shrugged half-heartedly, wishing it wasn't true.

"Take it from his momma, that woman is not meant for my boy. Why do you think I came to Dallas? When he told me he was dating her again, I jumped in my Caddy and burned some rubber. I drove nonstop from Little Rock, prepared with note cards and charts."

"I'd love to see those."

"Name the time, darlin'."

I wrapped my arms around her. "I love you, Miss June."

"Oh, sweet girl, I love you more than you'll know," she choked up. "I'm going to make it right, for everyone, even Tom. He's going to wake up, or so help me there is going to be hell to pay."

"He's going to need our fighting spirits. The odds aren't good," I stuttered.

"Honey, if there is one thing I know about Hamilton men, it's that they don't put stock in the odds, only themselves. Tom's a fighter. We just have to let him know we are all cheering him on."

"You know me—I love being a cheerleader."

"Dust off your pom-poms. We all have some tough games ahead of us."

"Games?" As in plural.

She wagged her brows. "Just promise me you're in it to win it."

"Win what?"

Her lips curled into a Cheshire grin. "What you know is yours."

I rubbed my chest. The voice couldn't be right. Could it?

Chapter Seven

Daddy brought me a change of clothes and a smoothie early the next morning. I couldn't bear to leave Tom alone. I knew he wouldn't be waking up, as he was in an induced coma; however, I worried about him dying all by himself.

It felt good to be in some warmer clothes: a pair of jeans and a mint pleated, flutter-sleeved blouse. Daddy had even thought to bring me a jacket. Bless him. It was freezing in here, though the nurse had brought me a blanket last night. Not that I'd slept much. There had been nurses in and out all night, checking his vitals and his temperature, even taking his blood. I would be living off adrenaline and Diet Pepsi for the rest of the day.

Daddy took a sip of his coffee while staring with concerned eyes at his best friend. "How long did June and Brooks stay?"

"They left around one a.m. June wanted to stay, but Brooks insisted she get some rest." More like he couldn't take the pressure any longer. He was fighting himself something fierce staying away from his daddy. He'd never ended up coming in.

"It was something else, seeing them after all this time."

"It sure was." I took a sip of my strawberry smoothie.

"Brooks grew up to be a good-looking kid." Daddy have me a crooked grin.

"He's all right."

Daddy lovingly stroked my hair. I had let it down and did what I could with it in the hospital bathroom, which was basically nothing. My hair didn't like to be tamed. So, I looked like a wild woman this morning. "Your heart never was the same after he broke it."

I whipped my head his way. "What are you talking about?"

Daddy leaned in conspiratorially. "I might not be the most attentive man, but I know my daughter."

I leaned my head against his. "You're the best daddy a girl could ask for."

"Only because I was blessed with the best daughter." He kissed my cheek.

"Do you think Tom will make it?" I whispered, pleading for him to tell me it would all be okay.

"He's in God's hands now."

"The doctor said if he doesn't wake up in forty-eight hours, we will need to discuss our options. Daddy," I cried, "I can't let him go."

"Shh. Let's not think like that. A lot can happen in two days. Maybe you should go home and get some rest."

"I don't think I could. It's almost like watching Momma all over again. Wanting to get in every last second, just in case."

"I know, honey." He wrapped his arm around me. "At least close your eyes."

I set my smoothie down, curled my feet under me, snuggled in the best I could on his shoulder, and rested my eyes. I saw flashes of Tom falling out of his chair and his eyes rolling back. I squeezed my eyes tighter. Then I replayed the conversation I'd had with Miss June, over and over again. The grief had made her high. It was the only explanation for her thinking I should fight for Brooks. Not happening. Now, if Brooks wanted to fight for me . . . nope. Nope. Not going down that road. It didn't matter that he had a great excuse for ditching me on prom night, he was still an arrogant jerk. And I didn't even know him anymore. You know, other than that he was beautiful. However, that wasn't a basis for a good relationship. Not to say it wouldn't help.

What was I even thinking? I was supposed to be here cheering for Tom and lending him emotional support, not thinking about ripping his son's shirt off so I could rub those broad shoulders again and asking him for pointers on kissing. Ooh, I bet he had some even better ones now. *Stop it, Gracie.*

I must have dozed off, because the next thing I knew, Daddy was kissing my head and saying, "Honey, I'm going to go wait in the waiting room."

"Huh?" I lifted my head.

"I need to go wait outside, since there can only be two visitors at a time." Daddy smiled.

I blinked several times, trying to comprehend what Daddy was saying. "It's only us," I slurred.

Daddy pointed at the door.

I turned my head slowly, and there stood Brooks, looking like he was dressed for court in his suit and tie. Holy crow. Could I ever run into him when I was wearing something sexy or at least had my hair done? Or better yet, my teeth brushed? I sat up straight. "I can go," I offered.

Daddy rested his hand on my shoulder, holding me in place. Which was an unusual move for him. "I think it would be best if you stayed."

I usually never disagreed with Daddy, but I had some serious objections. Yet, before I could voice them, Daddy was at the door and patting Brooks's arm. "Tom will be happy you're here." Daddy walked off without another word.

Brooks watched him go, and then he turned his sights on me. He ran his hand through his hair. "When did you get here?"

I uncurled my legs and let them drop to the floor. "I never left."

"Oh. I figured since you weren't wearing your magically delicious shirt, you went home." His lips twitched.

"If I wear it too long, it will lose its charm."

"I doubt it."

My brow raised, surprised by his flirtations.

Brooks hemmed and hawed at the door.

I patted the seat next to me. "I won't bite."

"How about squeeze my nose?"

I shrugged playfully. "We'll play it by ear."

With a smile, Brooks hesitantly took a step, then froze when he looked at Tom, who looked more machine than man right now. Brooks flexed his fingers several times. With each flex of his fingers, his face turned a deeper shade of red.

"He hates himself more than you will ever hate him," I whispered.

Brooks jerked his head my way. "I wouldn't be too sure about that."

"I don't want to argue with you again this morning, but you're wrong." Admittedly, I felt a tad guilty for being so salty the night before.

Brooks relaxed some. "I don't want to argue with you either."

"How disappointing," I teased. "Does that mean you think I'm right?"

"No." He strode my way as if he were daring himself to get closer to his daddy. He dropped onto the seat next to me. "I promised my mother I would be courteous to you if I saw you today."

I scrunched my nose. "What's with your formality? Mother? Courteous? Did they teach you that in law school?"

"I find people take me more seriously when I drop the accent and speak properly."

"Properly? You grew up in Texas, and we have mommas down here; and we aren't courteous, we have manners. The kind of manners where you wouldn't have to promise your *momma* you would be kind to me—that would already be a given."

His left eyebrow arched so debonairly I wanted to swoon. "Am I the only one expected to have manners?"

I slapped my chest. "Are you suggesting that I don't? I'm hurt." I smirked.

"You are just like I remember."

"And how would that be?"

"Infuriating but . . ." He paused.

"But what?"

He stared blankly at the monitor displaying Tom's vitals. "Never mind."

"Oh no, you can't make a statement like that and not finish it."

"Of course I can."

"Fine. I'll finish it for you. Let's go with infuriating but irresistible."

He chuckled while rubbing his neck. "I'll let you have that."

That made my pulse tick up a bit. "So, uh, how is your momma this morning?"

Brooks was looking everywhere but at his daddy. "She's resting now, and then she's going to pick up Carly and her family from the airport later."

"I bet she's excited to see her grandsons, at least."

Brooks flashed me a genuine smile. "We both are."

That surprised me. I wondered what kind of uncle Brooks was to Carly's boys.

"Are they all staying with you?"

"I suppose," he sighed, not sounding thrilled. "My condo isn't designed for houseguests."

Why didn't it surprise me that he lived in a condo? "You know, they could stay at your daddy's. I have a key, and the house is in great condition. Plenty of room for everyone. Besides, it's closer to the hospital."

One thing Tom hadn't let go of was the home he had raised his family in. It was almost sad how religiously he had kept it clean and just the way it had always been. Honestly, it looked as if it were frozen in 1999. The house was filled with big, clunky wood pieces. The entertainment center alone probably weighed a couple of tons. The floral furniture was so retro it was adorable. Tom had even covered it in plastic to preserve it. He loved telling us how June had dragged him around for months, going to every furniture store in Texas, until she had found the perfect living room set. He talked the salesman into giving them the set off the showroom floor so June didn't have to wait any longer.

"I don't know." Brooks seemed uneasy with the thought. Probably because it might mean that he would actually have to come home.

"Think about it."

"I will. So, what did you do all night here?" He seemed anxious to change the subject.

"Mostly talked to him and caught up on our book club reading for the month."

"I can't believe you and Tom have a book club."

I refrained from rolling my eyes. "Your *daddy* thought it would keep his mind sharp, and he likes to do it as a way to connect with Carly. This month we're reading *Twilight* because it's Carly's favorite book."

"The book about sparkly vampires?" Brooks cringed.

"You make it sound so bad." I grinned.

"I never understood the appeal. The main character sounded like a stalker, climbing through her window and watching her sleep at night."

"How do you know he did that?"

Brooks's ears tinged pink. "I dated a woman who was obsessed with it."

"Morgan?" I did my best to not snarl her name.

"No. She has more sense than to read such foolishness."

I tilted my head. "Why is it foolishness? Just because it isn't one person's cup of tea, doesn't mean that it doesn't have value. The book obviously filled a need, judging by its popularity when it first came out."

"What need would that be?" He sounded like he was putting me on trial.

"The need to be loved at any cost."

"That's a fantasy."

"Perhaps. Every relationship involves some risk—women want to know that the person they love thinks they're worth it."

He studied me for a moment, and a slight softness washed over his features, making me think he was beginning to understand. Until he opened his mouth again. "Men need to stalk women to prove this?"

I sighed loudly. "You're obviously missing the point. But . . . ," I gave him a crooked grin, "if I remember correctly, there used to be this boy who would crawl through my window at night unbeknownst to my daddy. Would you consider yourself a stalker?"

Brooks's face turned redder than the apple on the cover of *Twilight*. "That was innocent," he stammered. "We were friends."

That was true. Despite how badly I used to wish it wasn't all innocent. Each time he'd knocked on my window after climbing our trellis, this tiny shred of hope had appeared. Hope that maybe that night would be the night he would want to do more than just listen to music and talk. Brooks was an old soul who had loved artists like Cat Stevens and Eric Clapton. He would replay certain guitar riffs and give me the history behind the song. Unfortunately, he'd never appreciated Rick Springfield for the musical legend he was. Nor had Brooks known how I'd longed for his kisses, especially after he'd given me a taste of one. However, the kisses never came, and eventually he stopped coming too.

"Friends," I whispered. "You know, I should give you some time alone with your daddy. For some reason you seem to bring out my snarky side, and I would hate for you to break your promise to your momma." I stood.

Brooks unexpectedly reached for my hand. "Please don't go," he begged like a child.

I stood stunned for a moment by his actions before I came to my senses and registered his plea. I squeezed his hand back, feeling so many things. Everything from belonging to anger—anger at myself for still feeling so attracted and connected to him. "Brooks, you're going to have to face him sooner or later. And there may not be a later," I cried.

"I know. Please stay." He gently tugged on my hand.

I eased back onto my chair. He kept a hold of my hand, just like the night after my momma had died when I had needed his comfort so desperately. The way he held my hand told me he needed that same comfort now. As much as it hurt and confused me, I would give my old friend that.

"Thank you," he whispered.

"You're welcome."

There we sat in silence, other than the sounds of the machines, for the better part of an hour, watching over Tom. Occasionally Brooks would run his thumb across my hand, and I would have to stop myself from shivering. Yet we never said a word. In my mind, though, I was having all kinds of conversations with myself and the pesky voice that had decided to make an appearance again. The voice and I fought over all the reasons Brooks and I were wrong for each other, no matter how right it felt sitting next to him and holding his hand. My reoccurring argument was that he was dating Morgan and hated marriage, according to his momma. I was smart enough to recognize that those factoids didn't bode well for me. And Brooks had never seen me as anything other than a friend.

Amid my silent battle, Brooks abruptly stood and rushed toward the door. Once the automatic doors opened, he looked back, his intense gaze centered on me. "Grace . . ."

"Yes?"

He didn't respond, other than shaking his head before he strode out like the devil himself was after him.

I took Tom's hand. "Did that seem weird to you?" Mentally, I heard Tom give an emphatic yes. "I agree. Definitely weird."

Chapter Eight

"You are a knotty girl." Colette loved to make that joke when she rubbed my neck and back. She was truly a goddess among women, with the most magical hands on the planet.

I closed my eyes while Colette worked out the kinks in my back. I didn't care how strange it must have looked to everyone dining in the surprisingly nice hospital cafeteria. It was set up like a restaurant with circular tables, and the roof was glass, so it looked like we were in an atrium. They even had classical music playing in the background.

"Sitting up all night in a chair will do that to you."

Lorelai sat across from us, typing notes. We were multitasking. Not only were the two best friends ever giving me a much-needed break by bringing me dinner, but they were helping me plan my twenty-year high school reunion. It was less than two months away. I'd had a hard time recruiting any of my old classmates to help—except for a few who were unbelievably unreliable or lived out of town—so my girls jumped in. Sadly, people didn't want to help, though they were more than happy to come.

"Maybe you should go home tonight and rest," Lorelai suggested. "Let his family take the night shift."

My bed sounded glorious, as did a shower that lasted longer than the five-minute one I'd taken when I'd gone home earlier after Carly and June had arrived. I'd wanted to give mother and daughter time alone to be with

Tom and each other. Family relations, I think, were strained on all ends, even though both Carly's and Brooks's loyalties lay with their momma. Carly had recently inched the door open to repairing her relationship with her daddy, so I think this was hitting her harder than anyone. She had sobbed all over my head when we'd seen each other earlier—a real danger when you had tall friends, and hence the need for a shower. I'd never found snot to be a good hair product.

"I have to stay. They're going to start warming Tom's temperature back to normal tonight. They're also going to ease him off sedation. He might wake up," I said, more out of hope than anything. The odds were that he was never going to regain consciousness, but I had to believe. Tom wouldn't want me to give up on him like almost everyone else had. My heart couldn't take the thought either.

Lorelai reached across the table, took my hand, and squeezed it. "I'll be praying, darlin'."

"Thank you." I squeezed back.

Colette's hands moved up to my neck, where she skillfully kneaded the tense muscles. "Will Brooks be coming back?"

I shrugged.

Lorelai flashed Colette an impish grin. "Would you like me to make him date thirty-six? Perhaps you could use your feminine wiles on him and he'll change his mind about writing a poor review about our spa."

"No, thank you. He's not my type," I lied. "Besides, he's dating someone."

Lorelai laughed while Colette patted my head.

"Would you rather take hobbit boy to your reunion?" Colette asked.

"Y'all know our history. Because of him, I have some weird need to recreate my prom. No way am I letting him spoil my night, again. Besides, he hasn't even RSVP'd, and technically, since he was our class president, he should be spearheading this. But, according to the organizer of our ten-year reunion, he told her reunions were a waste of time," I whispered for some reason, even though I didn't expect Brooks to come back. In fact, his momma was madder than a hatter at him, because instead of being at the hospital, he and Morgan were attending some live TED Talk tonight about what happens when you donate your brain to science. June had quipped that she wished Brooks would get a brain and dump Morgan. I felt like that was a reasonable wish.

Colette removed her glorious hands from my neck and took the seat next to me. Her gorgeous sea-green eyes were all lit up. She was honestly the cutest thing, with her dark pixie-cut hair. Not many women could pull that off, but she had the best cheekbones on the planet and a sweetheart-shaped face. She was the youngest of the three of us at thirty-six. Like me, she had never been married or had children. She was more okay with it than me. At least she wasn't taking ovulation tests every month. "What if," she breathed out, "fate is giving you a chance at a full redo?"

"Ooo. Yes." Lorelai closed the lid to her laptop. "I can feel the powerful energy of that statement. I mean, what are the odds that he shows up at our spa? And not to be too morbid, but the timing of his daddy's illness might not be coincidental either. It's like the stars are aligning and pulling you together."

I loved Lorelai and honestly believed in energy healing, yet sometimes she took things too far. "Ladies, I love you both more than my signed *Working Class Dog* Rick Springfield album—the one he sweated on—but you're both a little nutty."

"I don't know. I agree with Lorelai. Something just feels right about all of this," Colette sighed dreamily.

"His daddy could be dying. There's nothing right about that," I said without any bite.

"No one is saying that, darlin'. However, God works in mysterious ways. And from the sound of it, I would say he's trying to kill ten birds with one stone." Lorelai was ever the optimist.

I waved them off. The only stone God needed to send was the one to knock me upside the head. I needed to forget about Brooks. "Let's change the subject, shall we? How many tickets have we sold?" I hated talking money or details at a time like this, but people were counting on me. And Tom and Daddy, bless their souls, had already donated a lot of their own money to the Class of 1999 Alumni Association, a.k.a. my pet project. Tom would want me to go through with this. I had to admit, I needed the distraction too. The last couple of days had been like an emotional hurricane.

Lorelai opened her laptop and pulled up the spreadsheet where we were keeping track of all the tickets sold and the expenses. She scrolled down. "To date, we have sold fifty-six single tickets and one hundred and two double tickets, including yours." She wagged her brows. "The question is, Who will your double be?"

I rubbed my temples. "I'm working on it. Do either of you have any other fresh bodies?"

Both ladies thought.

"My pastor is single," Colette chirped.

"Hmm. How does he feel about dirty dancing?" I teased, sort of. I liked to get up close and personal when I danced.

Colette giggled. "Well . . . he did give a sermon last week on how evil can be disguised as anything, including music. He probably wouldn't appreciate the playlist we gave the DJ. But he's pretty cute. He even has dimples." She was a sucker for those.

"Maybe you should ask him out, then."

"I can't take that kind of pressure. I would probably use a dozen four-letter words out of nervousness before we even made it to dinner. By the time dessert arrived, he would probably know every sin I'd ever committed. And the list is long, mind you." She winked. "Then I would have to find a new church, and I'm too lazy for that."

"So, no pastors." I smiled. "Lorelai? Anyone?"

Lorelai was scrolling through her contacts. "Let's see. Have I mentioned Dane Barret yet?" she hesitantly asked.

I had to stop and think. The list was getting ridiculously long. "I don't think so."

Lorelai nibbled on her bottom lip and contemplated. "He was one of William's old buddies," she whispered. "He's a bit rough around the edges. He was in the military for a long time, but he's been back for a while now. He's a professional cowboy."

"Intriguing."

"He's ruggedly handsome, and last time I saw him he was still in great shape. If memory serves me correctly, he has normal feet," she giggled. She never showed me pictures; I wanted to go in completely blind. I figured that's how the voice worked—by surprise.

"Perfect. How does he feel about blind dates?"

"After I show him a picture of you, I would say he'll be a big fan."

I ran my fingers through my uninhibited hair. "Don't snap any of me today—I'm a hot mess. The bags under my eyes need their own zip code." Even though I never wanted to see a picture of the men beforehand, I had no qualms letting them see me—just in case I repulsed them. This way they could back out beforehand.

"At least it's prime real estate," Colette quipped.

"Aww. Now if I can find someone who would like to move in permanently," I lamented.

"You will," Lorelai reassured me.

I nodded, somewhat hopeful. "Okay, now back to business. I talked to the graphic artist, and he should have some designs for us to choose from for the commemorative T-shirts that we'll have available for purchase. And I've narrowed it down to two photographers." I pulled out my phone to show them each photographer's website. "What do you think—"

"Hello, Grace," a debonair voice said from behind me.

I fumbled my phone before dropping it on the table. What was *he* doing here? I thought he was at a TED Talk.

Lorelai's and Colette's eyes lasered in on Brooks. Meanwhile I froze in place, not daring to turn around. Then I remembered I'd had poppy seed dressing on my salad. Surely Lorelai or Colette would have told me if I had a poppy seed or two stuck in my teeth. I wanted to flash Lorelai a smile to check for me, but she was mesmerized with the man who stood behind me. I couldn't exactly blame her; he was beautiful to look at.

I had almost gained enough courage to turn around when I heard a voice from the past that I could have done without. I began to silently pray she had gotten ugly or lost all her teeth. I hated myself for being like that. Momma used to say envy was 90 percent of what was wrong with this world. Specifically, she used to tell me that being jealous of Morgan was like a finger being jealous of a thumb. "The hand needs both to function properly," she would say. Then she would smooth my brow and whisper, "The world needs Gracies and Morgans."

I would reply, "But does Brooks need us both?"

Momma would smile and respond, "Yes, but I hope for his sake and yours, he'll see why he needs you more." That had always been my wish, although it was never coming true.

"Gracie Cartwright, it has been a long time." Her smooth-as-silk voice wafted in the air, making me want to barf up my dinner.

I had no choice but to turn around, making sure not to smile in case of a rogue poppy seed. "Morgan. Brooks. How unexpected," was all I could think of to say while I gawked at the pair. Brooks was still dressed in a suit and tie. Did he ever wear casual clothing? And Morgan, well let's just say she hadn't gotten ugly and she still had all her gleaming, straight, white teeth. On top of that, she matched Brooks perfectly in her board-room suit. Apparently, her love for the pencil skirt still lived on. And her voluptuous chest was accented by her tailored jacket. So maybe, just maybe, I saw a strand of gray in her mocha-colored hair. And, if I was being snarky, it didn't shine like it used to. Yet it didn't matter, because she was still beautiful. She and Brooks looked like the perfect power couple. Oddly, though, they weren't touching. If Brooks were my boyfriend, you better believe I would have my hands on him 24-7.

Morgan eyed me with the same interest as I had given her. I couldn't tell by her narrowed blue eyes if she found me to be a joke in my skinny jeans and *I Would Rather Be Watching General Hospital* sweatshirt, or if she loathed me. Maybe some of both, by the way her lips pursed together like she had just sucked on a lemon.

Brooks cleared his throat. "We came to check on my mother, and I thought she might like a cup of coffee."

"How nice." I turned toward my friends, who, by the looks of pure pleasure on their faces, were apparently enthralled with this entire scenario. "These are my best friends and business partners, Colette and Lore-lai."

Brooks was surprisingly well mannered and stepped forward to shake their hands. "Yes, I remember you both from the spa."

Morgan's microbladed eyebrows shot up. "Serenity Spa?"

"Yes." A smile a mile-wide spread across my face. I'd forgotten all about being embarrassed about possible poppy seeds. "We are the lucky owners."

"Well, you should fire your aesthetician, Jane. I'd heard such positive things about your place, but that woman sounded absolutely vile."

Brooks cleared his throat. "Morgan, that's probably an exaggeration."

FACIAL RECOGNITION

I wondered why he hadn't mentioned to Morgan that I was a co-owner or the aesthetician in question. "Oh, don't worry, Jane is history."

Lorelai and Colette giggled.

Morgan gave them a scathing look that made me flinch. Holy crow.

Colette didn't bat an eye. "You know, Brooks, we would love to make it up to you. Your next visit is on us, and this time we'll pair you with our best aesthetician . . . Gracie." Oh, she was wickedly good.

Morgan about choked on her tongue.

Brooks, on the other hand, gave me a half smile. "Perhaps I'll take you up on it."

"You never know," Lorelai sang. "You may decide to change your review afterward."

"Possibly," he responded a little too cockily.

Morgan grabbed his hand and held it like a vise. "I don't know if you'll have the time, Brooks. Our schedule is packed the next several weeks." She directed her attention to me specifically. "Maybe you heard—I'm the newly appointed vice president of my bank."

Why would I have heard that?

"And as such," she continued, "I have to go to a lot of community events. I'm the face of the bank."

"You should make sure to put that in your bio for the reunion," Colette backhandedly mocked her.

"Reunion?" Morgan's face pinched together.

"Our twenty-year high school reunion is coming up. We're the planning committee," I informed her.

Lorelai held up the laptop. "It looks like y'all haven't responded. You should get tickets now before they go up in price next week. Should I put you down as a double or single ticket?" she asked with a hint of evil.

Brooks and Morgan both looked appalled at the thought, with crinkled brows and sneers.

"I didn't get an invitation." Morgan sounded offended, though she stood taller, which was saying something, as she was already straight as a pin. "It's probably because I traveled so much with my last position. I've always been a highly sought-after asset. People just can't do without me."

I refrained from gagging on her self-importance. I might have accidentally left her off the mailing list. I mean, I didn't have a current address, and I thought sending one to her parents' home was a waste of a stamp. At least that was the story I was sticking to.

Her next statement proved me right. "However, reunions," Morgan scoffed, "are for people who peaked in their pasts. We," she yanked Brooks right up next to her, "are all about our futures."

I glared at Brooks, who looked a tad embarrassed at his girlfriend's over-the-top behavior, and then at Morgan, feeling every bit of the slight she'd tossed at me. "We will have to agree to disagree. I feel a person who forgets the past somehow never makes peace with their future." I swiveled back around. "Please mark them off our list," I said to Lorelai. To Brooks and Morgan I mumbled, "We'll make sure you don't get any correspondence from us again."

And don't worry, Brooks, I'm marking you off my list too.

"By the way, you have a poppy seed between your front teeth," Morgan threw in with such an air of haughtiness she was probably floating on cloud nine.

Of course I did. I wanted to respond that it was better than having a stick shoved between my buttocks like the big one she was sporting. Instead I went with, "Oh, thank you, Morgan. What would I ever do without you?"

Chapter Nine

"I hope you don't mind that I stayed," Carly whispered as we watched over her father late into the night. We had each taken a side and carefully held his hands, as he was fitted with so many tubes and IVs. The semidark room glowed with all the machinery used to keep Tom alive.

"Of course not. He's your daddy."

She tucked some of her long-bobbed, ash-colored hair back behind her ear. For being twins, she and Brooks didn't have similar coloring. Carly was fairer, with eyes that were much lighter, and they were softer than Brooks's.

"You've been more of a daughter to him. Whenever we did talk, he always mentioned how good you've been to him. I was both jealous and relieved."

"I know it's complicated. I'm glad you're here, though. I've missed you."

Her eyes misted over. "I've been the worst sort of friend. I went back on every promise I ever made, including having you be the maid of honor at my wedding. I'm so sorry, Gracie. Everything just got so messed up."

As hurt as I had been about that, it all didn't seem to matter in this moment that teetered on life and death. "Please don't apologize. You're here now, and that's what matters."

"Does it?" she begged to know.

"I think so."

"Brooks mentioned being able to stay at the house." She swallowed. "I think I would like that. I want my boys to know their granddad's house. My house."

"Tom would love that. He just had the pool cleaned, so it's ready to be used." I usually did laps in the morning come late spring and into the summer. There was a gate between our two yards that allowed me access.

"The pool." She grinned. "We spent a lot of good times there, didn't we?"

I smiled, thinking about all the ogling I had done of Brooks in his Hawaiian-style swim trunks. Then I reminded myself I wasn't going to think about him or Morgan anymore. "Yours was the party house." Almost every cheer team party we'd had was at their place. We had all loved to admire Brooks. And he'd made sure to come out and strut his stuff, insisting it was all in the name of safety. He had been our designated lifeguard. Man, how I had contemplated faking drowning. I'd wanted some mouth to mouth from him. Ugh, there I went thinking about him again.

"You were always the best party planner, though. Still are. The reunion sounds amazing, except I want to lose fifteen pounds before the big day."

"You look great."

She looked down at her tall body. She was thick boned like her momma, but she wore it well and confidently. It was a Hamilton trait.

"Not as good as you. Please tell me your secret. You haven't changed at all over the years."

"It's the dim lighting."

"I don't think so. You have Brooks in a tizzy, I'll tell you that."

I shifted in my seat. "I irritate him, is all."

"Right," she impishly gleamed. "I suppose that's why Morgan was reprimanding him earlier in the waiting room."

"She was? Why?"

"Something about how Brooks should have mentioned that you owned the spa, and she would have appreciated it if he would have backed her up more about not attending the reunion."

"Hmm. Well, they seem like a solid couple, so I wouldn't read too much into it."

"Ugh. Please don't say that. I'd hoped after twenty years Morgan would have mellowed, but she's just as controlling as ever. I've never understood why Brooks, who never lets anyone boss him around, has let Morgan call the shots with him."

"She is beautiful, and men seem to love the chase."

"Huh. I never saw her as very pretty. She has this coldness to her that makes her unattractive."

I could see what she was saying, but there was no question that Morgan was gorgeous.

"I only hope my brother realizes that before she leads him to another dead end and breaks his heart again."

I shrugged, pretending not to care whether he got his heart broken by Morgan. Yet, my heart broke a little knowing she had the power to wreck his. A power I'd never had nor would ever possess. Not that I wanted to hurt him. I had only wanted to love him and make him happy. Things, apparently, he didn't value. Which was why I really needed to stop thinking about him.

"Tell me how life in California is." I needed to change the subject.

She gave me a small smile. "Really good," she said almost guiltily. "Dillon's a portfolio manager and the best dad and husband around. I think our boys love him more than they love me, which is okay because sometimes at the end of the day, I'm ready to sell them on Etsy."

I chuckled. "Their pictures on Facebook are darling, so you could probably charge a decent amount," I teased.

She broke into fits of laughter. "Oh, Gracie, I've missed your sense of humor and your friendship. Momma and I were talking earlier about how we've all missed you."

"Not Brooks, which is fine," I made sure to add in.

She tilted her head. "That's not true. Honestly, when we were growing up, I was kind of jealous of the bond you two had. In some ways, I think you were more connected to my twin than I ever was."

I shook my head to disagree.

"No, it's true. I think Brooks felt safe to be who he really wanted to be around you."

"What do you mean?"

"Even though Brooks and I were technically minutes apart, he always took on the role of the oldest sibling. Type A all the way. He was all about reaching his goals. I mean, the only reason he ran for class president was because it would look good on his college applications. I think he would have preferred to skip high school altogether, if he could have. But you brought out this side in him no one else seemed to. And I know he was sneaking into your room at night."

I blushed, even though nothing had ever happened. "Um . . . we were only listening to music."

"I know. I spied on you a couple of times," she admitted.

"What?" I laughed.

She bit her lip. "I thought maybe you guys were having some secret love affair. I mean, you flirted with each other all the time."

"Not really. It was me, not him," I reluctantly admitted. I had never told Carly I was in love with her brother back in the day. It went against some unwritten code about not dating your best friend's brother. Even when I'd asked him to prom, I'd told her it was only as a friend. Though I wasn't sure she had ever believed it.

"No, Brooks was just always bad at flirting. But he was a better person with you. The nights I watched you two, I saw a side of Brooks I never had before. The way his eyes lit up when he was talking about music, which was something I hadn't even know he was into. He'd hidden it, almost as if it would make him seem weak or like a human. More amazing was seeing him listen to your music, and though he balked at it, I could tell it made him happy. You made him happy, Gracie. In a way I'd never seen then, nor since."

I tucked some hair behind my ear, begging myself not to believe her. It was detrimental to my heart and plans. "I'm sure Morgan makes him happy. Why else would he be with her?"

She let out a huge exasperated sigh. "That's a good question. One I've been trying to figure out since high school. At least he plans on never getting married, so I'll never have to have her as a sister-in-law."

I grabbed my stomach. Why did that feel like such a sucker punch? Probably because I heard strange voices. "I guess that's good."

"It's sad is what it is. He would be such a great daddy. You should see him with my boys. Not only does he spoil them rotten, but those boys use him for a jungle gym, and he loves it."

I could picture it, and it was adorable. Too adorable. So adorable, I shouldn't think about it.

"Maybe he'll change his mind," I offered her.

Carly stared at her daddy. "I don't know. When your hero falls, it does something to you. Not only does it make you see how weak that person is but how susceptible you are too. And for Brooks, that is more than he can bear. I think he believes that by not getting married, he can say he was always better than Daddy."

Tears pricked my eyes. *Poor Brooks.* It was a dangerous thought. I couldn't allow myself to develop feelings for him again—or more accurately, I couldn't let those feelings resurface. Being near him was only a reminder they hadn't gone away. Was it pathetic that the only time I'd ever really loved someone was in high school? I had really liked some men. I'd even had some long-term relationships along the way, but I'd never felt a connection like I'd had with Brooks. That had been all one sided, though. Or had it? No. No. I couldn't think like that. I had to find the perfect reunion date, and thoughts like that weren't going to help my cause.

"I really am sorry, Carly. Your daddy is too."

She turned my way. Tears filled her eyes too. "I just hope he wakes up so I can tell him that I forgive him."

"Me too."

Chapter Ten

"I know you're cheating." I flipped Tom's cards over for him. He had a royal flush. I showed Tom his cards, begging him silently to open his eyes. "You're on fire tonight; you should really wake up and take all my money."

Tom didn't move an inch.

"Come on now. We are way past being dramatic. You've made your point. You better wake up or I'm going to stack the deck." I gathered the cards together and began shuffling them. "Seriously, Tom, you have to wake up. You're family's all here. Even Ryker and Axel came. They can't visit you in the ICU, so you need to open those mischievous eyes of yours. Look at the cards they made you." I grabbed the two bright and colorful handmade cards and giggled. "Little Axel looks like he's choking you in this one, but I'm pretty sure he's hugging your neck."

"Please, Tom," I whispered. "It's been seventy-two hours. Thankfully the neurologist says we should give you more time. And good news, your EEG says you have brain activity. I bet you're arguing with yourself right now. Debating whether your life is worth waking up for. Well, it is," I cried. "June's been here, and let me tell you, she's looking pretty fine. She still has some meat to her, as you would say. And Carly, she's so sorry. She wants you in her life. She's even staying at the house. Isn't that great?"

I dealt us each a hand. "I know you're wondering about Brooks. He hasn't been by in a couple of days, but we don't need him. He's probably been going to TED Talks about how to properly tie your shoe, or something just as ridiculous."

I peeked at my cards. "Yikes. I should have worn my magically delicious shirt. I think you really are cheating."

The sliding door opened, and my head popped up. I was expecting to see Tom's overnight nurse; instead I was greeted by a familiar but surprising face.

"Knock, knock, I hope I'm not intruding." Julian Bronson, or should I say Dr. Bronson, Morgan's brother, walked in, wearing green scrubs and looking dog tired with red eyes and a serious layer of scruff on his chiseled jaw.

I set my cards down on Tom. I hoped he didn't mind that I was using him for our card table. "What are you doing here? Shouldn't you be in labor and delivery?"

He chuckled lowly. "Just came from there. I delivered a ten-pound baby tonight."

"Yikes. That makes my insides hurt." Not to say I wouldn't do it in a heartbeat. What I wouldn't give to pop out a chunky baby. The question still remained, though. What was Julian doing here?

His tired violet eyes livened up the closer he got to me. "Rumor has it you've been living here for the past few days."

I tilted my head. "Who have you been talking to?"

He flashed a smile reminiscent of his sister's. Big and toothy. They probably both had gotten caps. "Didn't you hear? I'm practically related to the Hamiltons now."

I accidentally inhaled the gum I had been chewing and started choking on it, sputtering and hardly able to catch my breath. While I embarrassed myself and tried to hack up my gum, horrible scenes flashed before my eyes of Morgan and Brooks walking down the aisle. Dang, did Morgan look perfect in her trumpet gown. Brooks was dashing in his black tux. Ryker and Axel were darling ring bearers, except they started fighting and the rings went flying. Carly dove to catch them in slow motion. Okay, that was pretty hilarious.

What wasn't funny was that I was choking to death. Julian rushed over to me and started pounding on my back. "Are you okay?"

I finally coughed up my gum and took a huge breath. "I'm fine," I eked out. You know, except my heart felt as if it had been bludgeoned to death. I thought Brooks had sworn off marriage.

"Good. For a minute there I thought you might need mouth to mouth." He wagged his brows.

I thought he was married. "Um . . . why are you here?"

Without an invitation, he pulled up the extra chair and sat next to me. "Brooks and Morgan mentioned last night at dinner that you'd been staying here."

So, Brooks was throwing dinner parties while his daddy was dying? Or maybe . . . "Did Brooks and Morgan get engaged last night?"

"Engaged?" he chuckled. "Let's hope not. Those two are like moths to a flame—eventually they'll go up in smoke. They always do."

Huh. That was an interesting take. One I would have liked to get more information about, but I was too busy internally breathing a sigh of relief. Which was dumb, as I had sworn off Brooks forever. "But I thought you said you were practically related."

He rested his masculine, missing-a-wedding-ring hand on my shoulder. "Figure of speech, darlin'."

I stared at his hand. "Oh. Well . . . how's your wife? I'm sorry, I don't remember her name."

Julian dropped his hand. "Our divorce was finalized last month."

Holy crow. Three divorces. "I'm sorry to hear that."

He shrugged. "You win some, you lose some." His eyes drifted toward the cards on Tom. "Looks like you are about ready to lose this hand."

"Tom's cheating," my voice cracked, betraying my emotions. I normally held it together during the day, but there was something about being here late at night, alone with just Tom and the nurses. Hope faded in the darkness.

Julian took my hand. It caught me so off guard, I numbly let him. It's not like I felt anything.

"Would you like to talk? I'm told I have an excellent bedside manner."

I couldn't tell if he was being sincere or propositioning me. Either way, I took my hand back. "I appreciate it. Although I'm sure you're tired and want to get home." It was nearing midnight.

"I'm happy to keep you company for a while longer. It's been a long time since we've caught up."

I narrowed my eyes at him. We had never been friends. Merely casual acquaintances, because in Pecan Orchard, that was the way of life. Everyone knew everyone. He had been three grades above me, and over the years all our interactions had been brief. "Not to be rude, but I don't remember us ever having anything to catch up on."

His eyes danced while he spat out a laugh. "My apologies. I would like to remedy that as soon as possible."

I wasn't sure what to say, and before I had to say anything, the door slid open, and in walked Brooks—with a purpose. Like he was practically marching our way, which I thought was unusual. Last time he had been here, he had approached with trepidation. Not only was I stunned by his sudden arrival, but his tight jeans and T-shirt had my heart betraying me and beating double time. Schnikeys, was he beautiful. I kept telling myself to look away, or at the very least not like what I saw, but it was hopeless, and apparently so was I. Why couldn't I just get over him? It had been twenty years, and he was dating the mistress of darkness.

Brooks's chocolate eyes darted between me and Julian, his scowl growing bigger and bigger. I guess he wanted to be alone. That was probably a good idea.

I popped up. "I was just uh . . ." Oh crap, I had lost all brain function. *Think of something, Gracie.* "Pepsi, yeah, Pepsi." *Holy crow, you sound like an idiot.* "I mean Diet Pepsi." *Yeah, that sounded better.* "I mean I'm going to get a Diet Pepsi." I practically tripped over my feet in my rush to get moving. I had to hold on to the chair before I killed myself. *Could I act more like a nutjob?*

Julian jumped up. "I'll go with you."

Brooks clenched his hands, and his face turned a lovely shade of crimson as he stared at Julian. "I need to speak to Grace."

No he didn't. That wasn't going to be any good for Grace. *Why was I thinking about myself in the third person?*

Julian looked between me and Brooks with a crooked smirk. "I'll wait for you, Gracie, and we can get that drink."

Why did I feel as if I were trapped in a no-win game?

"It could be a while," Brooks growled.

That wasn't helping my situation. At. All.

"I'm used to pulling all-nighters." It sounded like Julian was taunting Brooks.

This was getting weird.

"You know, maybe you two should stay. I'm sure you have some things to talk about." I scooted past Julian and was about ready to sprint past Brooks when he gently grabbed my arm.

His eyes zeroed in on my own, holding me in place. "Please stay."

Under his penetrating gaze, my resolve began to weaken. I saw the boy I had loved in his pleading eyes. I tried to grasp for all the reasons I should go. I kept trying to form words, but nothing was coming. When I couldn't respond, Brooks said, "Please, Grace."

There he went using my name again. Did he know the power that it carried?

"For a few minutes," I relented.

Brooks gave me a half smile before jerking his head toward Julian. "There are only two visitors allowed at a time. The nurse told me you would have to leave."

Julian gave him a look that said *touché* before setting his sights on me. "I'm sure we will see each other again. Soon, I hope. I owe you a drink. I'll throw in dinner too."

"Um, okay," I stuttered, before fully realizing what I was agreeing to. These men were throwing my brain out of whack.

Julian strode by, making sure to flash Brooks a wide grin. "Be sure to say hello to my sister for me." That sounded an awful lot like a warning. If Julian thought Brooks had any interest in me, he was sorely mistaken.

"Will do." Brooks let my arm go.

I faltered, then steadied myself. I ended up backed up against the sink the doctors and nurses used to wash their hands.

"Goodbye, Gracie." Julian waved.

I half-heartedly waved back.

Brooks watched Julian leave, and as soon as the door closed, he turned toward me and growled, "You should be careful around him. He has a less than desirable track record with women."

"Thank you for your concern, but Julian isn't the one for me." I was confused by his obvious irritation.

"Are you seeing someone?" His voice hitched.

"I try and go on one blind date a week."

His brow arched. "Why?"

"I'm testing out a theory," I admitted, a bit embarrassed.

FACIAL RECOGNITION

"What theory?"

"I like to call it facial recognition. I won't bore you with the details." More like we needed to quit talking so I could leave his overwhelming presence. He was proving my facial recognition theory right, and that I couldn't have. "Where's Morgan?" I asked, flustered.

"I assume at her apartment, but I don't know. I haven't seen her tonight."

I know it shouldn't have made me happy to hear that, but it did. "Why are you here?"

He ran a hand through his hair. "I couldn't sleep." His gaze landed on his daddy. "I've been thinking a lot."

"I'm sure you have. I'll give you some privacy."

"Grace," he turned back toward me. "I've been thinking a lot about you too."

I felt as if I'd been dipped in hot wax, warm and immobilized. "You're still mad about the facial massage?" I went the teasing route, because the way he was looking at me wasn't helping my resolve. Honestly, he looked like he might want to devour me, and I was going to let him order me off the menu.

He stepped closer to me. "Perhaps a little, but that's not what I've been thinking about."

I gripped the counter behind me. "What's been on your mind?" I stuttered, breathless.

"Our friendship."

My stomach dropped. Right. I sank where I stood. Friends. It's all we ever were. "It was a long time ago. No need for you to be worried about it now. I should go."

He inched ever closer. "Why won't you let me get out what I want to say?" he pleaded.

I closed my eyes, thinking for a reasonable answer because I couldn't tell the truth.

"Grace." He was close enough to feel. His warm, inviting scent filled my senses.

I slowly opened my eyes and was met with his imploring ones. "Didn't Morgan say neither of you like to live in the past?"

His shoulders rose and fell. "That came out more callous than she intended."

Please tell me he didn't believe that.

"My past is complicated, but, Grace, you were a bright spot in it. I could always count on you."

"Honestly, I'm surprised to hear you say that."

"Why?" He genuinely seemed shocked.

"Because if you'd truly felt that way, you would have come and told me the truth. You would have at least said goodbye."

"Don't you think I wanted to?" His emotions bled through. "You don't know how many times I thought about climbing up to your window, but I couldn't."

"What stopped you?" I begged to know.

"You."

"Me?" I pointed to myself.

He let out a heavy breath and began to pace in front of me. "I didn't want any reasons to come back to Pecan Orchard, and I knew you would have given me one. My world had just crashed around me, and I couldn't have you righting it in any way, like you always did when I would let you." He stopped and faced me, as if pleading his case to a jury. "No matter the situation, you had a knack for making it all better. If I lost a debate, you would take me out to ice cream and help me dissect where I had gone wrong and let me redo my talking points. You were the one who came up with my campaign slogan and made all the posters when I ran for class president. *Vote Brooks for a Better Outlook.* It was perfect." He grinned.

"I thought so."

"Grace." He took my hand, causing massive flutters. "You were my best friend."

The flutters died a painful death upon hearing the big F word. I could practically hear them wailing.

"You don't know how much I appreciated the way you would decorate my truck before every track meet. Or all the brownies you made me for my study sessions when I was trying to increase my SAT score. I don't think I said thank you enough. So, thank you." He squeezed my hand.

"You're welcome." I pulled my hand away from him.

His brow knit together when I severed our connection. "I'm sorry for not being a better friend to you."

If he said the F word one more time, I might start using some of my own F words. You know, like fudge, fondue, flan, and frosting straight out of the can.

I nodded because I couldn't think of anything to say. What I really wanted to do was run away and have a good cry.

Brooks rested a hand on my arm. "I hope we can be friends again, Grace."

I was definitely eating some fudge after this. Maybe even frosted fudge. Then I was going to go get a CAT scan to figure out why I was hearing voices. One thing I was for sure not doing, and that was becoming friends with Brooks again. I was about to tell him, but I could have sworn I saw Tom move. I sidestepped Brooks and rushed over to Tom. His hand was twitching.

"Do you see that?" I asked Brooks.

Brooks, without getting too close, took a peek.

Tom's fingers moved.

"I saw that," Brooks whispered.

I took Tom's hand. "Tom, squeeze my hand." I waited. "Please, Tom." I looked at Brooks. "Talk to him."

Brooks's eyes resembled a deer in headlights.

"Please, Brooks."

Brooks cleared his throat. "Tom," he stammered.

"Come on, Brooks, you can do better than that."

Brooks crept closer. "Father."

I threw him a crusty look, then softened it once I registered the fear in Brooks's eyes. "Brooks," I whispered, "I'm not going to pretend I understand what you went through or how you feel, but try to remember the man who came to every track meet and debate and cheered louder than anyone. The man who paid for every bit of your higher education, even though you loathed him. The man who gets tears in his eyes every time he talks about you. He loves you, and I know deep down you love him, or you wouldn't have even bothered coming here."

I reached out my free hand. "I'll help you."

Brooks reluctantly took a few steps toward me. "Grace . . ."

"I know. Forgiveness is a beast, and it scares me half to death. But we used to be able to conquer anything together," my voice cracked. "We can do this too."

Brooks gripped my hand and knelt near me. Tears pooled in his eyes. He swallowed hard. "Daddy, it's Brooks." He smiled up at me. "And Grace." He rested his hand over mine and his daddy's.

With Brooks's touch, Tom squeezed my hand. Joy pulsed through me, and tears poured down my cheeks. I knew it wasn't inevitable that Tom would recover, but it was a step in the right direction. I was so happy I lost myself. Without thinking, I grabbed Brooks's stubbled cheeks and pressed my lips against his. Oh. Wow. Like, snap, crackle, pop, wow. It felt like I had found the missing key to the lock I'd been trying to open for years. I should have backed away. Or he should have. But neither one of us made a move. Thankfully, my head kicked in and reminded me he was dating Morgan. Yet I only moved an inch, allowing us to share the same breaths. "Thank you," I whispered.

"You're welcome." He leaned away, his eyes blinking rapidly.

"I'm sorry. Sometimes I get carried away. But, I mean, friends kiss, right?" I spit out in a rush, sounding foolish again.

"Are we friends, Grace?" he asked, pleading.

My head was telling me to say no, but my heart—my heart had other ideas. "Um . . . yes."

Chapter Eleven

I fidgeted with the sleeves on my sundress, pulling them onto and then down below my shoulders while I peeked out my window at the scene next door. Brooks was playing football with his nephews on the front lawn of his daddy's house. To my knowledge, he hadn't entered the house yet, but I supposed this was a good start.

Daddy came and stood next to me. "You look beautiful."

"Thanks, Daddy." I kept my eyes on the man I had kissed a week ago. So much had happened since then. Tom had woken up and was out of the ICU but was still being monitored closely. He had a long road ahead of him, but his prognosis was good. He had no memory of the incident and was honestly quite incensed they were making him stay in the hospital, even though he was having a hard time remembering some words and he couldn't walk by himself to the bathroom. On top of that, he was having surgery in a few days to have a cardioverter-defibrillator implanted in his heart to correct an arrhythmia.

While Tom's heart was on the mend, mine was calling out for Brooks. It didn't help when he was behaving so adorably with his nephews, chasing them around the yard and letting them tackle him. I would have loved to get in on that action, but duty called.

"I should probably get going or I'm going to be late for my date." It felt weird going out at a time like this, but June was keeping Tom company tonight. Tom was thrilled. I wasn't sure if anything would come of it, but June seemed determined to make amends and bring her family together.

Daddy gave me a knowing smile. "You don't seem all that excited for it."

I stepped away from the window and smoothed my unruly hair that was making me look like a wannabe eighties music video star. "I'm sure it will be fun."

Daddy rested his hand on my cheek. "You deserve the break. You've been amazing these past couple of weeks, which is no surprise."

"You're biased."

"No, my dear, I'm truthful. I don't think Tom would be here if it weren't for you. He told me he could hear your voice in his head yelling at him to wake up and fight."

I smiled. "As much as I would love to take credit, I think it has more to do with his family."

Daddy patted my cheek. "You are his family."

That brought a tear to my eye. "Don't go messing up my makeup now. You never know, I could be meeting your future son-in-law tonight, and I want to make a good impression."

Dad glanced out the window. "Are you sure you haven't already met him?"

My eyes popped. "And who would that be?" I played coy.

Dad gave me a mischievous grin, which was unusual for him. "I was thinking about a young man who used to sneak into my daughter's room at night."

My jaw dropped to the floor. "You knew?"

"You weren't exactly quiet."

"Why didn't you tell me? Or ground me for going against your rules?"

Daddy tapped my nose. "Because I trusted both of you. And after your mother died, I knew you needed him, just like he needed you. Just like you need each other now."

A lump formed in my throat. "Daddy, he's dating Morgan." And he had been avoiding me since the night I kissed him. Though he had held my hand while the doctor assessed Tom after Tom had begun to stir. However, he hadn't been to see his daddy since Tom had woken up, and I had a feeling it had more to do with me than his issues with Tom. I had no idea what had come over me that night—it had just seemed so natural to kiss him. Part of me felt guilty since he was dating someone. Despite my not liking Morgan, I was never one to steal another woman's boyfriend. Although technically he did say they weren't exclusively dating each other, my guess was Brooks wasn't dating anyone but her.

"That can always change. Have a lovely time tonight." Daddy walked off, whistling to himself.

Right, tonight. A date with Peter, an insurance agent from Cherry Hills and a friend of Colette's. Dane, the guy Lorelai had offered up to me, wasn't interested in blind dates. Which was fine, but what was weird was Lorelai had seemed relieved. When I pressed her about it, she waved off my concern. I had a feeling there was a story to be told, but I would let her tell me when she was ready.

I took several deep breaths in and out, preparing myself to walk out the front door. I was berating myself for not parking my car in the garage earlier when I had come back from buying the perfect shade of nail polish to match my coral sundress. Laziness always had a way of biting me in the butt. Perhaps, though, Brooks would pretend not to see me.

"Bye, Daddy," I yelled up the stairs.

"Bye, honey."

I grabbed my purse and opened the door with gusto. Perhaps the voice would come back tonight. Hopefully a different voice, since the previous one was a big fat liar. I walked out into the warm May evening. The air smelled like lilacs and barbecue. It was a fantastic combination. It made me both hungry and nostalgic. My grandma used to wear a lilac-scented perfume.

I hustled to my car, trying to go unnoticed, but Ryker saw me and shouted, "Gracie!" That's what I got for buying the boys a boatload of Nerf and water guns during their stay.

I had no choice but to take a detour and walk over to the neatly trimmed hedges that separated our yard from the Hamiltons'.

Brooks dropped the football and stood frozen near the pecan tree in their yard while he stared at me.

Both boys ran my way. Axel, the youngest, was sporting a different smile. "I lost my two front teeth." He proudly showed off the gaping hole in his mouth. "The tooth fairy gave me ten dollars last night."

Whoa. That was a nice tooth fairy. I only used to get a dollar per tooth. "Wow. What are you going to do with all that money?"

"I'm going to take my dad out to get ice cream when we get home tomorrow."

That was sweet. Their dad had gone home a few days ago to get back to work. Carly and the boys were leaving tomorrow so the boys could finish out the last few weeks of school. They would come back after school was out. Tom should be home by then.

"That's very nice. I'm sure your daddy will love that."

"He will," Axel informed me.

"Are you excited to go home?" I asked Ryker.

"Yeah, but I'm going to miss Uncle Brooks and Grandma."

Brooks had decided to saunter our way by this point. He ruffled his nephew's blond hair. "We'll see each other soon, buddy." Brooks gave me a good once-over. "How are you, Grace?"

"Good. I'm headed out—on a date," I made sure to mention so he didn't think I was getting any more than friendly ideas. Not that I didn't have them, but he didn't need to know that. "How are you?"

He blinked several times as if he were trying to comprehend what I had said. It was odd, considering his profession, and I knew he had the skills to think on his toes. I'd watched every debate he'd ever participated in back in the day.

"I'm good," he stuttered after a long pause. "Morgan and I are going out later too," he threw in. "She's taking me to a human cadaver art exhibit."

"Um . . . that sounds kind of disturbing."

His tan cheeks pinked. "It's science."

"Well, you have fun with that. I'll see you later. Bye, boys." I waved to Ryker and Axel before turning around.

"Hold up, Grace." Brooks, in a surprising move, hopped over the hedge like he was seventeen again. He made my heart skip a beat or two. "Ryker and Axel, give me a minute to talk to Grace."

The boys took off, tossing the football between them. That left me stunned, staring at Brooks in his tight hug-my-butt jeans. He looked better now than back in high school. Which wasn't helping my situation any. I was supposed to be looking forward to Peter, but all I could think about was Brooks.

I bit my lip. "Can I help you with something?"

He let out a heavy sigh. "As a matter of fact, I was hoping you would meet me at the hospital tomorrow morning while my mother takes Carly and the boys to the airport."

I tilted my head. "Is everything okay?"

He swallowed hard. "I haven't seen my father and . . ."

"You want someone to hold your hand?" I guessed, giving him a crooked grin.

"Yes. I mean, figuratively, yes."

Ugh. Of course. These dang F words were getting on my nerves. "Why don't you take Morgan with you?" After all, they were dating, and since they loved going to see cadavers, the hospital should be a real treat for them.

He rubbed the back of his neck. "Morgan doesn't understand the intricacies of it all. And my parents never understood her, so bringing her would add more tension to the situation."

Oh, his parents understood her all right, that's why they didn't like her. It was Brooks who'd never understood her and how manipulative she was. For being so smart, Brooks was an idiot. If his girlfriend couldn't understand the details or importance of him trying to mend his relationship with his father, I would say it was time for him to get a new girlfriend. I had a suggestion of who that could be, but I wasn't sure I wanted to date an idiot.

He stepped closer. "Please, Grace, you understand the situation better than anyone. And since you're so close to Tom, I thought it would be best to have you there. I promise not to keep you long."

"Well, I was planning on spending most of my Sunday there to read *Twilight* to him; I suppose I could meet you there. What time?" I must be a masochist at heart.

"Nine? Is that too early? We could make it later, if you plan on having a late night tonight," he asked nonchalantly.

"We can only hope it will be a late night, but nine will work either way."

He rubbed the back of his neck. "Er . . . Great. Thank you."

"See you tomorrow."

"Is this another blind date?" he asked, seeming reluctant to say good-bye.

"They always are."

"Testing your facial recognition theory?"

I wrung my hands together. "Yep."

"What is that again?"

"I don't want to bore you with the details." Because they made me sound like a whack job. "I need to get going."

"Of course. Sorry I kept you."

"No problem. Good night." I turned to go.

"Grace, you look great. Your date is a lucky man," he rushed to say before hopping back over the hedge.

I turned back to face him, but he was already jogging toward his nephews. I watched him for a moment. He picked up Axel and swung him around. It was too adorable for words. Unfortunately, the dang voice was not as at a loss for words as I was. *He's the one.*

Please stop saying that! I marched toward my car, determined to hear a saner voice tonight.

All the way to the restaurant, I blared Rick Springfield, trying to get Brooks off my mind. Unfortunately, Rick was singing Brooks's and my song, "Affair of the Heart." It should be noted that Brooks didn't know we already had a song. I found myself playing it more times than I should have. I knew how silly it was. It had been twenty years, and I knew nothing about him now. Even so, I felt like I knew him better than most people in my life, and somewhere inside of him lived the boy I'd loved. Obviously, though, he loved Morgan. Why else would he agree to check out dead bodies?

I had to push him from my mind. I needed to focus on Peter. I changed the song to "Jessie's Girl" and instead sang "Peter's Girl" to see if it had a ring to it. I wasn't feeling it, but who knew, this date could be life changing for me.

FACIAL RECOGNITION

I sat across from Peter at this fantastic burger place in downtown Fort Worth. It wasn't too far from our spa and happened to be a favorite restaurant of mine. This was no run-of-the-mill burger place. We are talking they put fried mac and cheese on top of burgers. It was genius, and it spoke to Peter being fun. It was better than checking out cadavers. And they had the Texas Rangers game playing on ten screens. Total score. Although it did remind me of a certain someone who shall not be named who got me hooked on baseball and the Rangers when we were in high school. To be honest, I was surprised He Who Shall Not Be Named was watching cadavers over his beloved Rangers. Not thinking about it.

I glanced up from my menu and took in my date. He was handsome, with dirty-blond hair that was parted with precision. He had brown eyes with a touch of green and a round face that gave him a boyish sort of charm. He'd pulled out my chair when I'd arrived and complimented my dress and hair. He wasn't Brooks gorgeous, but he was easy on the eyes and had been polite. No voice yet, though the night was still young, so I was holding out some hope.

"Do you come here often?" I asked.

He looked up from his menu and smiled. "Never been here, but Colette mentioned it was one of your favorite places."

I liked that. It was thoughtful of him.

"She would be right. I hope you like it; everything here is fantastic."

"What would you recommend?"

"That depends—do like spicy or sweet?"

"Both," he said with a crooked grin.

Hmm. That was an excellent answer. I was liking him even more. "In that case, I would go with the sweet-and-spicy Hawaiian burger."

He set his menu down. "Sounds perfect. Have you been to Hawaii?"

I nodded. "Colette, Lorelai, and I took a girls' trip there a few years ago. It was amazing. We went snorkeling and jumped off waterfalls—"

He held up his hand. "I hate to tell you, but that kind of risky behavior isn't good for life insurance rates. You should probably consider some new hobbies."

"Uh . . ." I wasn't quite sure what to say.

Apparently I didn't need to respond, because he reached down and grabbed a tablet out of his attaché case and said, "Let me show you what I mean."

I had noticed the attaché earlier when I'd arrived. I had just thought he was metrosexual and comfortable with his feminine side, which was fine by me. However, I wasn't expecting what came next.

He pulled up a PowerPoint presentation on his tablet. "This is important information I give all my clients. It could save you thousands of dollars over the years. How old are you?"

"Thirty-eight."

"So, you basically have forty years left to live, if you go by the United States average for women." He pointed at a brightly colored chart.

Was this really happening? He was making me wish for hobbit man.

"Do you have life insurance?" he point-blank asked before reaching for a brochure. "If you don't, you should really think about it. You're still relatively young, and you look healthy. You don't smoke, I hope."

I didn't, but this date was going up in smoke fast.

He fanned out several brochures in front of me. "Take a look at these. I'm sure I can find the perfect plan for you."

No, Peter. I don't think so. On to date number thirty-seven.

Chapter Twelve

I was downing Diet Pepsi and popping chocolate donut holes into my mouth on the drive over to the hospital to meet Brooks. It wasn't a pretty sight, but after my date—I mean insurance appointment—I'd stayed up half the night bingeing General Hospital clips of Rick Springfield and my favorite couple ever, Frisco and Felicia. Sadly, Frisco and Felicia didn't make it on the show or in real life, but, man, were they the cutest. And oh, could they do a good kissing scene. Why couldn't I find someone to kiss me so passionately? Or kiss me at all, for that matter?

Brooks had probably had a better time looking at dead bodies. In fact, I would have had a better time looking at dead bodies than attending the insurance seminar disguised as a date. And can you really call it a date when you pay for yourself? Peter believed that all dates should be dutch unless you were sleeping together. So not happening. I needed to have a serious talk with my best friends about the guys they were setting me up with. I mean, I totally appreciated their efforts, and I understood they only knew so many single men. However, we needed to come up with a better screening process—feet hair check included.

Perhaps I should just be done with blind dates. I could only stay optimistic for so long. Going stag to my reunion was sounding better and better all the time. Okay, so it didn't sound good at all. Even so, I needed to give up on finding someone who made the voice appear. Yes, I knew the voice was speaking again, but it was confused, and I couldn't afford to listen to it. It had been wrong twenty-four years ago, and it was insane now. Brooks was in love with Morgan. Period. The end.

I pulled into the parking lot and flipped down my visor mirror. Yikes. I had chocolate all over my lips, and my eyes were so red it looked like I had gone on a bender last night. If you counted hours and hours of watching scripted love scenes, I supposed I had. I did feel hungover, or was that lovesick? I needed a Noah Drake or Frisco Jones in my life.

I wiped the chocolate off my mouth, took a big swig of my caffeinated beverage of choice, threw my shades on, and popped a mint. Dressed in my cutoffs and tank top, I wasn't even trying to impress Brooks. Why bother?

I hopped out of my car and told the voice in my head to keep its mouth shut. I spotted Brooks at the entrance pacing back and forth. The sun fell on him, making his golden-brown hair glimmer and illuminating how dang attractive he was in his white dress shorts and polo shirt. He looked like he was hitting the golf course later. Wow, did he have some fine, long, lean legs. *I wouldn't mind doing some rounds with him.* Oh my gosh, I needed to stop thinking like that. I was here to help him reconcile with Tom.

"Good morning," I tried to say cheerily, with heavy friendly undertones, when I approached Brooks.

He stopped pacing for all of two seconds and said, "Hello," before he went back to acting as if he were an animal trapped in a cage.

"You doing okay?"

"Not really."

I went to reach out and grab his hand to calm him down, then thought better of it. I was still thinking about the kiss I'd lain on him. Sadly, it was the best kiss I'd had in forever. Considering where my thoughts were, touching him was out of the question. In fact, I was never touching him again.

I shoved my hands into my pockets and told them to behave. "It's just your daddy."

Brooks stopped dead in his tracks, and his brooding brown eyes hit me with such force I took a step back. "You know it's more complicated than that."

"I realize that, but the longer you stay away, the more complicated it's going to get."

"I know." He started pacing again.

Against my better judgment, these imprudent words came flying out of my mouth: "Do you want to take a walk and talk before we head up to see your daddy?" What I really should have said was: "You're on your own, buddy. And could you please make yourself look more unattractive?"

He breathed out a huge sigh of relief. "I would appreciate that."

Of course he would. "There's a park near here with a lake we could walk around."

"Near the old county water tower?"

I was surprised he remembered. "That's the one."

He headed that direction, and I kept pace with him, making sure to keep my distance on the sidewalk that wended around the hospital and out toward the street we needed to follow to the park. Unfortunately, the gentle breeze was blowing his clean scent my way. He smelled like a spring rain shower, and I wanted to dance in it until I was soaked by him.

We both seemed nervous, me with my hands safely in my pockets as he walked with his behind his back, wringing them.

"How were the dead bodies?" I couldn't think of anything else to ask.

He shrugged and chuckled. "Let's just say I was the life of the party."

"That bad, huh?"

"The exhibit was . . . *intriguing.*"

"Sounds awful." I laughed.

"It was. But with that said, it was educational, and I appreciate that Morgan always wants to expand her knowledge."

"I guess that's a good thing." As a matter of fact, I read *Cosmo* and *Soap Opera Digest* to keep my mind fresh and up-to-date on all the latest fashion trends and *General Hospital* gossip. Not to mention I took all the quizzes in *Cosmo*. And, not to brag, but I always scored high. Oh, and how could I forget my subscription to *America's Spa*? A magazine specifically tailored for aestheticians. Did that count as expanding my knowledge?

"How was your date last night?" he asked.

"Well, the good news is I now have a half-million-dollar life insurance policy."

Brooks's brow scrunched. "What?"

"Don't even ask. It was one of my worst dates ever, and that is saying something." If I wasn't mistaken, his lips twitched like he was going to smile.

He cleared his throat. "So, did he prove your theory right or wrong?"

"I guess it depends on how you look at it, but it's neither here nor there. I think I'm going to call it a day on my scientific experiment. The only good thing that came out of last night was I got to see the Rangers trample the Astros. Did you get to catch any of it?"

He stretched his neck from side to side. "I didn't."

"You should definitely catch any replays. The ninth inning was AH-mazing. I won't spoil it for you, but trust me, you will be proud of our guys. I mean, your team." I was an idiot. In high school, we had always thought of the Rangers as our guys. We'd spent many nights on his couch cheering them on together and drinking root beer floats.

He stared out into the distance, fixed on the intersection ahead. "I'm trying to cut down on the amount of sports I watch."

"Have you become a couch potato?" I teased.

"Nothing like that. Hell, I work sixty plus hours every week."

"That sounds terrible."

"Nature of the beast, if you want to be the best."

I wasn't sure helping people dissolve their marriages was something you should aim to be number one at, but I didn't mention it. "What about downtime? I would think you would need some in your line of work."

"Yes, but Morgan has helped me to see it shouldn't be filled with mindless activities."

She was a monster. I shouldn't have, but I rolled my eyes. And yep, he noticed.

"You don't agree."

"Not at all. In fact, I have it on authority from an athletic trainer I once dated that watching sports is actually good for you. It increases your heart rate, respiration, and skin blood flow—which I'm all about. And you tend to have more friends and higher self-esteem. Which, judging by our latest interactions, you probably don't have an issue with your self-esteem, but I can't speak on the other areas." I smirked.

His eyes widened. "You aren't afraid to speak your mind, are you?"

"Have I ever been?"

He thought for a moment, and a smile began to slowly form on his beautiful face. "Overall, I remember you as being sweet, but now that I think of it, you were awfully opinionated."

"I think you meant to say right." I nudged him with my elbow. "But I am still mostly sweet," I threw in there.

"I'll give you that one."

My cheeks pinked. "Well, since you've given up on watching sports, I'll tell you that last night there was the prettiest grand slam you'll ever see."

"Really?" He sounded depressed.

"Honestly, the ball seemed to sail for days, and the way the players ran around the bases was like a well-choreographed dance. It was beautiful. Maybe you could sneak in a clip."

"Maybe," he whispered like he was afraid his momma would catch him and scold him.

Yep, Morgan had gotten to him again. Why, oh why, did he love that woman? Maybe he really did only love her for her mind. Though, let's be real, she had a rocking body. Perhaps I should have gone to college and enhanced my chest. No. That wasn't me. I wanted someone who loved me for who I am.

We came to the intersection and waited in silence for the crosswalk signal to give us the go-ahead. The park was in view. There was hardly a soul there. Only a couple of people walking around the lake. Most people were in church. Normally, I would have been too, but I felt like God would forgive me since I was doing a good deed. I would read the Bible to Tom before we started in on *Twilight*. Jesus, then vampires.

An uncomfortable tension hung in the air. After what seemed like fifteen minutes, the signal changed, and I hustled across the street, hoping to outrun the yucky feeling. Once on the other side, I took a deep breath and let it out. I reminded myself that I was only catching up with an old friend and to quit thinking in terms of what might have been.

"So, do you like your job?" I asked as we headed to the path that led around the lake. What a happy place it was with tulips galore and ducks swimming about. The sunshine felt good on my skin—I only hoped I didn't burn too badly in the midmorning light.

"I'm not sure *like* is the right word, but I get a lot of satisfaction from it," he answered matter-of-factly.

"From helping people get divorced?"

"I help people make course corrections." He defended himself.

"That's putting quite the spin on it."

His eyes narrowed. "I'm not spinning anything. Marriage is one of the most destructive forces on earth."

I stopped in my tracks and slapped my hand against my chest. "Whoa. That's some strong language."

"It's true. Marriage destroys more lives than disease."

"It's also beautiful and lifesaving at times."

"Very rarely, in my world." He stalked off.

"Maybe you should step out of your world for a while," I kindly suggested as I jogged to catch up to him.

"I doubt it would change my mind. I've seen firsthand what a seemingly good marriage can do."

"If you are speaking of your parents, you're looking at it all wrong," I said, my tone pleading for him to believe me.

He looked at me with such disdain.

He didn't scare me. "It's true. Your parents' marriage was as good as any. Even you have to admit that. Yes, your daddy made a huge, life-altering mistake, but it didn't have to permanently destroy anything. That was a choice made by your entire family."

Brooks's cheeks were so red, they looked as if I'd slapped him.

"I'm not defending what your daddy did, but he isn't the only one who made mistakes. Even your momma would admit to that. And by the way your momma's been behaving, I would say she wishes she would have given it a chance to work out. To create something beautiful out of the mess."

"My mother needs to be careful," he snapped. "And you have a very fairy-tale way of looking at that situation. But let me tell you, fairy-tale marriages and reconciliations don't exist. I've had plenty of clients try to quote, unquote *work it out* only to come back to me wishing they never had."

"Lucky for you," I zinged back as I gazed out across the lake. I loved watching the gentle ripples on the water and seeing a daddy help his son throw bread in for the ducks, though I was so disturbed by Brooks's outlook I couldn't even focus on the beautiful sight. I wasn't naive about love and marriage. I knew it had risks, yet in my heart I knew how wonderful it could be. My parents had shown me what it looked like to love someone so much that you cared more about their happiness than you did your own.

"Grace," Brooks interrupted my thoughts. "Why do I tick you off so much? I don't remember it ever being like this between us." His voice was melancholy.

I kicked a pebble on the path, not knowing exactly what to say without revealing how I had felt about him all these years. The best thing I could come up with was, "I'm sorry, you do seem to bring out the worst in me. I guess . . . I'm just disappointed that you didn't reach your potential."

He tilted his head. "Excuse me? I graduated with honors from one of the top law schools in the country, and I work for one of the most successful firms in the state."

"All admirable achievements, but at the end of the day, are you happy?"

He shoved his hands in his pockets. "Happiness is overrated."

"If you say so. I'm tired of arguing with you. Tell me why you're so nervous to talk to your daddy."

He looked down at his leather boat shoes and thought for a moment. "For a long time, I told myself I didn't care what happened to him, and then when I thought he was going to die, I realized that wasn't true."

"You still care about him."

He nodded.

"There's nothing wrong with that."

FACIAL RECOGNITION

"I know you might not agree with me, but he did destroy my world. I swore I would never give him that power again."

Against my better judgment, I tugged on his arm. Oh, wow, did it feel good. "Brooks, I understand your trepidation, but you, your momma, and Carly were and are his world. Believe me, he's just as scared as you are that he'll screw it up again. This isn't a power struggle. Maybe look at it more as building a bridge together as equals."

A softness washed over his face. "You always knew the right thing to say."

I dropped my hand and started to smile, but Brooks's head jerked up. "What does that kid think he's doing? He's defacing public property."

I followed Brooks's line of sight and saw a kid spray-painting a huge pink heart on the water tower. "That's so cute."

"He's breaking the law. I should call the police."

I rolled my eyes. The water tower had so much spray paint on it, the county officials hadn't bothered to repaint it in years. "Don't you dare. It's romantic. I always wanted some guy to paint my name on the one in Pecan Orchard."

"You wanted someone to risk having a misdemeanor on their permanent record just to prove to you they liked you?"

I shook my head, flabbergasted at how hardened he had become. The boy I'd known would have thought spray-painting your feelings for someone on a water tower was silly, but he wouldn't have wanted to call the authorities. Instead he would have teased me about what I would want my tribute to say. I used to think *Brooks Loves Grace* would suffice. "What happened to you, Brooks?"

He blinked a few times. "I don't know what you mean."

"Therein lies the problem."

Chapter Thirteen

"**A**re you ready for this?"

Brooks stared at his father's hospital room door, running a hand over his cleanly shaven face. "Maybe I should wait until he's home."

It was surprising how afraid the tough-as-nails lawyer was. "You haven't even been able to walk inside the house yet."

"I've been waiting for the right time," he growled.

I took a step back. "Okay."

"Grace," he sighed. "I'm sorry. I appreciate you being here more than you know."

"Remember when you decided to take your dad's car for a spin before you got your license and you hit the mailbox?"

Brooks grinned.

"You thought your daddy was going to kill you, so you hid over at my house. We watched *Clueless* like four times in a row."

"That was a punishment all on its own."

"Whatever. You loved it. You totally had a thing for Alicia Silverstone. But that's beside the point."

"What is your point?"

"When your daddy finally came looking for you, do remember what he did?"

Brooks became awfully interested in the tiled floor before he mumbled, "He wrapped his arms around me and told me I should never be afraid to come to him. It didn't matter what I had done, his arms would always be wide open for me."

"He meant that." I got a little choked up.

Brooks tipped his head up. "What if I don't need or want to be in his arms?"

I stepped closer to Brooks. "If that were the case, you wouldn't be having such a hard time walking in there. Maybe it's time to take the first step. No one will think less of you. Certainly not me."

"I can't let him destroy my world again," he whispered.

"Brooks, you might not like me saying this, but I don't think your world ever got put back together."

He opened his mouth, I'm sure to disagree.

I placed my finger on his lips. "Shhh. Don't ruin the moment." I smirked. "Trust your old friend. Not that I'm old, but you know what I mean. Now let's go see your daddy." I dropped my hand and shook off the feel of his lips. I was in way over my head. I opened the door, but before I could walk in, Brooks unexpectedly kissed my cheek. "Thanks, *old* friend."

For that I elbowed him in the gut. It felt like old times.

"Ugh," he groaned and grabbed his stomach. "You pack a punch now."

"Make sure you don't forget it." I stepped into Tom's room. It smelled of antiseptic and his turkey bacon and egg whites breakfast. It was certainly healthier than chocolate donut holes and Diet Pepsi.

Tom was sitting up in his bed, his tray of food in front of him. He had hardly touched it. I knew he was anxious to see Brooks.

I kissed his mangy head. "I think at this point we are going to have to go for the man bun."

Tom chuckled. "How are . . . you, G . . . Gracie girl?" His words were a bit stilted, yet he got them all out.

"I'm good. I brought someone to see you."

Brooks stepped closer, his Adam's apple bobbing furiously.

Tom took my hand and squeezed it, tears forming in his eyes. "Hi . . . hi, son," his voice cracked.

"Tom," Brooks replied.

I narrowed my eyes at Brooks but kept my mouth shut. He was here. I would at least give him credit for that, though it had Tom hanging his head a bit. Yet he still managed a small smile for his son.

"It's g . . . good of you . . . you . . . to come," Tom said. "Please have a s . . . s . . . seat."

Brooks took the couch farthest from us and sat so stiffly he looked like a wax figure.

I sat on the edge of Tom's bed, keeping a hold of his hand.

Neither man seemed to know what to say, so it was up to me. "Carly texted me and wanted me to give you both her love. She said she'll call when she lands in Burbank."

Both men nodded. The silence stretched.

I guessed I was going to need to up my game. "Oh, and I'm thinking about moving to Vegas with this male stripper I met last night."

Brooks actually jumped up, and Tom about flipped his breakfast tray over. I had to grab it before his food went flying.

"You will do no such thing, young lady." Tom sounded more author-itative than my daddy ever had, and his words flowed freely all on their own.

"But he's really fine, and he says he loves me." I busted out laughing.

Tom swatted me. "G . . . Gracie g . . . girl, my heart can't take that."

I kissed his head. "I'm sorry. I suppose y'all better think of something to talk about, then."

Brooks lowered himself back onto the couch, shaking his head at me.

Both men still seemed at a loss about what to say.

I pulled out my phone and googled great conversation starters while the men stared at each other. "All right, y'all, I'm going to help you out. Fifty-seven killer conversation starters, number one—"

Tom pushed my phone down. "D . . . Darlin', you've made your point." Tom let out a trepid sigh. "H . . . How have you b . . . been, son?"

"Good one." I nudged Tom playfully, making both men smile.

"I just made junior partner," Brooks replied.

Tom beamed. "That's w . . . wonderful. E . . . Equity or nonequity st . . . status?"

"Nonequity, but once I'm promoted to senior partner, I'll receive equity status."

"Ex . . . Excellent. I'm p . . . proud of you, son."

Brooks bristled and cleared his throat. "I didn't do it for you."

I gave Brooks the evil eye, but he didn't flinch.

Tom patted my arm, knowing I was about to get fired up. "I never ex . . . expected you to. That doesn't ch . . . change h . . . how proud I am of you."

Brooks pressed his lips together and simmered down but then threw out, "You don't know anything about me."

"H . . . How c . . . can I change that?" Tom begged to know.

Brooks ran a hand through his hair. "I don't know."

Silence creeped in again.

I clapped my hands together. "You know what? I think this was a good start. I'm proud of both of you."

Brooks and Tom gave me crooked grins.

"Now that we're done with the awkward first session, I have some important items to discuss with Tom about the reunion." I directed my attention to Brooks. "And since I know you find reunions distasteful, you can be dismissed."

Brooks's eyes widened.

"You're not going to the reunion?" Tom asked Brooks. "G . . . Gracie's put s . . . s . . . so much time and effort into it."

Brooks shifted in his seat.

"Don't pressure him, Tom." I patted Tom's hand. "He and Morgan believe only people who peaked in high school attend them."

"Non . . . Nonsense," Tom spouted. "Our G . . . Gracie girl is reaching new heights all the time."

Brooks let out a heavy breath. "I'm sure she is. That said, some of us don't feel the need to catch up with people we haven't seen in twenty years and probably will never see again. And, I'll be at a conference that weekend anyway."

"Perfect. More fun for the rest of us, then." Internally though, I was disappointed there was no chance of him coming. I knew it was a long shot. Yet, somewhere deep down, a tiny shred of hope burned that the old Brooks would appear and see we were meant to be. Then he would sweep me off my feet and give me the night we should have had twenty years ago. I shook off those thoughts and turned my attention back to Tom, expecting Brooks would leave, but he stayed put.

"D . . . did you f . . . find a date yet, darlin'?" Tom asked.

"No. I'm thinking of going alone. Or maybe you and Daddy can escort me." I winked, trying not to feel like a loser in front of Brooks.

Tom chuckled. "It would be a p . . . pleasure, but you d . . . don't give up yet. Surely there is a man sm . . . smart enough to make you his g . . . girl."

I shrugged and tapped on my phone to pull up the table settings the caterer had sent me to choose from. "I need your opinion. The girls," meaning Colette and Lorelai, "and I can't decide if we should go with the more elegant theme or something more on the fun side, like this one." I clicked on the picture showing the centerpiece made from yearbooks that had photo booth picture strips accented with flowers and the year we graduated. "I'm leaning toward this one. I think it shows a personal touch. What do you think?"

Tom's brow crinkled. He was giving it some serious thought. "Well, d . . . darlin', I say whatever you choose, it's going to be p . . . perfect."

I kissed his head. "You're no help, but thank you."

He chuckled. When he laughed, it made it obvious that he was still sick. There was an odd rattle to it, and it was subdued.

I handed him his water. "I think you've had enough excitement for the day. How about we read from the Bible and then *Twilight*? She's about to meet his parents."

Brooks stood. "I should probably get going."

That was probably for the best, I thought. "See you later."

Tom set his water down and gave his son a timid smile. "It was g . . . good to—"

"Knock, knock, knock, the doctor's here," a familiar voice interrupted us. Julian swaggered in wearing scrubs and carrying a vase full of cheerful daisies. How odd.

Brooks must have thought so too since he grimaced at Julian. "What are you doing here?" He dispensed with any pleasantries.

"Wishing Tom well, of course, and looking for you, actually. Morgan said you would probably be here." Julian didn't seem at all put off by Brooks's cold greeting.

Brooks's pursed lips said he wasn't buying it.

Julian paid him no attention and turned toward Tom and me. Julian's eyes lit up when he saw me. "Gracie, you're here too. What a surprise. It's so good to see you again."

"It's nice to see you too," I sort of lied, but what else could I say?

Julian set the flowers on the table under the TV. "Tom, you're looking good after your brush with death. I'm happy to see you pulled through."

Tom, like Brooks, looked confused as to why Julian was there. Tom squeezed my hand. "Thanks be to G . . . Gracie. I'm a l . . . lucky man."

Julian looked me over. "Yes, you are."

Brooks cleared his throat. "Did you need to talk to me?"

Julian reached into his pocket and pulled out two tickets. "I just scored some Rangers tickets for this evening. Home plate, brother. You in?"

Brooks stretched his neck from side to side. I could tell he was torn.

"You should go," I encouraged him. "Those are great seats, and they're playing the Astros again."

Julian grinned at me. "You a baseball fan?"

"A big one."

Brooks flashed me smile. He knew he was to blame for that.

Julian looked between Brooks and me with interest. "I know my sister doesn't understand the importance of sports, but she'll get over it. I mean, you might be in the doghouse for a long time, but it will be worth it," Julian taunted him.

Tom and I looked at each other and rolled our eyes. I knew we were thinking the same thing. Morgan was a controlling wench, and Brooks was an idiot.

Brooks blew out a deep breath. "I have court tomorrow, so I need to prepare. I'm going to pass."

Tom and I gave a collective sigh.

"If you're sure." Julian shoved the tickets back into his pocket before he set his sights on me. "Gracie, I believe I owe you dinner. How would you like to eat it at the ballpark tonight? Say, behind home plate?"

I bit my lip. "Um."

Brooks shot Julian a look of pure loathing.

Tom's eyes darted between Brooks, Julian, and me. A big ol' grin erupted on his unshaven salt-and-pepper face. "I think that s . . . sounds like a g . . . great idea. You should g . . . go, darlin'."

"Yes, darlin', you should come with me," Julian echoed.

I did love baseball. And with Julian I would have no long-term expectations because I already knew he loved himself more than anyone else and had been married way too many times for my comfort. So this would just be for fun, I reasoned. As an added plus, Brooks looked oh so agitated by it. His face was redder than his polo shirt, and he kept tugging on his collar. It was probably evil of me, but I found myself wanting to vex Brooks. "I would love to eat dinner behind home plate. Just so you know, I can eat a lot."

"That's my kind of woman. Have Brooks text me your number. I'll call you later to make plans."

"Okay."

"See y'all later." Julian waved. "I'm off to deliver a baby."

As soon as Julian closed the door, Brooks started in on me. "You're not seriously considering going out with him, are you?"

"You just heard me tell him yes. And it's not my style to agree to go on a date and then back out."

"Ouch," Tom whispered.

Yeah, I knew what a kill shot that was, and I should really just get over it, but I couldn't help myself.

Brooks growled, like actually growled. "We will get into the past later, but going out with him isn't a good idea."

"It's only a baseball game. One you should have gone to."

He blew a breath out of his nose like a raging bull. "You don't understand my life."

"You're right," I whispered. I didn't understand his kowtowing to Morgan and how hardened he had become.

"Just be careful around him." He stormed off.

"Wow. What was that all about?" I commented after the door slammed.

Tom chuckled. "You don't know?"

"What's so funny?"

Tom rested his dry, aged hand on my cheek. "G . . . Gracie girl, I h . . . have a f . . . feeling your life is about to get in . . . interesting."

"How so?"

"I'm th . . . thinking you're g . . . going to have some options on who to t . . . take to the reunion."

"Julian?"

"And Brooks." He wagged his bushy brows.

"I think the medication they have you on has made you loopy."

"I d . . . don't think so, darlin'. B . . . Buckle up. I think you're in for a wild ride."

I was thinking more like he was delusional.

Chapter Fourteen

I closed my eyes and leaned my head back, enjoying the light breeze and evening sun through my SPF 150. "It's perfect baseball weather."

"It's almost a shame they'll be in a climate-controlled stadium next year," Julian commented.

I flipped down my shades and turned toward him. "Almost, except when it's a hundred degrees and one hundred percent humidity."

"True," he chuckled.

I liked his laugh—it was masculine with a hint of mischief. And he laughed often, if you could judge that from the car ride over. Apparently, I was amusing. Or at least he thought my obsession with Rick Springfield was funny. I may or may not have given him a concert on the way over. I appreciated that he let me put on my playlist in his fancy car. Doctors must make a lot more money than I do. His car had more buttons than a fabric store.

"Are you hungry yet?"

"I'm trying to decide between the street tacos or bacon-wrapped wings. Decisions, decisions."

"How about I get the wings and you get the street tacos and we'll share?" he suggested.

"Ooh, I like the way you think."

He threw his baseball cap on backward. "I like you."

"Thanks."

"You don't like me?"

"It's still early in the night," I teased. Though it was true. I was holding out judgment based on what I knew about him and, admittedly, Brooks's warning. Brooks's multiple warnings. He had texted me twice reminding me that Julian had been divorced three times and how short-lived his marriages were. All less than two years. Definitely not a good track record. But like I said, I was just here for the fun. Julian and I weren't going to be a thing. I had texted Brooks back that I appreciated the warnings, but I didn't need him to play big brother. He'd texted back that he never wanted to be my brother, only my friend. Believe me, I knew. Tom was totally off his rocker thinking Brooks was going to want to take me to the reunion. He wasn't even going to be in town. And hello, he was dating Morgan, Julian's sister. Which was weird, come to think of it.

Julian leaned in closer. I noticed some gray in his stubble. It was kind of sexy, and so was he, if I was being honest. His minty breath wafted my way. "I'll see what I can do to tip the scales in my favor tonight."

"Food is always a good way to start."

"Food it is. I'll be right back."

"I can pay for my half." I thought I should offer since this wasn't a date, and after my last date, I wanted to find out if he thought we should be going dutch.

"Tonight's all on me."

"Thank you."

"Save my seat." He jumped up.

While he was gone, I soaked in the sun and savored the smell of the grass. I may have also checked out the butts of some of the players warming up on the field. Baseball pants were a special kind of pants. I got my phone out and took some pictures of the scenery, butts included, and texted them to Lorelai and Colette. Along with the picture I had snapped of Julian, unbeknownst to him. I had filled my bests friends in when I was getting ready for the game—which meant I threw on my pink Texas Rangers T-shirt and pulled my hair up in a messy bun—and they were curious about Julian and this turn of events.

I immediately got responses from them.

Dang, that Julian is yummy! And he's a doctor? He might not be the marrying type, but please make out with him, Colette responded.

Darlin', that is one fine man. Don't let your eyes fool your heart, Lorelai wisely counseled. *However, I agree with Colette. Lay a big one on him.*

I giggled at my friends, wondering what it would be like to kiss Julian. I typically didn't make out with men unless I saw some potential for a relationship. Not to say I hadn't kissed someone in the moment. With Julian, I knew there was no potential; but friends did kiss, like I'd told Brooks. And there I went thinking about Brooks and his lips again. This needed to stop.

Julian returned in no time, bearing some fabulous-looking and delicious-smelling food. The aroma of bacon from the wings and the al pastor chicken and lime from the tacos was making my mouth water.

"Which do you want first?" He showcased each item like he was Vanna White.

"Um . . . tacos."

"Excellent choice." He handed over the cardboard container filled with tacos.

"Thank you."

"You're very welcome." He settled back next to me.

I took no time tasting my chicken tacos. Holy crow, flavor explosion. "Mmm." I chewed and swallowed. "These are amazing. Take a bite." I held out the taco.

"We're sharing germs already?"

"Does that bother you, Dr. Bronson?"

"Not at all." He leaned in, his stubble tickling my fingers, and took a large bite. While he chewed, he groaned in pleasure. "That is good."

Some juice had dribbled down his chin. I instinctively wiped it with my thumb, and his brow quirked. "Um . . . you had some juice there. I didn't want it to stain your shirt." *Do not be seduced by his face*, I reminded myself. But up close he was very pretty.

"Thanks, darlin'." He leaned back and grabbed a wing.

I berated myself for being so touchy-feely and flirty, even though I found he made it so easy to interact that way. To recover from my eager fingers, I thought it best to get to know him. "What made you decide you wanted to be a doctor?"

"That's classified information," he said lightheartedly.

"Oh really. Like if you told me, you would have to kill me classified?"

"More like, I'd have to sue you if you ever divulged it."

"I'll take my chances; I know some really good lawyers."

He tilted his head side to side, deliberating. "Okay," he whispered. "This goes no further than here."

I played along and crossed my heart.

"My mom was a huge *General Hospital* fan when I was growing up—still is."

"Shut the front door, so am I." This news was practically life changing. The Bronsons were known for their propriety and pushing their children to be the best. Hence, they had a doctor and a VP on their hands. They were pretty standoffish, like their daughter. I could never imagine stuffy Mrs. Bronson watching a soap opera.

"I figured, from your Rick Springfield obsession. I'm embarrassed to admit this, but I thought the doctors were so cool and the nurses were hot. Who knew that they didn't really have a nurses' ball or a disco on the hospital campus?"

FACIAL RECOGNITION

I couldn't help but giggle. "Honestly, why doesn't every hospital have one?"

"I've tried to get one going at each hospital I had privileges at, but it's always been a no go."

"The question is, Who is your favorite *General Hospital* super couple? Mind you, your answer will determine whether we can be friends or not."

"Is this even a question? Felicia and Frisco."

Oh my gosh. It was like true love, but it wasn't, because it could never be. However, if true love could be based on that answer, Julian and I would be headed down the aisle. "Ding, ding, ding. You passed. We will now be best friends."

He laughed loudly. "Darlin', like I said, I do like you."

"You know, I think I might like you too."

Monday, I felt lighter than I had in the couple of weeks since Tom's death-defying episode. It had me getting into work early to inventory and restock the shelves with our skin care products and healing oils. I was lining the bottles of moisturizer up perfectly on our tiered display case when Colette and Lorelai unlocked the front door and rolled in together. They happened to live in the same townhome complex not far from the spa. On occasion, I thought about purchasing one too, but living alone never sounded all that appealing to me. Besides, who would take care of Tom and Daddy?

"Well, look at you, early bird," Lorelai sang.

I smiled over at my best friends, who always looked adorable in white scrubs with our logo on them.

"So happy too," Colette commented. "It must have been a good date."

I finished setting the last bottle out. "It wasn't a date, but it was a lot of fun." Surprisingly so. Julian was my kind of sports guy. He cheered loudly when our team did well, and he heckled the other team. He obnoxiously sang "Take Me Out to the Ball Game." Plus, he'd bought me a huge waffle cone sundae that we had ended up sharing. To top it off, he was a total gentleman. He'd opened all my doors, and when he had dropped me off last night, he'd walked me to my door and kissed my cheek.

Lorelai sidled up next to me. "Uh-huh, honey. You have good date written all over you."

Colette peered at me from across the display case. "Are you going out again?"

I bit my lip. "Yes. We're going to that Zero Gravity place."

"He's a daredevil." Lorelai nudged me. "I bet you like that."

"He's fun. That's all."

"You're still hung up on Brooks." Colette guessed right.

"I'm not hung up on him. I know Brooks and I will never be together. Same with Julian and me. I mean, the man has been divorced three times, and Morgan Bronson and I will never be related."

"Sister, you stick with that attitude," Lorelai growled. "After meeting her one time, I could tell I'd rather slam all my fingers in the door and break my nails than be around her for one second."

"Wow. That's saying something." Lorelai loved having her nails done, and there was hellfire to pay if one got chipped.

"Darn straight. I don't usually like to judge people by one meeting, but that woman is the she-devil herself. Her beauty is all on the surface."

"Truth," Colette chimed in. "And to be honest, if Brooks is that stupid, I don't think I want you with such a guy."

"I agree. Still, I think I'll have some fun with her brother in the meantime. You know, as friends only."

"Friends." Lorelai patted her heart. "Darlin', we'll see how long that lasts."

"I give it one more date." Colette wagged her brows.

"Y'all are being silly."

"How many second dates have you been on lately?" Lorelai asked.

"Well, none."

"Think about that." Colette beamed. "Maybe you should ask Julian to your reunion."

"Oh no, no. I'm still holding out for the voice or, you know, a different voice." Only Colette and Lorelai knew about my crazy voice.

Lorelai took my hand. "Maybe it's time to listen to your own voice. What do you want?"

I thought for a moment. "I just want to be seen and loved. Is that too much to ask for?"

"No, darlin'." Lorelai squeezed my hand.

"Oh, and no overly hairy feet and insurance seminars."

We all busted out laughing. When we stopped giggling, I looked between the best friends a girl could have. "Thank you, ladies. Honestly, I don't know what I would do without you."

Chapter Fifteen

"Tom's going to need around-the-clock care when he comes home, so between the three of us, we need to come up with a game plan." June patted both Brooks's and my knees as she sat across from us in the hospital waiting room. She had the spark of the old Miss June I remembered. Her eyes were bright, and her take-charge attitude was back in full force. Or maybe it was her new spray tan. She'd always said if you want to feel good about yourself, get a spray tan.

Tom's surgery to implant a defibrillator into his heart went well. He was expected to be released from the hospital tomorrow afternoon. Unfortunately, he was still having a hard time walking and remembering some words. He had severe fatigue too.

"I'm still running my gift basket business out of my house, which I can easily do from here, but that means in the evenings, I'll need you two to fill in once you're done with work." Miss June had been making corporate baskets for years. The woman could whip up some of the finest tasting and prettiest cookies you had ever had. Not to mention she had this knack for making everything look amazing.

"I'm available anytime you need me," I volunteered.

Brooks shifted uncomfortably in his seat. He obviously wasn't thrilled to be at the hospital or with the prospect of helping his daddy. "My caseload is heavy right now."

His momma swatted his arm. "Brooks Thomas, there's more to life than work. I know your daddy isn't your favorite person right now, but he's family, and from here on out we are going to act like a family and take care of each other."

Brooks pinched the bridge of his nose. "Fine. I can help on Thursday nights."

"Well, how generous of you, son." June rolled her eyes. "What about the weekends?"

"Morgan usually has plans for us."

"Heaven forbid you miss out on a TED Talk," June barked.

I snickered, and Brooks snapped his head my way. I smirked at him. "Don't worry, Miss June, I'm happy to fill in anytime. If I have a date, I'll just bring him. Maybe we can all listen to TED Talks together online." Miss June and I broke into fits of laughter.

Brooks wasn't amused. "You can gain a lot of valuable insights about improving your life and productivity by attending TED Talks and workshops."

"Whatever, darlin'." His momma wasn't buying it. "I find living in the real world and loving people will teach you a heck of a lot more than any workshop."

Brooks's lip curled up into a snarl, but he didn't argue.

June stood and stretched her back. "They should be done examining him and changing his clothes. I'm going to go check on him. Maybe you two should grab a bite to eat," she suggested, not so subtly. She was desperate for Brooks to ditch Morgan. She'd told me so last night when I had come to visit Tom. I'd told her and Tom it didn't matter if Brooks wasn't dating Morgan, he still wouldn't be dating me. Brooks loved throwing around the F word anytime we were together. Plus, he and I were opposites in almost every way now, and we had completely different life goals. He wanted to rule the world, unmarried and probably childless, and I wanted to experience the world with a husband and half a dozen kids. Good news, the ovulation test I took the night before said my eggs were still popping. And my gynecologist had told me at my last appointment that I had beautiful mucus in my lady parts, which was kind of gross and maybe more than I wanted to know, but she said it was a good sign.

Surprisingly, Brooks said, "I'm game."

I shrugged. "All right." We were *friends* after all.

Miss June beamed. "You two have fun and take your time."

I stood. "Do you want to try the new biscuit and limeade place nearby? I met Julian there for lunch today, and it's fantastic."

Brooks grimaced when I mentioned Julian's name.

"Why don't you like him? I mean, you could be related to him someday." I grabbed my stomach at the thought.

Brooks pushed himself out of his chair. "Neither Morgan nor I believe marriage is a viable institution," he scoffed.

"Right." I walked off toward the exit.

Brooks followed. "And it doesn't matter what I think about Julian. The question is, Why do you like him? He has completely different ideals than you. He's deathly afraid of having children, and he treats marriage like the jam of the month club. When he gets tired of one, he tries a new flavor."

"Good thing I don't plan on marrying him."

Brooks looked visibly relieved at my revelation. "Then why are you spending so much time with him?"

"Why do you care so much?"

"Because we're friends, and I don't want you to get hurt."

If only he knew how much he had and was hurting me. "Julian and I are friends too, and he's fun. A lot of fun. Besides, he understands all my *General Hospital* references, which is a huge plus for him." And when I said a lot of fun, I meant it. We had done every ride at Zero Gravity, from bungee jumping to the skycoaster that had us zipping through the air at sixty mph. Not only that, he had been very gentlemanly and friend-like. No kisses other than a kiss on the cheek when he walked me to my door or each time we parted. Sure, he was flirty and so was I, but he hadn't even tried to hold my hand.

Brooks snorted. "He probably studied up on that show so he could impress you."

"You say that like it's a bad thing. Heaven forbid someone try to impress me. But that's not what he did." He'd admitted during lunch that *General Hospital* was the one thing he could bond with his mother about. Besides that, it sounded like she was a taskmaster, always pushing him to be better academically and professionally. She'd pushed him to be an OB-GYN because they are well respected, and their family had a connection to make sure he was a partner in a practice straight off his residency. It made me sad and almost had me feeling sorry for Morgan. I was lucky enough that my momma always wanted me to do what made me happy. And we got to bond over *General Hospital* because we both loved it.

"You know, I probably know more about *General Hospital* than he does, after the way you and Carly used to talk incessantly about it in high school."

"I doubt it. He's well versed."

We walked out into the warm, muggy air. Summer was upon us. Memorial Day weekend was too.

"Ask me a question." Brooks was determined, it seemed, to best Julian.

"No. This isn't a competition."

"I still don't get his appeal," Brooks growled.

"Of course not, because you've forgotten what it's like to have fun."

He shot me a scathing glare.

"Don't look at me like that. It's true. Now where do you want to eat? I'm starving."

"Not the biscuit place. Morgan and I are on a low-carb, no-sugar diet."

I refrained from rolling my eyes. "You just proved my point. All fun foods have carbs and sugar."

"There's no such thing as fun foods. Food is for sustaining life. If everyone realized that, there would be less disease in the world."

He'd probably learned that from a TED Talk. I rubbed my hands over my cheeks. "I think maybe you should eat alone."

His shoulders slumped. "I'm not as bad as you think, Grace."

I took a moment to search his eyes. I noticed that the spark that used to be in them a long time ago was all but gone. "You're not bad at all, simply different. And honestly, I miss the old you. Have a good night." I turned and headed toward my car.

He didn't take the hint and followed after me. "We can go to the biscuit place, if it means that much to you. I'm sure they'll have something there I can eat."

"They don't." It was empty carb heaven. I picked up the pace to my car.

"We can go anyway. Please just stop."

I skidded to a halt and faced him. "What do you want from me, Brooks?"

He looked up to the clear blue sky and sighed. "I want us to be friends." He lowered his head until our eyes met. "I've come to realize how much I missed our friendship. You always brought out my fun side." He gave me a half smile, which was quite charming even if he was profusely using the F word.

"That was a long time ago. Maybe we should just admit we've grown up and grown apart. For your parents' sakes, we'll pretend in front of them that we like each other. You know, like when your momma used to tell you and Carly to pretend that you loved each other, but as soon as she turned her back, y'all were flipping each other off. I mean, we don't have to do that part." I laughed.

Brooks stepped closer and tugged on my ponytail. "Grace, I don't need to pretend. I do like you. A lot."

I swallowed hard, believing every word he said and trying not to get drunk on his amber scent and bedroom eyes. "Now that we've cleared that up, I guess I'll see you later."

"I thought we were going to have dinner together."

I pursed my lips together in thought. "I have a better, more fun idea."

Brooks's lip twitched. "Why doesn't that surprise me?"

"Are you in?"

He debated for a second or two. "Okay."

"I need you to be more enthusiastic than that."

He rolled his gorgeous eyes. "Fine. Okay!"

"That sounded like it hurt, but I'll accept it. Now follow me. I'm driving."

"I don't think so." He grabbed my arm and tugged me back. "I remember how you used to drive. We can take my truck."

"Hey, I've never been in an accident or hurt anyone."

"Which is a miracle," he quipped.

"I only hit the trash cans two or three times, tops."

"It was more than that. Not to mention you almost made the drivers' ed teacher retire. I heard the poor man had to start taking tranquilizers after you took his class."

I playfully smacked Brooks's arm. "You're lying. It was one Valium. And it wasn't my fault that squirrel ran out onto the road. I only swerved into the other lane for a few seconds. The oncoming car wasn't even close to hitting us."

Brooks chuckled deeply. "I don't think anyone else in that car remembers it that way."

"You can't believe everything you've been told. Don't they teach you that in law school?"

"Among other things. So where are we going?"

"You'll see."

"Why do I have a feeling I might regret this?"

"If you do, I'm going to be very disappointed."

We stopped at the edge of the sidewalk before we went across the parking lot.

Brooks smiled at me. "The last thing I want to do is disappoint you, Grace."

My insides shivered, even though I knew in the end, being disappointed was exactly what I was going to be. Yet, I proceeded. "Let's go have some fun, old *friend.*"

Chapter Sixteen

"I can't believe you talked me into this. I should be prepping for client meetings tomorrow."

"Don't you have a paralegal to take care of that?"

"I have one paralegal and two legal assistants."

"Wow. Color me impressed."

"I wasn't bragging."

"Well, you should. I'm proud of you."

Brooks's tan cheeks turned a nice shade of blush. It was adorable.

"But there is more to life than work. Look around you. It's a beautiful night, you are surrounded by the best people in the world, and you're getting ready to watch one of the most classic movies of our generation, *Back to the Future*. Not to mention, we have strawberry spinach salad—dressing on the side—for you, and peanut butter cups for me." I was taunting him. Peanut butter cups used to be his favorite candy, but they were on the no-fly list with Morgan. I swear she was trying to control every aspect of his life. I felt like I needed to save him.

Brooks looked around at the park near Pecan Orchard's town square. The park was filled with happy families sitting on blankets, all celebrating the end of the school year. A movie in the park was a tradition on the last day of school. I hadn't been to one in forever. The older I got, the more they kind of depressed me. I had thought by now I would have had some of my own kids in school.

"This place never changes."

"You say that like it's a bad thing."

He shrugged and grabbed a fork out of the bag.

Before I could tell him that a lot of people still cared about him in this town, the point was made for me. Our neighbor from down the street, Miss Ellen, spotted us. She was as cute as a button, wrinkly, and all of four feet, ten inches tall, with dyed pink hair. I wanted to be like her when I grew up.

She waddled over with her hand across her heart. "Look who it is. Brooks and Gracie together again." She threw her tiny arms around Brooks. Since he was so tall and she so short, there was hardly a height discrepancy with Brooks sitting down. She kissed his head. "Hubba, hubba, did you get so handsome. How are you, darling boy? We've missed you on Poplar Street. I still tell everyone to this day, no one ever mowed my lawn better than you."

Brooks seemed at a loss for words. I had to help him out. "He became a big-time lawyer."

"Just like your daddy. Bless his heart, we've all been praying for him. How is he?"

Brooks cleared his throat. "He's coming home tomorrow."

"It's a miracle. Thank the Lord for your quick thinking, sweet Gracie." She looked between the two us. "It's so good to see you kids. I always had a feeling you would end up together."

"We're not together," I spluttered.

"We're friends." Brooks loved throwing around that word.

Miss Ellen patted his head. "That's how it starts." She gave him another big squeeze. "Don't be a stranger, and don't let this one get away either," she said, pointing at me. "I'm off to see my grandbabies. Bye-bye." She scooted off before we could respond.

"Sorry about that. I hope it doesn't cause any trouble with Morgan." Miss Ellen, though wonderful, was a gossip.

Brooks flicked some grass off our picnic blanket. "Don't worry about it. Like I said, Morgan and I aren't exclusive. She doesn't believe in labels."

"Do you?"

"I find it easier not to. Girlfriends tend to want to become wives."

"Oh, the horror," I teased, though Brooks was breaking my heart with his attitude toward marriage.

Brooks stabbed his fork into a juicy strawberry. "I know you don't agree with me."

"I wonder if you agree with you . . . or Morgan."

He shoved the strawberry in his mouth, chewing on his food and thoughts. Once he swallowed, he let out a heavy sigh. "Morgan and I have both seen the damage marriage can do. Neither of our parents fared well. I appreciate her bold, out-of-the-norm attitude."

"You look down on mine."

"No. I envy yours."

I bit my lip. "You do?"

"Yes, Grace," he said my name so gently. "In fact, I'm surprised you're not married yet."

"That makes two of us." I reached into the bag for the peanut butter cups. I needed chocolate, stat.

"Just haven't met the right guy yet?" Brooks seemed hesitant to ask.

I grabbed a handful of candy and began unwrapping them as fast as I could. "No, I've met him."

Brooks fumbled his salad and barely caught it before he dropped it. "Julian?" The hitch in his voice begged me to tell him it wasn't so.

"No." I popped an entire peanut butter cup in my mouth, not believing I was having this conversation with the "right" man.

"Who, then?"

I took some time to savor the sweet ecstasy in my mouth. The mix of the salty peanut butter with the sweet milk chocolate was perfect. "It doesn't really matter," I said after swallowing. "He doesn't see me that way."

"Sounds like a real idiot."

"Oh, he is." I shoved another peanut butter cup into my mouth.

"Why do you want to be with him, then?"

I stared into Brooks's eyes. Hints of the boy I'd loved showed in the gold flecks. "Because the first time I met him, I knew he was the one."

Brooks's brow creased. "How is that possible?"

"I don't know. I don't make the rules. I just knew."

"But you didn't know anything about him." Brooks seemed to be concerned for my well-being. Perhaps even my mental health.

"Not at first, but I quickly remedied that."

"What did you think about him after that?" Brooks was awfully curious.

"That he was everything I'd hoped he would be," my voice cracked, betraying me. "You know, except the whole him not wanting me part."

Brooks rested a hand on my bare knee. "I'm sorry, Grace. Like I said, the guy must be a real idiot."

I peered down at his hand. It felt like fire against my skin; his touch called to my soul. "Regardless of what he is, I moved on." Well, at least I thought I had. "I want someone who's going to wake up every day excited to see me. Someone who appreciates me and all my quirky obsessions. Someone who wants to go on adventures with me." I pulled my knees up to my chest, making Brooks's hand drop. His touch made me long for him to be the person the voice and I knew he could be. That *someone*.

FACIAL RECOGNITION

Brooks flexed his fingers. "I hope you find the right man for you. You deserve that." He sounded sincere.

"Thanks." I had no idea what else to say. Brooks had no clue I was talking about him, which kind of said it all.

"Was he part of your facial recognition theory?" Brooks asked.

"I suppose he was the catalyst. But I was wrong about the theory, like I was about him."

"And what is the theory?"

I rested my head on my knees. "You'll think it's silly."

"Probably, but you should tell me anyway." He gave me a sweet smile. The kind of smile he used to give me. The one that could coax anything out of me.

His powers of persuasion won me over. I sat up. "When I met—let's call him 'The One'—I heard this voice tell me that I would marry him."

"A voice? As in you're hearing things?"

"No. My inner voice. The voice that you can't quite explain, but something deep within you knows it's right."

"But you said it was proven wrong."

"I said he was wrong and the theory was wrong, not the voice." Though I had questioned the voice and its sanity, more like my own sanity. Yet deep down, I knew the voice hadn't lied. It had just failed to recognize Brooks's free will in it all.

Brooks tilted his head. "He was wrong for you or about you? I don't understand."

Believe me, I knew he didn't. "He was just wrong. That's beside the point. My theory was—since I'd heard the voice the first time I saw 'The One'—I was hoping that maybe if I went on several blind dates, with no prior knowledge of what the men looked like, perhaps the voice would speak to me again."

Brooks chuckled. "How did that work out for you?"

"Not so well," I sighed. "If it had, the man I'd hoped for would be sitting across from me right now, sharing my peanut butter cups and whispering things in my ear that aren't appropriate for all the kiddos running around to hear."

Brooks's cheeks reddened. "Is that what you really wish for?"

"Pretty much. Plus a guarantee he'll adore me forever." It's not like I wanted the moon.

"What are you going to do if you never hear the voice again?"

"Who says I haven't heard the voice again?"

Brooks's eyes widened.

"Yeah, it's annoying, like a broken record. Apparently, it's really hung up on 'The One' for some reason."

"Are you?"

I lowered my head. "I wish I wasn't. Anyway," I reached for my salad, "enough about me."

"Grace." He rested his hand on mine. "While I don't think it's good to believe in 'The One,' I do hope you find who you're looking for." He spoke in hushed tones. He brushed his thumb across my skin before lifting his hand. "I hope it's not Julian." His tone went from sweet to brusque.

"Why don't you like him?"

"I like him fine, but he doesn't have a healthy outlook on relationships."

"The same could be said about you."

"You're right. And I would never wish myself upon you either. You deserve better than that." Regret seeped through his words. Or was I imagining that? Either way, I sat stunned. Was he saying he had thought about us being together? Or was that wishful thinking on my part? Unfortunately, I didn't have time to mull it over. The night was about to get more awkward. Our prom king, Sean Devereaux, spotted us. He wasn't the typical prom king who was the best looking or most athletic. In fact,

FACIAL RECOGNITION

Sean was the president of the chess club back in the day. Currently, he was balding with a paunchy stomach. Yet, he was one of the nicest guys around and could make anyone laugh. All reasons he was voted to be the prom king and why he was a great car salesman. He'd sold me my new car a few years back. He and his wife, Lily, had been married for a good seventeen years and had four kids, ranging from sixteen to four.

Sean landed on our blanket and looked between the two of us. "Wow. I have to say, I never thought I would see you two together."

I guess he didn't share Miss Ellen's opinion.

He patted Brooks's back. "It was savage the way you left poor Gracie at prom." He wasn't wrong, but he didn't need to say it out loud.

Brooks gave him a scathing look, all while tugging on his collar.

Sean wasn't reading the signs and continued on. "Man, you should have seen the tears in her eyes. And you really missed out, buddy; Gracie was a vision that night." He smiled at me. "Still the prettiest girl in town, besides my Lily, of course."

"Thanks, Sean. The movie is about to start," I said, hoping he would get the hint and skedaddle before Brooks punched him.

Sean reached into his pocket, took out a business card, and handed it to Brooks. "If you ever need a new car, give me a call. You can ask Gracie here. I'll give you a good deal."

Brooks slowly shook his head no, as if to say it would be best for him to leave.

Some concern crept into Sean's eyes.

I tried to smooth it over. "Brooks has two vehicles already." I knew that because I was surprised that Brooks drove a truck, and not a new one either. I'd asked him about his "old" truck on the drive over, and with pride he'd told me how it was the first vehicle he had ever purchased on his own, right after he'd landed his first job for a firm in Houston. However, Morgan wasn't fond of it and admonished him to be more eco-friendly, so he'd bought a BMW hybrid. He only drove the truck when Morgan wasn't around. I wanted to ask him if that seemed odd to him but didn't have the courage. And let's be real, if I asked, it would only be my jealousy talking.

Sean slinked the card back into his pocket and jumped up. "Sorry to bother y'all. Have a good night." He disappeared into the maze of people.

Brooks pressed his lips together and stared at me thoughtfully. "Did you really cry that night?"

I nodded, embarrassed.

"I'm sorry, Grace." This time there was no mistaking the regret in his voice. "Like I said, I would never wish myself upon you."

Funny. He was all I'd ever wished for.

Chapter Seventeen

"You're quiet tonight." Julian walked beside me as we crossed the arched bridge in the Japanese Garden at the botanical garden.

"Sorry." I smiled over at him and admired how handsome he looked in his khaki shorts and blue polo shirt that brought out his vibrant eyes.

He tugged on my hand and led us to the side of the bridge to look over the rails at the massive koi pond surrounded by cherry trees and Japanese maples. It was lovely, even if the humidity was making my hair frizz. Julian kept ahold of my hand, and we interlocked fingers. He smiled at me. "Can I hold your hand, Grace?"

I nodded, feeling a tiny spark. Don't get me wrong, I was attracted to Julian, but it wasn't this overwhelming, I-can't-live-without-you feeling. Not only that, Brooks's words of warning kept buzzing around in my head. In fact, all of Friday night haunted my thoughts. I had meant for Brooks and me to have some fun together watching an old movie, but it ended up with us mostly staring aimlessly at the screen, hardly saying a word. And the darker it had gotten that night, the more the tension seemed to tighten between us, like we should have been doing what Julian and I were doing now—holding hands and gazing into each other's eyes. Allowing the sparks to possibly ignite. Brooks's hand had inched over all night, but each time, he would pull it back. Mine would do the same, as if we were playing some cat-and-mouse game to see who was brave enough to catch the other person's hand. It had all come to nothing.

"Do you want to tell me what's wrong?" Julian's voice shook me out of my head.

I peered out over the water and watched the large koi fish swim in circles just beneath the surface. "Nothing is wrong per se, just thinking a lot about my life."

"Wondering where I fit in?"

I nudged him with my shoulder. "It's a little early for that, don't you think?"

"Darlin', I'm teasing you. I'm just looking to spend some time with a beautiful woman. No strings, no commitments. Is that all right with you?"

Brooks was shouting in my head to say yes to no commitments with Julian. More like he was telling me to run the other direction. But Julian seemed harmless, as long as we kept it no strings attached. And his honesty was kind of refreshing. "Yes, but—"

"There's always a but, and it's usually painful."

"I promise, I'll only hurt you a little."

He pulled me closer. "Don't excite me like that."

"Behave," I playfully responded.

His laughter rang through the gardens. "I'll do my best, but admittedly, you aren't making that easy."

Some heat rose to my cheeks.

"Blushing?" He ran the back of his hand down my cheek. "You are adorable, and I think I'll need to be careful around you."

A man hadn't touched me so tenderly in a long time. I found I longed for it. Yet, I wasn't sure if I should crave Julian's touch.

"I haven't gotten to the *but* yet, so you might want to reserve your judgment."

He squeezed my hand. "I do like you."

"I like you too, which is why I wonder how you feel about relationships. Not that I'm looking for one with you." I made sure to put his mind at ease. Yet, I needed to know if he really did have unhealthy attitudes toward relationships, as Brooks had warned me. Sure, I was all for having some fun, but I was smart enough to know that it wasn't all fun and games. Anytime men and women mixed, there was the potential for trouble to brew.

"Are you looking for a relationship?" he asked.

"I'm thirty-eight years old, and I'd like to have a baby before I'm a contender for the *Guinness World Records'* oldest mother. And I just went on thirty-six blind dates, most of which were either plain awful or laughable. So the answer is yes. I want to be in a relationship."

I could see his body tense.

"Not with you," I added.

He cocked his brow. "What, am I not good enough for you?" he teased.

I let go of his hand and shook his shoulders. Nice broad shoulders, I might add. "You said you didn't want to be in a relationship, and you're avoiding my question."

He sighed. "You're different than I thought you would be."

"How did you think I would be?"

He pursed his lips together. "Just different," was all he would own.

"Different in a good way or bad way?"

He leaned in, close enough for me to inhale his minty breath. "Very good." His eyes drifted toward my lips.

I placed my hand on his chest to make sure he kept his distance. Not to say I wouldn't ever kiss him, but I needed to be sure about his character. And I worried I would like the way Julian kissed. Confident men tended to innately know how to set your lips on fire and make your head spin. I didn't need that added confusion right now.

Julian placed his hand over mine, pressing it firmly against his solid chest. Oh, wow, was it hard. Probably not as defined as Brooks's, but if I was a betting woman, my money would say I would probably drool a little if I saw the doctor shirtless.

"Gracie," Julian whispered. "No matter what happens between us, please remember I never set out to hurt you."

"Are you going to hurt me?"

"Sooner or later I've ended up hurting every woman I've had a long-term relationship with."

"Oh."

"Relationships aren't my family's strong suit."

Even Morgan's? I wanted to ask, but when I was with Julian, I did my best not to mention her. I didn't think I would be able to hide my distaste for her.

He brushed his thumb across my hand. "My parents raised protégés, not human beings." The bitterness in his tone was undeniable.

"I'm sorry."

"Don't be. And promise me, Gracie, you won't let me make you sorry for the time we spend together."

"How can I do that?"

He glanced down. "By keeping me at arm's length."

I dropped my hand and let out a deep breath. I was beginning to wonder if every man I was attracted to wanted me to keep my distance.

After Julian had walked me to my door and kissed my cheek, I had no desire to walk inside. Instead I sat on the porch, listening to the crickets chirp and the neighborhood teenagers play football in the road under the glow of the streetlights. It was in moments like these that I desperately missed my momma. She would know what I should do about Brooks and Julian. I was beginning to think those two needed to start a tormented men's club or something.

I looked over to the Hamiltons', and it struck me that there was a momma there tonight. June had practically moved in yesterday when Tom had come home. She'd made sure to mention she was sleeping in the guest bedroom. All I know was that Tom was one happy camper, even if he had to use a walker and was on a strict diet and several new prescriptions.

It was only nine thirty. Julian had dropped me off early because one of his patients had gone into labor. Surely Miss June would still be up and could talk with me. Unless she and Tom had decided to rekindle their romance. Yikes. Would that make Tom's heart stop again? Maybe I shouldn't go over there. Except I really needed to talk to someone. Not that I couldn't talk to Daddy, but the man wouldn't care if I ever left home. Honestly, I think if I got married, he would say we could just move in with him. Very Mr. Woodhouse–like. If only my Mr. Knightley would show up and not have a load of baggage like Brooks and Julian seemed to carry with them. Not that I wouldn't help carry another person's luggage, but they had to be willing to let me get close enough to do it. I was willing to assist them in unpacking, but they had to open their suitcases up to me first.

I stood and decided to go for it. I needed a woman's and a momma's opinion. I practically tiptoed down our brick path to the sidewalk. From there I leisurely strolled while listening to the boys in the street call out plays and children laughing in the distance. Someone was even shooting off fireworks. Tomorrow was Memorial Day, not the Fourth of July, but whatever. They were pretty in red, white, and blue. I loved this neighborhood. Though some neighbors had come and gone over the years, it still had the feeling of home and all things good in the world.

Tom's yard was proof of the goodness that existed. "Welcome Home" signs dotted the lawn, and someone had hung a banner across the wraparound porch. It had brought Tom to tears yesterday when Miss June and I had brought him home. People had lined his walk, cheering him on as we drove up. Even Daddy had shed a couple of tears, so happy his best friend had made it. Tom wasn't completely out of the woods yet. The next year would be telling, but Miss June was determined to get him in shape and force him to live.

There were lights on in the house, which I took as a good sign. I knocked on the heavy oak door that was plastered with paper hearts.

In no time, I heard footsteps and saw Miss June peeking out of one of the small windows framing the door. Her face lit up when she saw it was me.

Miss June swung open the door, showing off her floral nightgown and the fact that she wasn't wearing a bra. Wow, did her babies hang. But, boy, did they still fill out the bustline. "Hey, darlin', did you come to make sure we weren't fornicating?"

I laughed instead of gagging like I wanted to do. "Uh, no," I stuttered.

She smiled and reached for my hand. "I figured my son had sent you over to check on us. I got quite the lecture from him yesterday about living under the same roof as his daddy."

I took her hand. "He does seem to give his opinions freely."

She shut the door behind me and beamed. "I bet he has some for you about the handsome doctor."

"That he does."

She waved her hand in the air. "The boy is awfully opinionated for someone who wouldn't know what a good relationship was if it bit him in the butt. Not that I don't blame myself for that, but he's a little too high and mighty for a man who's dating a woman who wants to be introduced as his intimate. What does that even mean?" Miss June was so fired up she didn't even take a breath to let me answer. "And get this, he's supposed to say it as inti-mate."

Mate? I could hardly breathe. "They're mates, as in mating?"

Miss June grabbed her heart. "Oh, darlin', don't ever say that. If Brooks procreates with that woman, I'm going to rent my clothes and cover myself in sackcloth and ashes."

She made me snicker. "From the sounds of it, I think she's not interested in bearing babies, so you're probably safe." I rubbed my heart, begging for that to be true. I knew I shouldn't care, but if he had a baby with Morgan, that was it. Game over.

"Child, let us pray." She clapped her hands together and looked up to the popcorn ceiling.

You know, praying wasn't such a bad idea. I threw up a silent one for the cause. Maybe it was sacrilegious to pray for such things, but after my time with Brooks and Julian, I had a feeling Brooks would have a miserable life if he got permanently entangled with that family. On the other hand, I had a feeling Brooks would be a great daddy. I loved watching him with his nephews.

As soon as Miss June said, "Amen," she focused right back on me. "How about some iced tea and a talk?"

"How did you know I needed to talk?"

"Oh, darlin', I remember that look on your face."

My eyes filled with tears. "A talk and some tea would be perfect."

She took my hand and led me to the kitchen that was still decorated with wallpaper that had lemons on it. "Let's talk in here so we don't wake up Tom. He's still mighty tired."

"He did good this afternoon walking to the mailbox and back." It wasn't much, but it was a start. I had followed him while he'd used his walker. He had fussed at me the entire way, embarrassed he couldn't stand or walk on his own and that he got so winded going there and back.

"He did, but, boy, did he cuss about it after you left. At least he didn't lose the dirty part of his vocabulary." She laughed. "Take a seat, honey." She pointed at the table in the breakfast nook. The old tablecloth matched the wallpaper. There were lemons everywhere in the large, once top-of-the-line kitchen.

I sat down, and so many good memories hit me. There was no telling how many times I had eaten dinner here growing up. Or how many school projects I had done on this very table while Miss June told us stories of the boys she used to date in high school. On this very table I had made Brooks's campaign posters while he had done his homework. I remembered him looking up several times and smiling at me. I loved his smile. I still did.

Miss June set a large glass of iced tea in front of me. She sat across from me and flashed me a Cheshire grin. "You need to talk about boys?"

I held on to the glass for dear life. "Yep. Boys."

"Are you falling for Julian?" She seemed hesitant to ask. More like hoping my answer would be no.

I ran my finger around the rim of the glass. "Not really. Don't get me wrong, I like him, and we have a good time together. But . . ."

"You have feelings for Brooks."

"I shouldn't."

She slapped the table. "Why ever not?"

"He's dating Morgan." Or should I say *mating* Morgan? I internally cringed. "And he told me he would never wish himself upon me. Then Julian practically said the same thing to me tonight. The crazy part is, when I'm with either one of them, it's the first time in a long time that I've found myself feeling connected and longing for a man's company. Even if Brooks and I fight most of the time, we're together."

Miss June's eyes lit up like the fireworks going on outside. "This is excellent news."

"It is? Because I've been thinking it isn't."

"Darlin', don't you see how badly Brooks is fighting against his true nature? When he was young, all that boy ever wanted to do was grow up to be like his daddy, right down to going into corporate law and living on the same street as him. Then he became a teenager and Morgan filled his head with stupid ideas. He rebelled a bit, like all kids do. His rebellion was rejecting our ideals. Toward the end, he was coming back around, but unfortunately, the divorce happened at the worst possible time and caused him to cling to his contrary ideals. And you, sweet girl, represented everything he then told himself he'd never wanted in the first place. Everything he wants so badly now but is too stubborn to admit it."

"I don't know, I think he likes driving a tiny car, eating salad, and incessantly listening to TED Talks and podcasts. They're enriching his mind," I mocked.

Miss June rolled her eyes so much I got a little dizzy. "One day he's going to wake up and realize how ridiculous he's being." She paused. "I hope that he'll recognize what he could have with you before it's too late."

I twirled my ponytail. "He doesn't want me. I'm not sure anyone does," my voice hitched.

She stood and walked over, taking the chair next to me. She wrapped me in her arms, and I sobbed like a baby into her bosom.

"I'm going to die an old maid, probably in my dad's house, surrounded by Rick Springfield posters, with *General Hospital* on replay because I won't remember which episodes I've watched."

Miss June rubbed my back. "Shhh. It's going to be okay, darlin'."

"I don't know if it will be. I'm beginning to think there's something wrong with me. Why do I keep scaring men away?"

"It's not you, it's them. Brooks and Julian. I think those men are more alike than they want to admit. They both know being with a woman like you will require change. And change is scary for men who like to pretend they have it all figured out, when in reality they haven't got a clue. Brooks hates to admit he's wrong. He always has. He comes by it honestly," she admitted.

"What do I do?" I whispered.

"I don't know if I have the right answer. All I know is don't you change yourself. If these men can't recognize what a gem you are, they don't deserve you. You let them come to you."

Huh. Maybe she was right. I'd felt like all I had done lately was look for Mr. Right. Maybe it was time to let him come find me. Even if it meant not getting my perfect reunion night. Even if it meant not listening to the voice anymore.

Chapter Eighteen

"Wake up, buttercup, you have a visitor." Lorelai knelt next to the round ottoman in the "executive" bathroom—where I was closing my eyes and contemplating my life—and poked my arm.

I turned my head and groaned, "I don't want to see anybody." My plan was to hide in the bathroom forever, or at least until it was time for my next appointment.

"You might want to rethink that. This visitor is fire engine red hot."

I bolted up. "Brooks is here?"

Her face dropped. "No, darlin'."

"Oh." I ran a hand through my hair, feeling more disappointed than I should. I had been having delusions of grandeur about Brooks finally realizing it was me he should be chasing. Even though I hadn't seen him or talked to him since last week when I dragged him to a movie at the park. "Who, then?"

She sat next to me on the ottoman. "I'm afraid to tell you now, for fear you will be disappointed."

"I'm pathetic. But I'm done chasing the ghost of Brooks. Who's here?"

She forced my head onto her shoulder. "You're not pathetic. That first love is magical and tough to get over. Especially when they walk back into your life."

"Are you speaking from experience?"

Lorelai paused, then sighed. "Yes, ma'am."

"Is it that guy you tried to set me up with? Dane?"

She softly laughed. "You are perceptive."

"Why would you try and set me up with someone you have feelings for?"

"Darlin', it's more complicated than a woman's brain. Let's just say, it would be best for both Dane and me to forget each other."

She had me so curious. "Did William know you had feelings for his friend?"

She rubbed my arm. "Gracie," she whispered, "there are hurts that run so deep it's best to keep them buried. Regardless, Dane deserves happiness, and I know you would be up for the job."

I let the inquiry into her past drop for now. "I'm not sure I'm up to making anyone happy."

"I beg to differ, and I think Julian would too, judging by the size of the bouquet he just brought you."

My head popped up. "Julian's here?"

"Uh-huh." She grinned. "Maybe I was wrong when I told you to be careful about him. Perhaps you should throw some caution to the wind. He's even more handsome in person."

"That he is. But he himself warned me to keep him at a distance. Not to mention all of Brooks's warnings about him."

She pointed at my heart. "What is this telling you?"

"I don't know. When I'm with Julian, I always enjoy myself. He makes me smile, and I even get a little fluttery around him. And he's been a total gentleman, which I like."

"But he's not Brooks," Lorelai suggested.

"It's more than that. I just can't put my finger on it."

"Well, it's probably his evil sister."

"Probably," I snarled.

"Honey, if I were you, I would go out there and see what the man has to say for himself. At least snag the flowers. They are the prettiest white roses I have ever seen. And you know they symbolize new beginnings. Maybe you both need one."

"Well, I do like flowers."

She stood and took my hand to pull me up. "All right, darlin', you get out there and see what the man has to say. By the way, he looks mighty fine in his jeans. Me-ow."

I straightened out my scrubs and laughed. "Do I look okay?"

"Honey, you are prettier than every rose in Texas. Now get going."

I gave Lorelai a quick hug before I scooted out the door and toward the check-in desk. I took lots of deep breaths in and out. I hadn't seen Julian since our date on Sunday. That was four days ago. I'd figured he was blowing me off. Honestly, I was kind of okay with it. I was a little tired of men, as of late. However, I was going to claim my flowers. And maybe check out his butt one more time. It was a lovely sight.

Demi, one of our part-time attendants, was manning the check-in desk when I arrived. The young woman was gazing dreamily at the doctor as he browsed our line of skin care products. Julian was carefully holding a square handblown vase filled with a large bouquet of roses that was bursting with greenery. It was as stunning as he was in his tight jeans and button-down, his Ray-Bans resting on top of his head.

When Demi noticed me approaching, she blushed and quickly turned to look at the computer on the desk just as Julian saw me. He smiled while looking me over in my scrubs.

We met in the middle of the lobby.

"Hey there," he crooned.

"Hi. What are you doing here?"

He held out the gorgeous flowers. "I was in the neighborhood and thought you might like these."

I took the flowers, which were quite heavy, and breathed in their heavenly scent. "These are lovely. Thank you."

"You're welcome." He seemed nervous, shoving his hands in his pockets.

"So you were . . . just in the neighborhood?"

A crooked smile appeared on his face. "I finished up my appointments for the day and I'm not on call, so I thought I should see what you were doing."

"You could have called."

He stepped closer, allowing me to breathe in his musky scent. Mixed in with the fragrant roses, it was kind of intoxicating. "I could have, but I wanted to see you."

"You did?"

He brushed my hair back, off my shoulders. "I found I've been missing you."

My stomach did a little swoop, but I played it cool. "Oh. That's nice."

He gave me a wide grin. "Do you know what else would be nice?"

"What?"

"I was hoping you would join me for a night of painting, chocolate, and wine. There's a great studio downtown that does date nights, and I made reservations for tonight, if you're amenable and available."

I tilted my head side to side, pretending to debate. The man had me at he'd been missing me. "What kind of chocolate?" I teased.

"Any kind you want, Gracie," he whispered.

The swooping in my stomach got bigger. I swallowed hard, trying to remember to be cautious. Though maybe Lorelai was right, I shouldn't overthink it, just see where it went. After all, he had come to find me. "I would love to, but I have one more client today and I didn't bring anything to change into."

"I happen to be partial to scrubs. And you're beautiful, regardless of what you're wearing." He was good. Maybe too good to be true. Yet, this didn't have to be anything serious. I mean, he admitted to being terrible at long-term relationships. So perhaps we could just be two people who enjoyed each other's company for the time being.

"Okay. I should be done by five."

"Then I will be here at five." He leaned in and brushed my cheek with his lips before whispering in my ear, "Just so you know, I intend to taste the wine on your lips tonight."

A little shiver went through me. "I prefer white wine."

"Good to know." He kissed my cheek one more time. "See you soon." He strutted off.

I watched him go, finding myself very much looking forward to our lips meeting.

Demi interrupted my thoughts. "You're so lucky."

Maybe for once I would be.

I held in my laugh while staring at Julian's copper moon painting. It looked more like a block of deformed swiss cheese.

"It's awful, I know," he lamented.

"I wouldn't say that. I think it's an abstract take on it."

"You're just trying to be nice."

"Maybe." I grinned.

He forcefully dropped his paintbrush in the provided cup of water, making a splash, looking sincerely disgusted with himself for not being good at something. The guy had graduated from UCLA with honors, and he was a well-respected doctor. It was weird that a painting would rattle him. I was beginning to think the Bronsons had totally screwed up their kids. I almost felt the tiniest bit bad for Morgan. Almost.

I took his hand and pulled him close to me. "Hey, I'm having a really great time tonight."

He peeked over my shoulder at my painting resting on the easel, which I had to say looked pretty amazing and closely resembled the copper moon our instructor had painted while teaching us.

"At least your painting turned out well."

Using my finger, I gently turned his face back to mine. "That's not why I'm having fun. It may have something to do with the company, but possibly more to do with the dark chocolate." I smiled.

He returned my smile with one of his own.

"That's better."

"Not quite." He drew me closer, his lips hovering merely an inch away from mine. "I did tell you I planned to have a taste of you tonight."

Holy crow. My heart was pounding double time. "You did give me fair warning," I whispered, inviting him to close the distance.

He tucked some hair behind my ear. "You are more than I bargained for, but I'm glad," he said before his lips barely brushed mine. His kiss didn't feel like fireworks, yet a burst of tiny tingles erupted down my spine.

"What did you expect from me?" I asked before his lips found mine again.

"Not this," was all he said before his lips pressed against my own. It was as if he were soaking me in and feeling me out. His lips stayed steady, never trying to part my mouth. And despite the tingles I was feeling, I was happy Julian kept it classy since we weren't alone.

His lips slid off mine, and he lightly kissed my cheek. "I do like you, Gracie."

"I like you too." And I did. He was always attentive when we were together, and he could make me laugh and even fascinate me with his knowledge about the weird things our bodies were capable of. Plus, he totally got all my *General Hospital* references.

My phone started buzzing loudly in my bag. At first I ignored it, as I was on a date and didn't want to be pulled away from Julian, but the phone began ringing again.

"Why don't you see who it is," Julian graciously offered. "I'll clean up while you do." He was my kind of man.

"Thank you." I grabbed my bag from where it sat near the easel and reached in for my phone. I found it was Miss June calling. Worry bubbled in my stomach before I could answer it. "Hello."

"Hi, darlin', I'm sorry to bother you."

"It's no bother. Is everything okay?"

"Tom's fine," she was quick to say. "He's a bit restless tonight. I think he's getting frustrated."

"Is Brooks with him?" It was his night to help.

"No, darlin', that's why I'm calling. He never showed up."

"What!"

"Don't get in a tizzy, honey. I'm riled up enough about it for the two of us. Unfortunately, I have an order that has to go out tomorrow and I'm behind. Is there any way you could come over and sit with Tom? I need to pick up some supplies at the grocery store."

"Of course. I'm in Fort Worth now, but I'll head straight there."

"I don't want to interrupt any of your plans. I can try your daddy."

"Don't worry about it. I'm on my way." I was so fired up about Brooks's failure to appear that I needed to leave. I knew I wouldn't be the best company after that news. What was wrong with him?

I tried to calm my agitation, and as soon as Julian returned from cleaning our paintbrushes, I said, "I'm so sorry, but I need to cut the evening short."

"Is everything all right?"

I debated about what to say. Dating Julian was tricky since our lives were tangled up in odd ways. Such as the fact that I hated his sister and I was beginning to despise the man she was dating. He better have a dang good excuse for not showing up. My anger over the situation won out.

"That was Miss June calling. This was supposed to be Brooks's night to help with Tom, and he was a no-show."

Julian rubbed the back of his neck. "He must have forgotten. I believe he's with Morgan at a charity event for a dog shelter."

Brooks was definitely in the doghouse with me. I ripped off my smock. "Well, his momma needed him tonight," I fumed.

Julian cleared his throat. "I could call him or Morgan," he offered.

"Don't bother. I'm going to head over there as soon as you drop me off at the spa." I carefully took my painting off the easel.

"Gracie," Julian's tender tone had me stopping in my tracks.

I gave Julian my attention.

"Is there something going on between you and Brooks?"

I swallowed my heart down. "No," I stammered. "Why would you ask that?"

"Darlin', you're way too emotional for there not to be some feelings toward him."

I didn't have time to debate with Julian, nor did I want to on this subject. "The only feelings I have for him right now are disappointment. He's better than his actions." Though I was beginning to wonder if he was.

Julian shifted his feet. "Aren't we all."

I tilted my head. "I suppose so, at times."

Julian gave me a strained smile. "Gracie, don't be too hard on him. My sister can be quite persuasive."

"Believe me, I know," I scoffed. Boy, did I know.

Chapter Nineteen

I walked up the Hamiltons' porch steps as I called Brooks. He was getting a piece of my mind. All the way home I had mulled over calling him, and I'd finally decided that if I didn't, I would stew about it all night.

After the third ring, he answered. "I know what you're going to say," he said with no other greeting.

"I don't think you do," I snapped. "Do you know how lucky you are that your daddy survived? Do you know what I would have given to have my momma live another day, to get her miracle?"

"Your relationship with your mother was much different than mine and my father's," he defended himself.

"That's been your choice." I was getting angrier at him by the second.

"Grace," he sighed. "It's complicated. I'm sorry if I let you down in some way, but I had told Morgan a while back I would go to this charity event with her—"

"Let me stop you there." I leaned against the porch rail and gripped my phone like a vise. "I really don't care what you promised Morgan. Any girlfriend worth having would have understood you not attending her precious event so you could help take care of your daddy. You do realize your daddy's chances of surviving this next year aren't good, right? You heard the doctor," I cried.

He let out a heavy breath. "I made a commitment to Morgan. I'll make it up to my mother." He sounded a bit remorseful.

"You just don't get it, do you? You may never get the chance to. Why in the world are you letting Morgan run your life?" I'd had it with that woman, and I wasn't keeping my mouth shut any longer.

"She doesn't," he growled.

"Are you blind? She tells you what to eat, which car you should drive, how to spend your time. I mean, you can't even enjoy your favorite candy because she told you not to. And if you think you love going to TED Talks, charity events, and seeing dead people all the time, you're lying to yourself. You'd rather be watching baseball and eating a steak. And you know it."

He paused for a moment. "She has my best interests at heart." Not even he sounded like he quite believed it.

"I don't think so. She has her own agenda, just like she always has. She's selfish and so are you. All your momma needed was a few hours of your time. And all your daddy wants is a chance to make it right with you. But you're so busy pretending to be something you're not that you've forgotten who you are. I just hope you figure it out before it's too late. Goodbye." I didn't give him the chance to say anything before I hung up. Before he could hear the tears in my voice and the longing for the boy who'd brought me cookies and sneaked into my room.

I took several deep breaths of the warm night air, trying to get my emotions under control before I headed into the house. On one hand, I felt better for getting those things off my chest. On the other hand, I felt awful because my old best friend was a jerk. And to top it off, I was upset because I had missed out on what was likely going to be a serious make-out session, judging by the goodbye kiss Julian had given me when he'd dropped me off at my car. Holy crow. He had used his lean, muscular body to push me up against my car while he trailed kisses up my neck before capturing my lips like he would his last breath. I'll admit to gasping when he parted my lips, and his tongue gently swept the inside of my mouth. I knew he would be able to kiss well, and he didn't disappoint. Except for how short it was.

I needed to quit thinking about men. They were ridiculously confusing. Even Julian was acting mysteriously with all his strange comments about how different I was from what he'd expected. He was different too. In a good way. In ways that had me thinking perhaps I would ask him to come to the reunion with me. First though, Tom. One of my favorite men ever.

I turned and knocked on the door. Miss June opened it in no time, inviting me in. She greeted me with a hug. "Oh, darlin', you are a lifesaver. I would have pushed off the order, but it's from my largest account. Besides, I think Tom needs you after my worthless son didn't show his face. That boy and I will be having some words."

"I just had some with him."

She leaned away from me with a satisfied smile. "That's my girl. You have a better chance than anyone to get through his thick head."

"I doubt it. But I said my piece."

She tapped my nose. "You're disappointed."

I nodded. "That's life."

"It can be, darlin', but don't give up hope yet. How was your date?"

"Good."

She gave me a sad smile. "You make sure that Julian Bronson treats you well, or he'll have to come talk to me."

"We're not serious about each other."

She seemed relieved.

"I better head to Tom's room."

She lifted my chin with her finger. "Chin up, honey. You'll figure it all out."

I hoped so.

"I'm going to run to the store. Thanks a million."

"See you later." I shuffled off to the den, where Tom was staying since his bedroom was on the second floor and he couldn't go up the stairs without major assistance. The stubborn fool had fallen twice trying to walk without help from either his walker or one of us.

I knocked on the french doors before walking in to find Tom propped up in the full-size bed we had moved in, watching *The Nanny*. "Good episode," I commented.

Tom flashed me a disgruntled look. "I don't need you to b . . . babysit me."

"Darn it. And here Miss June promised me five dollars an hour. Now I won't have enough money to buy that new CD I've been saving up for."

Tom chuckled. "It's good to . . . see . . . you, Gracie girl." He stumbled on some of his words.

I walked over and kissed his head. "It's good to see you. It looks like you got a haircut today and shaved." He smelled good, too, like Old Spice. It mixed nicely with the smell of all the old books that filled the built-in shelves lining two of the walls.

His ears pinked. "June c . . . cut my hair and . . . she helped . . . me shave."

"Ooh. That sounds romantic. Spill the beans." I sat in the chair next to the bed and took his hand, which was still riddled with colorful bruises from all the IV lines.

Tom squeezed my hand the best he could. He didn't have a lot of strength yet. "I'm w . . . working on her," he stuttered.

"Oh really. What's your master plan?"

He thought carefully. I wasn't sure if it was because he couldn't think of the words or if he wasn't sure what his plan was. "I'm g . . . going to marry her," he finally got out with some force.

"Wow. That's quite the plan. Are we thinking summer or fall wedding? I look really good in peach and coral, so summertime would work well for me. Though I can rock some gold and even some warmer reds, so fall could work too," I teased him.

He patted my hand. "G . . . Gracie girl, you m . . . make this old man smile."

"I'm glad. But you didn't answer my question. I need to start shopping."

"We're t . . . taking it slow," he admitted.

"So she's on board with your plan?"

He gave me an impish grin. "She let me k . . . k . . . kiss her last night."

"That's a start."

"She told me, though, that I need to get my fat b . . . butt in shape."

I laughed. "That sounds like Miss June. I guess you better work extra hard during physical therapy so we can start doing Zumba together."

"I'm not g . . . going to shake my b . . . butt like you girls do."

"That's probably a good call. How about we'll start with walking around the neighborhood?"

He nodded, but tears pooled in his eyes.

"What's wrong?"

With some effort, he pulled my hand up and kissed it. "You've been like a d . . . daughter to me," he stammered. "You never g . . . gave up on me."

"Of course not." He had me choking up. "I love you."

"I l . . . l . . . love you," his voice cracked. Once he'd composed himself, he asked, "D . . . do you think Br . . . Brooks will ever forgive me?"

I tossed my head from side to side. "Honestly, Tom, I don't know. I think Brooks lives in his own world right now."

"I just want my family b . . . back," he cried.

"I know. I want that for you too."

"What d . . . do I do?"

I thought for a moment. "You know, Miss June gave me some good advice about men. She said I needed to let them come to me. I think that's what you have to let Brooks do. You've done all you could over the years to keep the door open and beg him to walk through it. Now it's his turn to knock and turn the knob."

Tears trickled down Tom's clean-shaven, weathered face. "I miss him, G . . . Gracie girl."

"I miss him too." Now more than ever, since I wasn't sure the real Brooks would ever come back again.

Chapter Twenty

I carefully walked down the stairs in my sparkly, strappy heels that went perfectly with my halter-neckline dress. The knee-length dress had a tight sheath underlayer with a translucent teal overlay that subtly glittered in the light. Julian was taking me to Manresa's, an overpriced fancy restaurant outside of Dallas. I'd told him that wasn't really my style, but he'd insisted I would love the food and atmosphere.

Daddy stopped in his tracks as he came out of the living room and grabbed his heart. "Wow. Honey."

I met him at the bottom of the stairs. "Do I look okay?"

"You, my love, are the spitting image of your mother. She always took my breath away."

My eyes got misty. I missed Momma so much. "Thanks, Daddy."

"Are you sure you want to go out looking so beautiful?" Daddy teased.

"Don't worry, I think I'm destined to be a spinster and live in this house forever. But just so you know, as soon as you kick the bucket, I'm repainting the robin's-egg–blue kitchen and your pink room." I winked.

Daddy chuckled. "The house is and will be yours to do with as you please. Though I have a feeling you won't be living here forever," he sighed.

I wrapped my arms around him. "If I ever do leave, I won't go far."

He gave me a good squeeze. "Don't let me hold you back."

"You've only ever lifted me up. I blame you for my high expectations."

He kissed my head. "You're a good girl. Make sure you choose someone who deserves you."

I nodded, hoping I would have some choices someday. Then the doorbell rang. "I guess that's my cue. Good night, Daddy."

"I'll wait up."

He had no idea how much that always meant. "Love you," I called before I opened the door to find Julian rocking a black suit and tie. Holy crow was he dashing. My jaw literally dropped. Move over, Dr. Noah Drake, there was a new doctor in town. Ye-ow. Now, if he could sing "Jessie's Girl," I would elope with him tomorrow.

Julian seemed just as stunned with me as his eyes roved over and over me. "Gracie," he said breathlessly. "You are a vision."

"I was thinking the same thing about you."

Julian pulled me to him and held me tight.

I snuggled against him. He smelled amazing, like a spice cabinet.

He took in several deep breaths and let them out slowly, clinging to me.

"Are you okay?"

"It's been a rough day, but you're making it better already."

I leaned away just enough to look into his beautiful eyes. "What happened?"

He closed his eyes. "I had to deliver a stillborn baby today. It's not the first time, but it never gets easier."

I rested my hand on his warm cheek. "I'm so sorry. Do you want to come in and talk? We can go out another night."

He leaned into my hand and opened his eyes. "A night out with you is just what the doctor ordered."

"Are you sure? I feel awful."

He pressed a gentle kiss to my lips. "Don't. I'm sure."

"Let me grab my purse and we can go." I fluttered back into the house, grabbed the silver purse that went well with my ensemble, and headed out the door with Julian.

The car ride was a pretty silent affair. I could tell Julian was lost in his thoughts as he held my hand and deftly weaved in and out of the ridiculous Monday night traffic. I couldn't imagine having a job that dealt with life and death. The most joyous occasions and probably some of the most heart wrenching. I wished I knew what to say or do to make it better.

When we arrived at the restaurant and before the valet was to us, Julian turned to me. "Would you mind driving home tonight?"

"Um . . . no."

"Great. I have a feeling it will be at least a two-glasses-of-wine night."

Before I could respond, the valet was to us. I wasn't sure how to feel about this turn of events. I wasn't against people drinking—occasionally I partook—but I wondered if he regularly used alcohol to cope. I, at least, appreciated him not wanting to drive intoxicated, and maybe he would only drink a couple of glasses, which was no big deal.

Julian held me close as we walked into the opulent restaurant that dripped extravagance. The ceiling was covered in live flowering vines, and the chairs were made of a deep burgundy velvet. Each table was lit by candlelight, and even though it was summertime, a large fireplace lowly burned in the center of the restaurant. I was completely blown away. Never had I been in a more romantic setting.

"Right this way, Dr. Bronson and Ms. Cartwright." The maître d', dressed to the nines in a tux, led us to our table. I felt out of place, like Julia Roberts in *Pretty Woman*. You know, except I wasn't a paid escort. The place screamed top one percenters. I felt like I had a big sticker on my head that advertised I didn't have a college degree and I drove a domestic car.

FACIAL RECOGNITION

We were barely seated before Julian ordered a bottle of wine. I was still trying to give him the benefit of the doubt. He smiled at me so sweetly from across the table, and it reminded me of how wonderful he had always treated me each time we had gone out. I had no reason to suspect tonight would be any different.

"This place is gorgeous."

"It pales in comparison to you."

"Have I mentioned how much I like you?"

"Please don't forget that."

He made the oddest comments sometimes. "What do you—"

"Julian," the most grating voice in Texas interrupted me. "What a coincidence. I didn't know you would be here." The wicked witch landed at our table with her flying monkey, a.k.a. Brooks.

Holy crow, I'd thought Julian rocked a suit and tie, but he had nothing on the broody Brooks, dressed to kill in his charcoal tailored suit. I wanted to kick myself for being so drawn to him. It was the tousled hair, I kept telling myself. I had a thing for it. And him, let's be honest. Unfortunately, I couldn't forget the boy who lived inside the man. Too bad Morgan looked like a goddess in her red evening gown that showed off all her curves and highlighted that voluptuous chest of hers.

I looked at Julian to gauge his reaction, and while his pinched features said he was miffed, he didn't look all that surprised.

"How are you, Grace?" Brooks grabbed my attention.

My name on his tongue warmed me in ways it shouldn't. Especially since I didn't particularly like him. Plus, I was on a date and so was he. How awkward was that? I turned to find his soulful brown eyes zeroed in on me. "I'm well." My tone was cool and steady.

Morgan didn't seem to care for the way Brooks kept staring at me. She yanked his arm to pull him closer, but if I wasn't mistaken, he didn't budge. Was there trouble in paradise, or should I say hell?

Morgan spat out a fake laugh. "Isn't this fortuitous?"

"I wouldn't say that." I kept it real.

"You were always such a joker." Morgan gave me a razor-like smile that said she would love to cut my throat.

"We're sorry to interrupt," Brooks spoke up. I could tell he, too, felt awkward about the situation.

"Brooks, I think it would be nice if we all dined together," Morgan suggested out of the blue. Was she high? "Weren't you just saying how you needed to talk to Gracie? Now here's your chance." It was like she was daring him.

Her voice was so freaking intimidating it gave me the chills while I contemplated why Brooks wanted to talk to me.

"Not tonight, Morgan." Brooks held his ground.

Morgan wasn't deterred. She looked to her big brother. "Don't you think we should all eat together?"

Julian looked between Morgan and me, his shoulders slumping and a heavy breath escaping him. My eyes begged him to refuse, but he paid them no heed. "Yes," he said half-heartedly.

Uh. Didn't I get a say in this? Before I knew it, Julian was moving next to me on my side of the table, and Morgan slid into his seat with a smile, like she was stealing home plate. Brooks stood, unsure what to do.

"Brooks, you're making a scene," Morgan admonished him.

Brooks resigned himself to his fate and took the seat across from Julian.

Julian squeezed my knee under the table, as if to say he was sorry. Oh, he better be. Honestly, if he hadn't had such a rough day, I would have pushed his hand off and left.

Morgan smiled toothily with her capped teeth. "Isn't this nice?"

I was going with no. I supposed the men felt the same way, since they didn't answer either. Thankfully, the waiter showed up with our menus and some goblets of sparkling water, making it so we didn't have to talk to each other for a few minutes. The tension around the table was palpable. Julian's wine showed up too, and he wasted no time downing the glass that was poured for him.

I buried my head in my menu and tried to comprehend the names of the food. I was tempted to get my phone out and type the items into Google Translate. I got distracted, though, when Cruella de Vil started in on Brooks about what he should order.

"I think you should get the tabbouleh."

I wanted to say, *Bless you*. It sounded like she'd sneezed the name. What I should have said was, *Oh my crap! He's a grown freaking man. He can order for himself*. I peeked over my menu to look at Brooks, willing him with my eyes to grow a backbone around this chick.

"Bulgur has a lot of fiber in it," Morgan droned on while Brooks stretch his neck from side to side.

Not sure what bulgur was, but it sounded disgusting. I knocked that off my list of items to order.

Brooks and I locked eyes for a moment, and Morgan caught us. She narrowed her eyes at me. "Gracie, did you need some help ordering? I know these kinds of places can be intimidating." If she'd said that any more condescendingly, she would have needed a higher horse to sit on.

"I'm fine, thank you for your concern."

"I usually get the chicken souvlaki. It comes with marinated vegetables and feta tzatziki," Julian piped up, I think trying to help me out. You know what would have really helped me out was for him to have kicked his sister to the curb earlier. What was it about Morgan that made men do her bidding? Was it the boobs? Hopefully that wasn't the case with Julian or we would be dealing with way bigger issues than I was comfortable with. It was already awkward enough eating dinner with Brooks—my supposed future husband, according to my inner voice—and Julian, who

I was considering opening the door for. That was, until he made me have dinner with his sister.

"That sounds great." I closed my menu, not sure what the heck I was going to be eating.

"There are a lot of calories in that dish," Morgan commented.

"Perfect. That's my kind of food."

I saw Brooks's lip twitch.

Morgan, on the other hand, didn't appreciate my comment. She sat up ridiculously straight. "Let's hope you don't become a thin-fat person."

"Excuse me?"

"You know, people who look skinny but are really unhealthy."

Who did this woman think she was? "I just call them happy," I replied with a snide smile.

Brooks barked out a laugh but hid it as a cough when Morgan whipped her head toward him.

Julian poured himself another glass of wine while trying to steer the conversation in another direction. "How's work?" He gave his sister a pointed look.

His drinking was starting to worry me. He was on his second glass and we hadn't even ordered yet.

Morgan's face lit up like a pyromaniac. "I've recently been tasked with reviewing the adequacy of our risk management procedures and methodologies. I minored in risk management." She directed her last comment toward me.

"How nice."

"You didn't go to school, right?" she purred, obviously trying to prove a point.

"Not the traditional kind, no."

"To each their own," she said as an insult.

"Morgan," Brooks said as a warning.

FACIAL RECOGNITION

I didn't need him to defend me. "I find it funny how women like you look down on what my friends and I do for a living, yet you make up most of our clientele. You even brag about what a privilege it is to use our services. I never hear about people getting excited to go to the bank, but they are always happy to visit us. So, maybe I didn't get a fancy degree, but what I do is important, and I'm proud of it." I didn't even try to hide the bite in my words.

Her mouth fell open.

That's what I called a mic drop. If she wanted to go tit for tat, she'd better get ready for a long night.

Chapter Twenty-One

Oh, what a dreadfully long night it was. It was apparent, as the dinner wore on, that Morgan was hoping to highlight my deficiencies. It was almost like it gave her a sick thrill. I was beginning to think she was a narcissist. After she'd brought up my lack of a degree, she'd moved on to how I still lived at home and in the same town we all grew up in. She'd droned on and on about the dreariness of Pecan Orchard and how she had lived in places like LA and Manhattan. Of course, she did it all backhandedly so she didn't come off as a total witch. The question was, Was it Julian or Brooks she was trying to convince of my undesirability?

I did find it interesting, though, to watch the way she and Brooks interacted. There was some definite tension between them. Brooks hardly said a word while he ate his salad, and anytime Morgan touched him, he flinched. Quite often I found him staring at me as if he were trying to figure me out. I was trying to work out some things too, like why he wanted to be with someone as manipulative as Morgan. Where was his brilliant lawyer mind when it came to her?

I also began to question why I was there with Julian. I had lost count of how many glasses he'd had. I knew he'd had a rough day, and he'd asked me to drive home, which was the responsible thing to do; however, I didn't want to be with someone who used alcohol to deal with their problems. I wasn't the only one who noticed. Brooks's eyes seemed to be searing into Julian, and the way his jaw was clenching was like he was forcing himself to keep his mouth shut.

Morgan, as always, was concerned with only herself. She, more than anyone, should say something to her brother. Instead she was holding up her phone and looking at herself in it. "Did anyone listen to Simon Sinek's TED Talk about how great leaders inspire action?" she asked after our dinner plates were cleared, but it looked like she was talking to herself into her phone.

No one responded right away, so I said, "I didn't, but I did take the latest *Cosmo* quiz, and, good news, I totally got A-plus kisser."

Morgan lowered her phone and gave me a sneer that could melt the butter on every table in the place.

Brooks chuckled, then stopped once Morgan hit him with her dirty look too.

Julian swirled the wine in his glass before downing all its contents in one gulp. As soon as he set his glass down, he began to pour himself some more. "I have to say I concur with the quiz. Your lips are sweeter than the wine."

I blushed, not wanting him to talk about the kisses we had shared, especially in front of Brooks. I knew it was ridiculous. Brooks was my *friend.* Or at least he used to be. Yet deep down, I still wanted him to be more. No matter how much fun I'd been having with Julian. I was connected to Brooks in a way I couldn't be with anyone else. Brooks had helped me through the death of my mother, and my sweetest childhood memories included him.

"Who knew," Julian continued, "when Morgan begged me to ask you out how much I would end up enjoying myself?"

Every head whipped in his direction.

My heart dropped to my stomach. "What did you say?"

"He's drunk," Morgan stuttered. "Don't listen to a word he has to say." She was shooting daggers at him with her eyes.

Julian waved off his sister. "I may be drunk, but I'm lucid." He turned toward me. "Morgan is jealous of you and thought Brooks would leave her for you, so she asked me to seduce you."

Bile rose to my throat. I had to swallow it back down before I vomited.

"Shut up, Julian," Morgan hissed.

"No, Julian," Brooks seethed. "I think Grace and I would like to hear what you have to say."

Julian gave Morgan a sinister smile as if he would like nothing more than to spill the beans on his sister. Meanwhile, Morgan was trying to take Brooks's hand, but he pulled away from her.

"Brooks, it's not what you think," Morgan pleaded with him to believe her.

"It's definitely what you think," Julian growled. "She hates Gracie. Always has. She was pissed, back in high school, when you said you would go to prom with her. But it all ended up okay in the end, right, sis? Brooks ditched Gracie for you, and you lost your virginity to him that night, am I right? I find it hilarious that you found girls who did that to be so cliché. You were even careless enough not to use protection. You got lucky there." He held up his glass as if to toast her.

I grabbed my stomach and faced Brooks, tears welling in my eyes. I knew I shouldn't care, as it was so long ago, but it hurt. I pushed my chair back and stood.

"Grace." Brooks threw his napkin down and stood. "Please, listen to me."

"I don't want to hear another word from any of you. You all deserve each other," I spit out with all the vitriol I could muster.

"Please, don't go, Gracie." Julian tugged on my hand. "What we have between us may have started out as a favor to my sister, but honestly, I haven't felt like this about a woman in a long time. Besides, you haven't heard the best part yet."

I couldn't care less what he had to say. I grabbed my purse, ready to order an Uber, when Julian spouted off, "Brooks, if I were you, I would go with Gracie. My sister is certifiable. Hell, my entire family is. Morgan about drove her ex-husband to the brink of insanity trying to control his life."

"Ex-husband?" Brooks spewed. "You said you were never married."

"She also said she moved back here for a promotion." Julian took another long sip of his wine. "Her little bank gives out vice president titles like the candy they give to their drive-through customers. But she was demoted."

"Just shut up," Morgan pleaded with tears in her eyes.

"I don't think so, sis. You wanted me to orchestrate this night with Gracie, so here you go."

This was all a setup? I stood there stunned and unbelievably hurt. I had thought Julian really liked me.

"And you want to know why she's been tasked with internal audits?" Julian soldiered on. "Her boss has had a few too many complaints about how she interacts with their biggest clients. She can't help but shove her ideas down everyone's throats. She just can't stomach the thought that she's less than perfect." He glared at Morgan.

"Brooks," Morgan spluttered, "I think it would be best if we went somewhere and discussed these over exaggerations."

Brooks looked down at her as if she were the scum of the earth. "I'm not going anywhere with you. I think you should take your brother home, and I'll make sure Grace gets home safely."

Oh no he wouldn't. "No thanks." I threw the valet ticket at Julian before spinning around and marching toward the door as several patrons gave me looks of pity. I truly felt pitiful. No doubt we had all made a terrible scene. Not that I cared. I would never be coming back to Manresa's. I would keep my all-American food and real friends, thank you very much. I grabbed my phone and, through blurry eyes, clicked on my Uber app.

I flung myself through the door and into the sultry night air, walking as fast as I could away from the restaurant. The tears finally began to fall and covered my cheeks. I was an idiot to believe that maybe I'd had Julian pegged all wrong. Worse, I had spent too many years foolishly loving someone who never had any intention of loving me back. Brooks had lied to me, humiliated me, and hurt me at a tender age. However, I'd still opened the door to him when he'd come back into my life, despite the fact that he hadn't even recognized me. And here I had felt sorry for him because of the truth he had discovered on prom night. Yet he had only used it as an excuse to do what he had really wanted that night—to sleep with Morgan. He never gave me a thought. Ever.

"Grace." Brooks gently grabbed my arm.

I yanked myself away from him. "Don't touch me. Don't talk to me. Just don't," I cried.

"Please, let me take you home."

I took a good long look at him, truly recognizing him for who he was—a selfish, self-centered jerk. "I never want to see you again."

"Grace, I was eighteen years old. You're going to hold that against me? You have no idea what I went through that night."

"You're right, because you never gave me the chance. And that's the difference between you and me. I gave you every chance to see I was the girl who truly loved you and wanted you to be happy. But you were too blind to recognize it because all you ever see is yourself. Did you ever once stop to think about how much you hurt me? Do you ever stop to think about anyone other than yourself?"

His mouth opened as if he were going to speak, but all that came out were a few splutters.

"Save your breath. There's nothing you can say to me that's worth hearing. But let me thank you for sparing me from wasting any more time on you. Goodbye, Brooks."

Chapter Twenty-Two

"Oh, Momma. I'm done with men." I dropped to my knees on the grave of my mother, in my evening gown and all.

The Uber driver thought it was creepy to drop me off at the cemetery, but I think he was more than relieved to have me out of his car after all the weeping and wailing I had done on the forty-five-minute drive back to Pecan Orchard. The cemetery was only a few blocks from our house and a place I frequented. Especially when I was upset. Momma was a good listener.

I outlined her name on the heart-shaped headstone that was embraced by a granite angel. *Fiona Cartwright. Beloved Wife to Stephen and Mother to Grace. General Hospital's Biggest Fan.* I giggled every time I read that last line. I swore I sometimes heard Momma laughing along with me. Just like I could feel her heart break for me now.

"What did I do to be treated so cruelly?" I landed on my butt, kicked off my sparkly heels, and began to pick the cool grass around me. The sun was about to go down, and the last rays tickled the headstones all around me, making them glitter. Not like vampires per se, but in a beautifully muted way.

My stupid phone kept going off with texts and calls from Julian. I finally reached into my bag and turned it off. There was nothing he could say to me to excuse what he had done. He had been like the butcher tonight, leading me, the lamb, to the slaughter. Okay, so I was a cheeky lamb and I'd held my own pretty well, but still.

Now all his cryptic comments made sense. He'd been playing me on behalf of his sister. That family needed some serious therapy. Like the shock kind. I was probably going to need some counseling after my brush with the Bronsons. And Brooks definitely needed to set up a therapy session, stat. How could he be so taken in by Morgan, now and back in high school? I was ill thinking about them together the night he'd stood me up. I knew it was twenty years ago, but he was supposed to have been my friend, and he had thought only of his own desires with no thought for me and my feelings. Perhaps I'd failed back then to recognize how selfish he was. Maybe I'd been blinded by love. The shades, though, had come off, and I would no longer be fooled by him. Or any man.

"Well, Momma, at least Daddy will be happy. Though I'm not sure you are ever getting a grandson named Noah." I brought my knees up to my chest and cried into my dress, not caring that I was leaving mascara stains on it. After several minutes of my personal pity party, I heard the snap of twigs and crunch of gravel over my sniffling and sobbing. I turned my head to see Brooks walking my way, undoing his tie as he went. How did he find me?

"Go away." I turned from him. I meant it—I never wanted to see him again.

He didn't listen and came within a few feet of me. His tall body towered over me. "Grace."

"Leave me alone. You had no right to follow me." Like a child, I turned my body away from him.

"I didn't follow you. I had a feeling you would be here. You always came here when you were upset."

I was surprised he remembered that. Regardless, he wasn't welcome. I went back to hugging my knees, intent on ignoring him.

He had other plans. He knelt in front of me, taking in my pathetic state. I probably had puffy, red raccoon eyes by this point with streaks of mascara down my cheeks. He lowered his head and let out a heavy breath. "Grace, please let me explain," he begged with such conviction.

Not happening. I grabbed my shoes and stood. I was going to look like a deranged prom queen marching home barefoot in my dress. It was apropos, considering our history. Tonight's sting was a little more acute, though. I got played by two men in one night this time. Two grown men, I might add.

Brooks wouldn't leave well enough alone and came after me, grabbing my hand.

I ripped it away as fast as I could.

"Damn it, Grace. Don't you think I feel terrible about what happened tonight? About what happened twenty years ago?" he added in quietly.

I took a second to scowl at him before trudging across the cemetery.

The jerk followed. "You don't have to say anything, but please listen to me," he pled like his life depended on it.

If it wasn't too childish, I would have covered my ears and loudly said, *La la la la la*. I had to settle for turning my head away from him as I continued to march past the headstones.

"I'll start with tonight." He wasn't deterred. "First of all, I had no idea you were going to be at Manresa's with Julian," he growled. "Morgan," he spewed her name, "told me she'd made reservations there for us several weeks ago. I had wanted to discuss our relationship with her, so I agreed to go. Your words last week cut me. Made me reflect on who I had become. I think she knew I was thinking of taking a step back, which is probably why she asked Julian to bring you."

That piece of information, unfortunately, had me betraying myself. I stopped in my tracks, my head snapping in his direction involuntarily as my mouth flew open. "Right, so you could see what a catch she was in comparison to lowly, uneducated me."

"Probably," he conceded. "Little did she know that it was the worst thing she could have done. I couldn't keep my eyes off you tonight, wondering how I had been so blind," he said as if he were angry at himself. "You are the most beautiful woman I know, both inside and out." His tone softened. "You left no doubt who the superior woman is."

My heart skipped a few beats. Thankfully my head kicked in. *Girl, do not fall for this fool's line.* I walked on. "Thanks for clearing that up. Good night."

"Grace." He started after me, vigorously rubbing his temples. "You were right about Morgan . . . and me. She is selfish and controlling."

"Let's not forget a liar." I couldn't help but say that. Who lies about being married and their career? I'll tell you this, she had done a good job covering it up. I had looked up her social media profiles, and they were all glowing reviews of herself. Not once did I see any hint of her being married or demoted. She was the best wordsmith around.

"That too," Brooks groaned. "I don't know how I got so taken in by her."

"Obviously, you're an idiot," I fired back. I kept up my steady pace, even though we had hit the paved walkways now and it wasn't feeling all that great on my bare feet.

"I am." He grabbed my hand. This time he held on tighter, pulling me to a stop and making it harder for me to twist away. "Please, Grace, let me have my say."

I looked between our clasped hands and his pleading eyes. The love I'd had for him bubbled to the surface. I pushed it back down where it belonged. "What difference will it make?" I stood my ground.

"Probably none, but you need to know the truth." With his thumb he gently wiped some tears off my cheek.

I turned my head from him. "Don't touch me."

He dropped his hand and sighed. "Grace, I never meant to hurt you."

I ripped my hand from his. "I don't believe you. You lied to me when you said you couldn't face me after prom because I would have given you reasons to stay in Pecan Orchard. The truth was, you never wanted to take me to prom. But worse than that, I can't believe you so callously used me so you could sleep with Morgan that night. Why didn't you just say no when I asked you?"

He closed his eyes and ran a hand through his hair. "I didn't plan on having sex with Morgan that night. It was a heat-of-the-moment, careless decision. My world had just come crashing down around me, and I needed someone to talk to. Someone who understood what I was feeling. Morgan's parents never had a good relationship, so she could sympathize with me. Before I knew it, one thing led to another."

He began to pace, breathing out hard as he went. "Grace, I couldn't face you after what we had done. You don't know how guilty I felt. Those next few weeks were hell for me, worrying that I might have gotten Morgan pregnant all while having to pretend my family wasn't falling apart. And the one person I needed the most—you—I couldn't go to." He stopped and met my eyes. "Grace, I had no idea how you felt about me."

My skin broke out in a tidal wave of red. Why had I told him I'd loved him? I hightailed it out of there. At least, I tried. I really should have put on my shoes. I stepped on a sharp rock and screeched, "Holy freaking crow!" into the night, hopping on one foot.

Brooks was to me in no time, lending me someone to lean on.

"I don't need your help." I tried to push him away.

He wasn't having it. He easily swept me up into his arms, like he was Prince Charming or something. More like Prince Not So Charming.

"Put me down," I demanded.

He pulled me closer instead. "No," he refused so adamantly, I stopped fighting him.

We locked eyes, and I noticed his had a sheen of moisture in them. I inhaled his amber-and-vanilla scent and had to fight against the urge to sink into him and stay awhile. All of me wanted all of him. And I hated myself for it.

"I didn't know you were in love with me," he whispered. "I thought we were friends."

"We *were*," my voice hitched. "Now let me go."

He didn't comply. "Grace, I'm sorry I've been so blind."

"I am too." I wiped the tears out of my eyes. "I wish I would have never asked you to prom. I don't even know why you said yes."

The corners of his mouth twitched. "When you tried on your prom dress for me, I couldn't resist. I'd thought it would be our last hoorah before I left for school. And I hoped I would get the chance to kiss you again."

"You wanted to kiss me?"

He nodded. "I may have been oblivious to your feelings, but I wasn't blind to how beautiful you were . . . are. I'd often thought of what it would have been like to date you, but I didn't want to ruin what we had."

"And you loved Morgan."

He let out a heavy breath. "Maybe I did. I don't know. She certainly had me under her spell. Honestly, I'm not sure I've ever truly been in love with anyone, except maybe myself."

That pierced my soul. "Great," I cried. "Can I go now?"

"I'm not saying that to hurt you. You always deserved better than me. I even knew that back in high school."

"That's where you're wrong. I deserved the boy who brought me cookies when he found me crying on my lawn. The one that helped me pass calculus. And I definitely deserved the boy who let me cry all night onto his chest the day my momma died and held my hand during her funeral." I paused, taking a deep breath. "I deserve that boy, but he no longer exists." I forcibly pushed myself out of his arms and landed on my feet. Before I marched off, I took a moment to gaze up at him. That sheen of mist in his eyes had turned to pools of tears.

"I don't know where that boy went or how to get him back," his voice cracked, but he cleared his throat like he was embarrassed by the emotion he'd shown.

I admit, he had me wanting to comfort him, but I couldn't. Not anymore. "Only you would know. Goodbye, Brooks." I turned from him.

"Grace, what if I found him?"

I refused to face him. I feared if I did, I would say things I would regret. Things like, *Please find the boy I loved. I miss him. I want him.* Thankfully, I held strong. "I think your family would love that."

"What about you? Us?"

I rubbed my chest. It was as if I could feel my heart breaking. "There never was an us."

"Could there be?" He said it like it was his last shot of hope.

I grabbed my stomach, holding back the sobs and my true feelings. "No, Brooks," I whispered.

Chapter Twenty-Three

I finished arranging my two signs on the front desk. The one for Lorelai read, I donut want to go to my reunion with anyone but you. I placed it above a huge box of letter-shaped donuts that spelled out REUNION. For Colette I had a venti espresso and a sign that said, This is hard to espresso, but I'll take a shot. Reunion?

After I got home last night and bawled my eyes out to my ever-faithful daddy, who had waited up for me, I stayed up half the night looking up cheesy ways to ask my two best friends to my reunion. Then I worked on the signs. The other half of the night, I watched my beloved Noah Drake tapes. And I might have consumed an entire pan of brownies. After a night like that, I looked dreadful this morning and would be treating myself to my own facial today. The day also called for lots of caffeine, not only in my eye cream but in the six-pack of Diet Pepsi I'd already halfway consumed. I'd peed like ten times this morning. But, hey, at least it meant I wasn't dehydrated from shedding gallons of tears last night.

I kept telling myself that last night was a good thing. It was like a reset button. Now I never needed to worry about Brooks or the voice again. In fact, I might never worry about men, period. I was thinking of adopting a puppy and a baby. Or maybe hitting up a sperm bank. After all, I did have beautiful lady part mucus, and my ovaries were still working. I mean, why not? We could convert the extra bedroom into a nursery. I wondered what Daddy would think about that.

Actually, Daddy had surprised me last night. I'd thought he would be happy, or at least relieved, that I had committed fully to being a spinster. Instead he suggested that I not be so hasty. That perhaps Brooks would surprise me. Daddy had said he'd always had a feeling about Brooks and me. Yeah, so had I, and it hadn't turned out very well.

I'd spent over half my life waiting for the voice to reappear. Waiting for a man to make me feel the way Brooks had. Come to find out, my old best friend was a bigger jerk than I thought. I was still sick thinking about him sleeping with Morgan while I was standing alone and devastated at prom. A few guys had asked me to dance, but I could tell the girls they had brought weren't fond of the idea, so I had declined. My only dance that night was the obligatory one with the prom king. Of course, my girlfriends and I threw down a few numbers, but most of the night I felt small and humiliated. I had even worried something bad had happened to Brooks. I guess something awful had happened to him—Morgan. I shuddered thinking about the pair.

I needed to stop dwelling on this. I had things to look forward to, like dating my best friends and putting the final touches on the reunion. Sure, it was turning out a lot differently than I thought it would, but at least I knew I would have fun with Colette and Lorelai. There would be no worrying about whether there would be a good night kiss or if the date would lead to more dates. Brooks and Julian had given me a gift. It had come in a crappy package, but at least I knew the truth about them both before I wasted another second with either one of them.

A minute after I had everything neatly arranged, my best friends walked in, all smiles and looking like they had gotten a good night's rest.

"Good morning," I sang. It sounded pretty croaky, since I hadn't slept a wink last night.

"Good morning," they both responded, looking intently at my setup. They walked closer, reading the signs. They both kept looking between me and the words, confusion etched on their faces.

I leaned on the welcome desk for support. I wasn't a spring chicken anymore, and the sleepless night was getting to me. "Well, don't leave me hanging. Will y'all be my dates?"

They tiptoed toward me as if I were a wild caged animal.

Lorelai delicately ran her fingers down my puffy, waterlogged face. "What happened, darlin'?"

My eyes betrayed me and started watering. "I'm fine. I just got slapped with the cold hard truth last night. But that's a good thing. Better to live the truth than a lie."

Colette wrapped her arms around me. "Tell us what happened."

My head fell on her shoulder, and the sobs came next. I seriously thought I would be out of tears by now. "It's so humiliating. Think prom two point oh."

"This sounds like we better use the 'executive' bathroom," Lorelai recommended.

"Grab the donuts," I was able to get that out through my howling. Like I needed more sugar. I was seriously going to have to detox after this ordeal.

My friends got me settled on the ottoman with two donuts and a Diet Pepsi. I must have looked so pathetic. They both knelt in front of me and rubbed my legs, which were still smooth from all my prepping last night. Now I wished I hadn't put so much effort in for my date that had gone south—more like to hell in a handbasket. I still had no idea what that meant. I should probably google it. Regardless, the date was bad. Like, the worst.

After some more sugar and downing another Diet Pepsi, I was able to recount last night's events.

Lorelai and Colette gasped and cussed at all the right moments. When I finished my ugly tale, they were both fuming.

"So whose house do we toilet paper first?" Colette asked.

"That's too kind," Lorelai responded. "I was thinking more along the lines of doing a billboard to call them out. Or a social media smear campaign."

I managed a weak laugh. "They aren't worth it. My only hope is to forget about all of them."

"Even Brooks?" Lorelai patted my knee.

"I have to," I choked out.

"What about the voice?" Colette asked.

"With every piece of my soul, I know it was right, but people change."

Lorelai gave me a crooked smile. "Yes, they do. Maybe your daddy is right. Perhaps Brooks will surprise you."

I couldn't afford to think like that. It had already cost me twenty years. "I don't think so. Besides, I'm done with men. So, what do you ladies say to being my dates? Uteruses before duderuses, right?"

We all broke into fits of laughter.

They each took one of my hands.

"Are you taking us out to dinner first?" Colette asked.

"Of course. You know that means we are at least going to get to first base," I teased.

"Don't excite me." Lorelai giggled. "It will be the most action I've seen in years."

I squeezed their hands. "I love you, ladies. Thank you," my voice went all pitchy.

"Honey, don't give up hope on Brooks—the Lord loves to work with the broken," Lorelai preached.

"What we had can't be fixed. Honestly, I'm not sure we ever had anything."

"If that were true, you wouldn't be so torn up about it," Colette wisely gave her two cents.

She was right. "Even so, it was all one sided. He never saw me as anything more than his friend."

"That's not true," Lorelai disagreed. "No man sweeps a woman up into his arms for no reason. And I saw the way he looked at you when we met him at the hospital."

Like I said, I couldn't go down that road. I took some cleansing breaths. "I have to let him go. Especially now that I snagged the hottest dates for my reunion." I couldn't say I wasn't disappointed that I wouldn't be dancing the night away with a beautiful man, but at least this way I knew I wouldn't be stood up. And I was guaranteed to have a great time.

"We are going to throw it down," Colette roared.

"Hopefully we won't throw out our backs." Lorelai snickered.

"I'll keep the Advil handy," I offered. I let out a heavy breath. "I think I'm ready to face the day now."

They smothered me in a Gracie sandwich. "You got this, Gracie," Lorelai whispered in my ear.

I wasn't sure about that. My only saving grace, no pun intended, was that I was certain Julian and Brooks would disappear from my life as quickly as they had drifted in.

So, I was wrong. Again. It was becoming a bad habit. One I really needed to quit. There I was after work, minding my own business and grabbing the mail from the mailbox before I walked into the house, and guess who showed up. Brooks, the prodigal son.

While I checked to see if I'd won a million dollars from Publishers Clearing House, he pulled up next to me in his truck and scared the holy living crap out of me when he said, "Hey." I jumped out of my skin, and my mail went flying everywhere.

Brooks hopped out of his truck and chased some of the mailers that had blown away in the light breeze. One piece gave him a bit of trouble and flew all the way into his daddy's yard before he could stomp on it and pick it up. A few weeks ago, I would have laughed at the scene and found him heroic for saving my junk mail, but now all I could think about was why he was here and how much it panged my heart to be in his presence. He was supposed to have disappeared without a word to me, like he had twenty years ago.

He ran back to me and handed over my mail. His soulful chocolate eyes tried to penetrate my own, but I wasn't having it. I grabbed the mail without a word of thanks and turned to go, refusing to acknowledge how fantastic he looked in his dark dress shorts and white polo shirt. And his five-o'clock shadow was begging for someone to caress it.

"Grace."

The unseen power of my name on his lips made me freeze in place, my back to him.

"I know you don't owe me anything, but please listen to me for one minute. I want you to know I'm going to try my best to make things right with my family." He paused. "With you."

I grabbed my stomach. A swarm of butterflies had taken flight against my will. "Just do right by your family," I stammered out, like I couldn't catch my breath.

"Grace, I went home last night with every intention of letting you go so I couldn't hurt you anymore. But I realized, there is no letting you go. You're part of me. A part I had buried, but it's the best part of me."

FACIAL RECOGNITION

Tears trickled down my cheeks. He had no idea how long I had ached to hear him say that to me. How it killed me now.

"When I look back on my life," he continued, "the happiest I've ever been is with you."

I felt the same way, but it was too late. I wasn't going to be second choice or an afterthought. I couldn't afford to hope this time he would truly be mine. "I have to go." I hustled toward my house.

"I'm not giving up on you, Grace," he called out. "I'm used to facing tough opponents. I'll plead my case to you for the rest of my life, if I have to."

Well, he'd better get used to losing. I was done with men. Especially ones who lied to me and never put me first. How could I ever trust him?

As I marched up the porch steps, I wiped my eyes and took several deep breaths. I only wanted to go inside, smile at Daddy, and pretend my little episodes with Brooks and Julian had never happened. After that, I was going to go to bed early and pray that when I woke up in the morning, I wouldn't love Brooks anymore. That what he had just said to me meant nothing. So basically, I was going to need an alien abduction tonight where they scrambled my brain.

I threw the door open, armed with the biggest fake smile ever, to find Daddy in the foyer surrounded by dozens and dozens of roses in a variety of colors and vases. It looked as if we had opened a floral shop.

Daddy grinned. "Looks like you have some admirers."

"Admirers?"

"As far as I can tell, the peach bouquets are from Brooks and the rest of them are from Julian."

I rubbed my face. This was so not happening. Okay, maybe it was sweet that Brooks remembered my favorite flowers were peach roses, but I wasn't falling for it. And as far as Julian went, he was dead to me. He'd

182

knowingly used me. Not to say the evil half of me wasn't happy to see him take his sister down, but still.

Daddy carefully walked around the jungle we had going on and handed me several cards I assumed had come with the flowers. "Looks like you have some interesting choices to make, my love."

I took the cards. "Did you read these?"

Daddy kissed my cheek. "I'm only looking out for you. Good luck." He chuckled to himself as he walked off.

I stared at the tiny cards in my hand. I tossed the ones from Julian. I'm sure they weren't any different than what his voice mails had said. Something to the effect of, *I'm so sorry. I know things didn't start out like they should, but I honestly think we could have something. I've never felt for a woman like I do for you.* I'd finally had to send him a text that said, *I listened to your messages, and I don't believe you. Please don't contact me again.* Honestly, there was nothing Julian could say to me to make what he'd done better. Not like Brooks had a better shot, but there was something about him that made it so freaking hard to let go. Like our souls shared the same ingredients or something.

Against my better judgment, I opened up the first card.

Dear Grace,

The first flower I ever bought for you was a peach rose. You don't know how sorry I am that I never gave you that corsage. If I could go back in time, I would have asked you to prom myself. I wouldn't have let anything get in the way of me taking you to the dance and holding you close all night long.

I flipped the card over.

I would have recognized what was right in front of my face the entire time. Grace, I see you. I'm sorry it took me so long.

Love,

Brooks

I looked up to the ceiling, tears streaming down my face. "Oh, Momma, I wish you were here. Do you know what this reminds me of?

FACIAL RECOGNITION

Remember when Felicia thought Frisco was dead and she married the man who'd tried to kill him? But then Frisco comes back, and Felicia gets amnesia, which makes her realize that Frisco is the man for her. So they get remarried even though Felicia hates that Frisco is a spy and leads a dangerous life. Okay, maybe my situation isn't exactly like that. But remember how happy we were every time we watched those reruns? Remember when you said there was nothing like a second-chance love story? Is that true?"

I lowered my head, angry with myself. Pretty words and flowers shouldn't be swaying my resolve. Brooks was my past. I was going to look forward to the future. Alone.

Chapter Twenty-Four

I opened the door, happy to see two of my favorite people. Tom and June were cute as could be standing on the front porch, him clinging to his walker and June's hand resting on top of his.

"Come in," I sang.

"Darlin'." June smiled. "I'm just dropping off this old geezer. I'm going to be late to my spray tan appointment if I don't hurry. Momma needs her some color." She pecked Tom on the cheek. "Be good and don't cheat."

"If you're not ch . . . cheating, you're not trying hard enough." Tom slyly stole a kiss on her mouth.

Old love was the best and, at my rate, the only kind I had a hope of obtaining.

She swatted his butt. "See you later."

"D . . . Don't excite me like that, honey," Tom laughed. His speech was getting better all the time. Maybe he just needed some sexy talk to up his game.

"Bye, June." I waved.

"Give the men hell tonight." She waved back.

Oh, I planned on it. I was so thrilled when Tom had called and asked if we could reinstate poker night. I wasn't sure his mind was up for it. However, it was normal, and I needed normal after the last month. I wanted my routine back again. Except no more fried food Friday. I was proposing fish Friday or maybe fajitas with whole wheat tortillas and fruit on the side.

I grinned at Tom. "You look good." His face was slimmer, and he looked like he was in a smaller size of pants. Plus, he had this glow to him that I hadn't seen in twenty years. I wondered if it had more to do with June or the fact that Brooks had been over the last couple of nights. Which, of course, meant I had stayed away. Not only had I wanted to give father and son some time, but my heart needed the distance from Brooks. I was curious, though, how it was going with the two of them. My plan was to get the scoop while we played poker.

Tom's ears pinked from the compliment. "No mushy stuff t . . . tonight. I plan on winning."

I playfully shrugged. "We'll see."

Tom, with effort, maneuvered his walker over the threshold and walked in. I made myself not help him. He didn't like to be babied. He had snapped at me a couple of times on our walks to his mailbox and back. Of course, he was quick to apologize, but he hated feeling like less of a man.

Daddy came out of the kitchen carrying a tray filled with fruits and veggies, and glasses of water with lemon. No more beer and chips during poker night. Besides, I could use some fiber in my life after all the sugar I'd been consuming, trying to force myself into a carb coma in hopes of forgetting a certain someone. Which wasn't going so well, considering I'd kept all the beautiful flowers he'd sent. I hated to waste them. I mean, peach roses were my favorite. Julian's I'd tossed in the garbage. I'd also blocked the moron's number after he kept calling and calling, begging for me to give him another chance, saying what we had was special. Um. No. It was all a lie.

"Steve," Tom rumbled in greeting.

"Tom," Daddy's voice cracked a bit. Daddy wasn't an overemotive guy, but I knew he'd feared for a while that he would lose his best friend.

"Ready to lose some money?" I tried to give the men an emotional out.

"Not tonight, G . . . Gracie girl," Tom chided. "I have a secret weapon."

My brow quirked. "If you think I'm going easy on you because you've been sick, think again." I pointed to my lucky *I'm Magically Delicious* shirt.

Tom painfully walked toward me with an impish grin. "I'm not sure you're l . . . lucky sh . . . shirt is going to cut it tonight."

"Did the nurses teach you some mad skills while you were in the hospital?"

Tom shook his head. "Nope."

"I think I'm safe, then."

The doorbell rang.

Daddy dashed into the living room, and Tom's impish grin grew. "I think you should answer that. I need to sit d . . . down."

My men were behaving oddly, but okay, I would answer the door since it was my house. I sauntered over to the door, expecting to find the pizza guy delivering contraband, which I would have to refuse. No empty, greasy calories tonight. Instead I opened the door only to gasp and choke on my own saliva. I began coughing and sputtering while Brooks stood there looking like he was posing for *GQ*, leaning on the doorframe in his tailored dark suit with a smolder to melt my insides.

"Are you okay?" he asked.

I slapped my chest several times, trying to get my coughing fit under control. The answer was, no, I wasn't okay. I was about to slam the door on him when he walked in without an invitation, kissed my cheek, and whispered in my ear, "I love that shirt. I have no doubt you're magically delicious."

That stopped the choking, but now I couldn't breathe.

"Shall we play cards?" He strutted past me, smiling at the bouquets he'd sent me that I'd placed on the entryway and sofa tables. Oh man, did he smell divine. No. No. No. I wasn't going to be taken in by him and his sexy ways.

My brain finally started functioning. Boy, did he have a lot of nerve. I wanted to kick Brooks's tight butt out of there, even though it was a heavenly sight. Holy crow. "Why are you here? I don't remember inviting you."

"Darlin', I did," Tom rang in with a joviality I hadn't heard from him in forever. He was so happy it gave me some pause.

Brooks loosened his tie and took off his jacket like he intended to stay for a while. This was not in my plans. Where was this Brooks twenty years ago? Heck, even a month ago? Now, though, I knew too much. That was a good thing, right? I steeled myself as I walked past the infuriating man, totally prepared to stick to my guns. Some flowers, a beautiful card, and a few flirty words weren't going to sway my resolve.

I took my seat at the card table and realized there were four glasses of water, which meant my daddy had betrayed me too. He'd totally known Brooks was coming and didn't tell me. I gave Daddy and Tom the evil eye. Both men had the audacity to laugh at me. I thought they were on my side.

Brooks sat to my right, closest to his daddy. "Father," Brooks struggled to say.

I suppose *father* was better than *Tom*, but you could tell it still cut Tom. However, Tom rallied with a smile. "G . . . Good to see you, son."

It wasn't like I had expected father and son to automatically fix all that had been broken. There was a lot of water under their bridge that had to be waded through. I would at least give Brooks props for coming, even if it tortured my soul.

"What are we playing tonight?" I decided to get the show on the road so I could get Brooks out of the house and my life. Though I had a feeling he was going to make both difficult.

"Why don't we let Brooks decide," Daddy offered.

I refrained from rolling my eyes.

"How about five-card draw?" Brooks responded.

"Amateur." I played with my chips.

Daddy and Tom chuckled while Brooks hit me with his enigmatic eyes. "Would you like to up the wager, then?"

"What do you have in mind?"

"I happen to have scored two front-row seats to the Rick Springfield concert next month."

No freaking way! I shouted in my head. On the outside, I remained calm, cool, and aloof. "How nice. I have tickets too."

"Yes, but are they in the front row?"

I rubbed my neck, seriously salivating for those tickets. "No."

Brooks leaned in, giving me a taste of his minty breath. "How's this? If you win, I'll give you the tickets. If anyone else at this table wins, you go with me."

Oh, that was so dirty. Like sexy dirty, but still rotten. I internally debated. I was a good poker player, and five-card draw was like a child's game. Yet skill was such a small part. It was mostly luck. And it was me against three of them. But, I really, really wanted those tickets.

I sat up tall and straightened my shirt. "Okay, fine, but you're going to have to win if you want me to go with you." It wouldn't mean anything if we went together. We would drive separately, and I would ignore him while I sang every single song and prayed Rick Springfield would reach down and touch me. Maybe pull me up on the stage and serenade me with "Jessie's Girl."

Tom clapped his hands together and hooted. "I l . . . love your fire, Gracie girl. Let's play." He grabbed the deck of cards in front of him. He was always the dealer. Except when he went to shuffle, his hands wouldn't work right. The cards kept slipping out of his fingers, yet he kept trying, cussing as he went. It was painful to watch, yet Daddy and I knew better than to interfere.

After several attempts, Brooks placed his strong hand over his father's. "Let me do it for you."

Tom stopped and met his son's eyes. Tears leaked from his own. "Thank you, son."

It was the most tender thing I had ever seen, so much so my eyes welled up with tears.

Brooks took the deck and, without another word, began to deftly shuffle the cards.

"No cheating," I threw out there to stop myself from kissing him for being so sweet to his daddy.

"I plan to win you fair and square," he zinged back.

"I'm not anyone's prize," I snipped at him.

"I think he meant to say you are a treasure," Daddy betrayed me and helped the fool out.

I faced my father in shock. Seriously, whose side was he on?

"That's exactly what I meant," Brooks agreed with Daddy.

"Let's just play cards." I was annoyed with all of them ganging up on me. "Ante up."

Brooks tossed a large pile of chips in the center.

"Um, you realize each of those chips represents real money, right? We don't mess around here."

Brooks flashed me a dazzling smile. "Neither do I, and I'm feeling lucky tonight."

Holy crow, he needed to stop with the alpha male vibe that admittedly turned me on like a floodlight. "We'll see."

"Yes, we will." Tom took a sip of his water.

Brooks dealt us five cards each. I picked mine up and held them close to my chest. I had to stop from grimacing. I had a pair of jacks and three crap cards. This wasn't good news. My only hope was to turn in the three meaningless cards and pray for a miracle. I looked around at my opponents, mainly Brooks, who was already grinning at me. I had to stop myself from smiling back. It was almost a reflex to this playful side of him that I'd thought was long gone. I couldn't let him get to me. I was here to win my Rick Springfield tickets. I averted my eyes. What I found was Daddy and Tom looking at each other conspiratorially. On an unseen cue, they both put down their cards and in unison said, "I fold."

"What! Let me see your cards," I demanded.

"Honey, that's not how it works," Daddy said reasonably. But there was no reason to any of this.

"Daddy." I used my *please, I'm your little girl* voice.

He patted my knee. "I think this is better left between you and Brooks."

"I second that m . . . motion." Tom grabbed a handful of grapes.

I couldn't believe my men had turned on me.

"Are you still in?" Brooks taunted me.

With determination, I threw several chips in the pot. If anything, I was way overconfident. Brooks matched my chips.

I scowled at him before discarding three of my cards and taking another three from the dealer.

With delight, Brooks counted each card out succinctly and slowly.

I picked up my cards, silently praying for another pair of jacks or three of a kind. I was gifted with a couple of twos. Two pair. It wasn't a good hand at all. Sure, I could win, but it was the third-worst hand to have in poker.

Brooks took two cards. His face was stoic and unemotive. He had a much better poker face than his daddy. After looking at his cards, Brooks tossed in a buttload of chips. Oh crap. Maybe he was bluffing? Please, let him be bluffing. I didn't care about the money. It was having to go to the concert with him. Not that long ago it would have been a dream of mine. Now it filled me with terror. How could I trust myself to keep it platonic? Because, I'm not going to lie, Rick does something to me when he starts singing. And Brooks only has to look at me and I go a little wobbly in the knees. This would not be a good combination.

I swallowed hard and pushed all my chips into the pot. "I'll see your bet and raise you fifty dollars." *Please let him be bluffing.*

With a smirk, he tossed in fifty bucks' worth of chips. Then he laid his cards out. The man had a straight flush.

I let out a long sigh and dropped my losing hand for the world to see.

Tom cheered, and Daddy squeezed my knee.

"Let's go double or nothing," I pleaded with Brooks.

Brooks leaned toward me and whispered, "Not a chance."

"What do you have to lose?" I begged.

He stole a kiss on my cheek. "Everything."

Me too.

Chapter Twenty-Five

"Here you go, ladies." June handed Carly and me each a strawberry daiquiri while we lounged poolside, our feet dangling in the cool crystal-blue water. It felt like perfection on a hot Texas summer night. The Hamiltons' backyard was lit up by strung bistro lights, and the waterfall in their pool made for the perfect background noise. It felt like the good old days when Carly and I were best of friends in high school. I was glad she was able to come back for the reunion taking place next weekend, as well as to spend time with her family.

"I was going to go nonalcoholic but added a little something something to celebrate our girls' night." June giggled. I think she might have been partaking already.

I took the pink drink in its fancy-shaped glass. "Thank you." I immediately took a sip and had to stop myself from coughing. Um . . . her little something something was going to make us all tipsy. It tasted like she'd used a half a bottle of rum. I set the drink down near me.

June plopped down on the other side of Carly and indulged deeply. "It's so nice we get to have an evening to ourselves."

"Amen." Carly downed a large sip. "I love my boys, but I'm happy to let them spend time with their daddy."

FACIAL RECOGNITION

"I just love that all my boys are together and mostly getting along." June splashed her feet in the water. Apparently Brooks's company had a suite at the stadium, and he was treating them all to a Rangers game.

"Is Brooks saying more than a few words at a time to Tom now?" I leaned back on my arms, enjoying the warm evening breeze.

"About as many as you say to Brooks," June teased me.

Carly nudged me. "Yes, I've heard you've been playing hard to get."

"She's been playing it smart." June held up her glass to me.

I thought about the last couple of weeks. I wasn't sure how smart I'd been. If anyone was playing it smart, it was Brooks. It was like he knew all the right things to do. More like he knew me. Not only had the man been having lunch with my daddy, but he'd helped Daddy weed our flower beds. Daddy refused to divulge what they talked about, other than to say Brooks had potential. Then I'd caught Brooks reading *New Moon*, the next book in the Twilight saga, to his daddy last week to catch him up on our new book club selection because Tom's eyes were having some issues and it was still hard for him to process information. When Brooks had noticed me, he'd hastily switched to the John Grisham book he'd brought. That was good because I'd almost planted a big one on him after witnessing how sweet he was being with his daddy. And, man, did *New Moon* sound sexy coming out of his mouth.

If that wasn't enough, he'd come to the rescue a few days ago when our DJ for the reunion up and quit on us, refusing to give us back our deposit. Brooks had heard me lamenting about it to Tom. Like Superman, he'd swept in and threatened the DJ with his lawyer powers. We got the deposit back, and Brooks called a friend of a friend who happened to be the most popular DJ in the Dallas/Fort Worth area. Which meant he was ridiculously expensive and out of the reunion's budget. Not to worry though, Brooks had picked up the tab. And made sure the man had plenty of Rick Springfield songs ready to go.

It was getting almost impossible to resist him. I was clinging to my principles and no-man policy by a thread.

"I'm still livid with that boy," June growled. "Having sex with that girl on prom night."

"Momma, it was a long time ago," Carly countered. "Haven't you been the one lately preaching about forgiveness and letting go of past hurts?"

I rubbed my neck, not liking the sense Carly was spouting.

June downed some of her daiquiri and stared out at the gently lapping water before throwing her daughter the stink eye. "I will be mad at that boy until he makes things right with this girl." She pointed at me.

Yep, definitely not liking where this was going.

Carly flashed me a wide smile. "How long do you think you can hold out?"

"I'm not holding out. I've turned over a new leaf. No men."

Both ladies giggled.

"Uh-huh." Carly wasn't buying it.

I leaned over so I could address June. "How have you reconciled with Tom after his betrayal?"

June gave me a knowing look. "Darlin', we're still working on it. I would be lying if I said it was easy. There are moments when I still want to slap him. Especially when I think about the repercussions it had on our children. Not to say I don't bear some of that blame. Yet, when I think about how my life was with him and without him, hands down, it was better when we were together. Love is the hardest work around." She winked.

"But what if, hypothetically speaking, the person you love doesn't want the same things as you? What if, for most of their life, they didn't even want you? At least Tom has never wavered in his devotion to you."

FACIAL RECOGNITION

June reached over and took my hand with her neatly manicured and fake-baked one. "Darlin', Brooks has always wanted the same things as you; he's just never known how to get them, so he lied to himself. Same thing with you. He never saw you as an option because he didn't believe he was worthy of you."

I let go of June's hand and tucked some hair behind my ear. "I never said I was talking about Brooks."

"Right," June and Carly roared simultaneously.

"I'm serious—the man in question told me marriage was not a viable institution. Let's not forget he was dating a woman who he called his intimate. And while we're on the subject of Morgan . . . He dated Morgan. Enough said."

June and Carly rankled at the mention of her name.

"I can't be with someone who doesn't believe in marriage. I'm too old to be someone's perpetual girlfriend. And I sure as heck don't want to be an inti-mate. My ovaries, while still functioning, are past their prime. I need a man who's willing to act quickly. The right man, mind you."

"You mean Brooks?" June didn't pull any punches.

"I admit, for a long time I thought he was the one, but come to find out he never even thought of me. That's not an easy pill to swallow. I mean, the man didn't even recognize me when he came in for his facial massage."

Carly patted my knee. "I'm not saying this to excuse him, but honestly, for a long time, I don't think my brother even recognized himself. Sometimes it was even hard for those of us closest to him to see the real him. You don't know how happy I was yesterday when we arrived," she got all choked up. "It was the first time in a long time that I saw my brother. When he wrapped his arms around me, I knew he was different."

I swallowed down my emotion. I had seen a difference in him too. The boy I'd fallen in love with had come back, but it scared me. "Do you think it can last?" I whispered.

"The question is, Do you think so?" June wisely responded.

That was a good question.

It was a question I thought about all night long, even after I went home to work on the name tags and photo booth props for the class reunion. I was using old yearbook photos that I had paid someone on Etsy to format with our high school mascot—an eagle—and our motto, *Soar Ever Higher.* Of course, I couldn't leave well enough alone and had decided I needed to embellish them with sparkly silver cardstock. Then I'd bought little buttons that sounded like cheerleaders when you pushed them, shouting our lovely motto. Hey, once a cheerleader, always a cheerleader. I looked at the name tags as precious mementos. Okay, so I was nuts. Although, I had to say the props for the photo booth were stellar. They had sayings on them like, *Reunited and It Feels So Good.* I even made one that said, *Still Lives at Home.* I would be sporting that one, unashamed.

As much fun as it was preparing for the reunion, thoughts of Brooks overshadowed everything. I had given up on avoiding him; he wasn't going to let me. After all these years, he was finally chasing me, and I wasn't sure if I wanted to be caught. Maybe that wasn't exactly true. It was more like I was wary. Was he really over Morgan for good? Would he continue to try to mend his relationship with Tom? Could he love me? Love me enough to give me everything that I ever wanted? To be his bride and bear his babies?

I sighed while using my hot glue gun to adhere the cheer buttons on each name tag as I watched my beloved Dr. Noah Drake break hearts. While I was deep in contemplation and wielding my glue gun like a pro, I heard a tapping on my bedroom window. At first I ignored it, thinking I was hearing things. I hadn't heard a tap on that window in over twenty years. Then the tapping became a desperate rapping, so much so I thought my window might break. I dropped my hot glue gun, rushed over to the window closest to my bed, and parted the gray ruffled curtains to find Brooks clinging to the trellis with a look of terror in his eyes. It was kind of adorable.

I unlocked the window and pushed it open. "What are you doing?" I heard some creaking and cracking in the wood.

"I wanted to see you, but I fear I miscalculated how sturdy the trellis was after all these years."

"I guess you better go back down before you get hurt," I grinned evilly.

He grimaced. "I just scaled your house and you're not going to let me in?"

"You know the rules: no boys in my room," I teased.

The trellis cracked and creaked some more, making Brooks hold on to the windowsill for dear life. "How about men?" he said as if he were out of breath.

I bit my lip. "Well, that depends on what kind of man he is."

"How about the kind willing to risk his life for you?" He clung tighter.

"Maybe." I grinned, watching him struggle.

His eyes bore into mine. "What about a man willing to risk it all for you?"

Oh. That pierced my heart. I was so confused. A large crack rent the air as the trellis gave out under his weight, leaving Brooks dangling from my window. "Grace?" he pleaded.

"Okay." I reached for him, making sure he didn't go the way of the trellis, crashing into the rosebushes below, while I prayed my heart would survive this.

Chapter Twenty-Six

I pulled Brooks through the window, and we both landed with a thud on the wood floor, Brooks on top of me. It was a good thing Daddy slept with a sound machine on nowadays.

Brooks was a lot heavier than I remembered, but it was pure muscle. Nice-feeling muscle, up against my own skin. I had forgotten I was only in a nightshirt. I hadn't been expecting company at eleven o'clock at night.

Brooks made no attempt to move, even though he was lying on me. He only brushed my bangs to the side. "You're so beautiful, Grace." His lips played barely above my own, tempting me. So, so tempting me.

"Brooks, maybe we should get up."

"I'm happy where I'm at." His lips inched closer.

My resolve was weakening at a furious pace. "We should talk." I was desperately trying to think of any excuse as to why we shouldn't kiss.

"We will." His breaths became my breaths.

I closed my eyes for a half a second, not wanting to fight the magnetism pulling us together and aching for our lips to become one. Still, a tiny bit of reason flickered in my brain, reminding me that Brooks and I had some very different views about life. Views that needed to be reconciled—like me forgiving him among other things. I opened my eyes, wriggled my arm free, and pushed against his yummy chest. "No, really, we should talk. Like lots of words."

He let out a disappointed breath. "You win." He settled for a kiss on my forehead before removing his godlike body from mine and standing up.

I needed a moment on the floor to stare up at him. Holy crow, he looked fine in his tight baseball T-shirt and athletic shorts.

Brooks reached out a hand to help me up. I took it, and our connection felt more real than it ever had. The voice was shouting, *He's the one!* I wasn't denying it, but the voice had to understand that I needed time. And we needed answers.

Brooks easily lifted me. When I was upright, he took the opportunity to pull me close and wrap his arms around me. I gave in and rested my head against his chest, listening to the steady pound of his heart.

"How was the game?" I asked.

"Rangers lost by one run, but we had a good time."

"You did?"

He leaned away. "Believe it or not, I do know how to have fun."

"You're going to have to prove that."

"I plan to." His sultry tones were going to be the end of me.

"You can start by helping me make name tags."

He looked around my room, which had doubled in size since the last time he was here. "It looks a lot different than it used to—except for your homage to Rick Springfield has remained, I see."

I lovingly gazed at my shrine to Rick, though I had to say Brooks was more attractive than him. "Rick is my one true love, besides chocolate and Diet Pepsi."

Brooks's brow raised. "Room for anyone else on that list?"

I shrugged. "Maybe."

He ran a finger down my cheek, leaving a trail of sparks so hot I thought my cheek might catch fire. "I'll see what I can do about that."

"We shall see. But first, reunion name tags."

Brooks caught my hand before I could flee to the safety of my couch. "Grace, I'm in earnest." He was as serious as he had ever been, which was saying something for him.

"There you go, using fancy words again." I grinned.

"I mean them." He squeezed my hand.

I wanted to believe him. I kept ahold of him and led him toward my couch, which was covered with tissue poms in our school colors of silver and navy. I'd ended up having to make some of the decorations to save money. I let go of Brooks and made a spot for us to sit, as I had been sitting on the floor before his unexpected arrival.

Brooks looked around at all of my handiwork. "I'm sorry you've had to bear the brunt of all the planning. I know, technically, it should have been my job."

"I've had a good time doing it, with the help of my friends. Besides, you won't even be there."

He rubbed the back of his neck. "I would come," he stammered, "but I'm doing a presentation about the dissipation of marital assets at the conference."

"Sounds riveting," I teased before plopping down on the couch. "Don't worry about it. I know you find reunions trite and for people who peaked in their pasts."

He sat next to me and let out a heavy sigh. "I didn't say that."

"You also didn't disagree with Morgan when she spoke for both of you on the subject."

"I wish I would have. You were right when you said that people who don't face their past can never make peace with their future."

"You remember that?"

"Grace, ever since you walked back into my life, I can't think of anyone but you." His sincerity was going to be my undoing.

But I still had some fight in me. "Uh-huh. Which was why you continued to date Morgan."

"It's why I was going to end it with her. But can we not talk about her?"

"That is always my preference, but you should know, she RSVP'd to the reunion." I couldn't believe it when her reservation came through on our system. I didn't know whether to laugh or cry. She was more hypocritical than I'd ever dreamed. What was she playing at, exactly? Especially after her sanctimonious speech about reunions. And the fact that I knew what a facade her life was.

Brooks's eyes widened. "Are you serious?"

"Like my love for *General Hospital.* She's bringing an Olivander Kennedy. If that isn't a pretentious name, I don't know what is. She obviously moved on from you pretty fast."

Brooks chuckled. "That brings you some pleasure."

"Maybe."

He leaned in closer. "You should know, Olivander Kennedy claims to be a cousin of the Kennedy family—as in JFK—yet can never produce any solid proof. He was also charged with embezzling a fortune from his father's insurance company, though he was let off on a technicality."

"How do you know him?"

"I represented his wife in their divorce last year."

"Why would Morgan date him?"

"Like her, he talks a good talk and can make himself look better on paper than he is in real life."

"I almost feel sorry for people like that. Almost."

"Don't. People like Morgan and Olivander never think for one second about anyone but themselves."

I tilted my head. "What about you?"

"I'm trying to be better. Trying to right my wrongs, though it's hard, and I admit I still harbor ill will toward my father."

I rested my hand on his thigh. "I know he appreciates your effort. How did it go tonight?"

He gave me a crooked smile. "Ryker and Axel did their best to make friends with my colleagues, entertaining them with ridiculous jokes that made no sense, yet somehow they made them sound hilarious." Brooks beamed with uncle pride. "When the rug rats let someone else get a word in, Dad enjoyed talking shop. He might have lost some memories, but he's still pretty sharp."

My brow quirked. "Tom has been promoted to Dad?"

Brooks smirked. "Don't act so surprised."

"I think it's you who is surprised."

"Right again." Brooks scrubbed a hand over his face. "He does like to talk about you, which plays in his favor."

"Is that so? What does he say?"

"That you're headstrong and wonderful."

"I concur," I laughed.

Brooks tucked some of my unruly hair behind my ear. "He also said I've been a fool for a lot of years."

"I agree with that too," I whispered.

"Me too."

"Brooks, I'm so happy you're trying to work things out with your daddy and, admittedly, that you've dumped Morgan. But . . . people don't just change. Not to say people can't change. But you have some pretty strong opinions about relationships and marriage. Opinions I don't share. And . . . you really hurt me."

He scooted closer, worry etched in his beautiful eyes.

I held still, though I was tempted to shy away from him. He had this way of encompassing me and making me forget why I shouldn't be jumping onto his lap and kissing his face off.

"Grace, I'm sorry I hurt you. For all the time we've lost. But you're right." He rested his hand on my cheek, and I couldn't help but lean into it. "I've seen what marriage can do to two people, and I shudder to think of you and me becoming like that. The bitterness, abuse, and dissatisfaction I see on a daily basis from my clients makes me hesitant. Not to mention my own family's situation."

My head tilted upright. "So, marriage is a definite no go for you?" I bravely asked, not really wanting the answer, yet knowing it was necessary that I hear the truth.

His chest rose and fell several times. "I don't know, but do we need to focus on that right now? I only want to spend time with you and figure things out as we go."

I inched back away from him. "Fifteen years ago, that would have been great. Now, honestly, it may sound cliché, but my biological clock is tick, tick, ticking like a bomb ready to explode. I don't have a lot of time left before the pin is pulled and I lose my chance to have a family. I want babies and a man who wants to be their daddy and my husband."

He swallowed hard, making his Adam's apple bob. "Grace, the night you took me to the movie in the park . . ."

I froze, having an idea what he was going to say and kicking myself for being so honest with him that night.

"You mentioned," he continued, "that you knew who the one was for you." He pointed at my heart. "That it came from a place deep inside."

I bit my lip. "What's your point?"

"Was it me?" he whispered as if he were making a wish.

I cleared my throat. "Wow. You threw that right out there."

"Grace, you're not answering me."

I tried to avoid eye contact.

"Grace." He pressed his forehead against mine.

"Brooks, I've known you were the one from the first moment I saw your head peek over the fence," I whispered. "You don't know how much I wanted you to recognize me as the one for you. But you never did. And then you disappeared."

His hand cupped my neck. "I was a teenager. My frontal lobe wasn't connected yet."

"It seemed to work for Morgan. And maybe it always will. Maybe she is your one, or someone like her." The thought made me ill.

He leaned back, his eyes ablaze. "How can you say that?"

"Brooks, whether you want to believe it or not, you like the pomp and circumstance of women like Morgan. Think about it. I was the one cheering for you at track meets and doing all the cutesy things like decorating your truck and baking you cupcakes with little mini tracks on them. And you liked it, even appreciated it, but you never wanted me. On the other hand, Morgan never did anything for you, never even came to your meets. Yet when she came calling, all she had to do was flash you a charming smile and say something like she wanted to study for the SAT. I saw in your eyes how much she excited you. How quick you were to ditch Carly and me for her." My stupid eyes betrayed me with a sheen of tears.

I composed myself before I full on started to bawl. "Even now, you like her bold, out-of-the-box thinking. It fits with your narrative, your world. I don't. I didn't even go to college, and I still live at home. Do you really want to introduce someone like me to your colleagues? Do you see yourself living somewhere like Poplar Lane and raising babies and weeding the flower beds for the rest of your life?"

He looked as if I had sucker punched him. He'd even placed a hand across his defined abs. "Grace, I would never be ashamed of you. You're an accomplished woman."

I laughed. "No one has ever accused me of that before. Don't get me wrong, I'm not ashamed of who I am or what I do. In fact, I'm proud of Serenity Spa. But I know I'm loud and sometimes obnoxious. Occasionally I snort when I laugh, and I'm obsessed with soap operas and an old teen idol. However, I want to be loved for all those things. I want a man who gets ridiculously happy when he sees me and wants to wife the heck out of me."

Brooks ran the back of his hand down my cheek. "You make me happier than I've been in a long time."

"That may be, but for how long? What happens when you wake up and realize I wasn't the one?"

I could see the wheels spinning behind Brooks's eyes, but he didn't seem to have an answer.

Hurt, I turned from him and grabbed my remote to turn up the TV. Dr. Noah Drake was about to play his real-life self, Springfield, and sing "Jessie's Girl" at the nurses' ball. I slid down onto the floor and retrieved my glue gun so I could get back to work, acting as if I didn't have a handsome man staring at me. As if my heart weren't breaking in two.

"I didn't know Rick Springfield came back on the show," Brooks commented. That wasn't what I wanted to hear. I wanted him to tell me I was wrong, then take me into his arms and kiss me until we were both breathless.

"He did for a short while."

"I'm really looking forward to taking you to his concert when I get back from my conference."

"Yeah." I squirted some hot glue on the silver cardstock I had already cut out.

Brooks joined me on the floor and gently, with his finger, tilted my head toward him. "Grace, please, give me some time to figure this out."

"Will it really matter?"

"You matter to me."

I let out a forlorn sigh, not knowing what to say. I wasn't naive, though part of me kind of wished I was. "If you're going to stay, you have to work." I handed him some scissors. "Cut these out, following the lines."

He stared down at the pictures of our old high school classmates. "I should have paid better attention to you back in high school."

I shrugged. "Stick to the lines."

"Maybe it's time I lived life outside of them."

My head snapped toward him. "That's not your style."

"Do we have to exactly match?"

"No, but there are things we need to be on the same page about."

"I just barely opened the book—give me some time to catch up to you," he pleaded his case.

"Very clever." I nudged him.

"Please, Grace," he begged.

"I'll see how well you do tonight, and then I'll decide." I flashed him a wicked grin.

"Deal." He pecked my lips.

I touched my lips—they felt sparkly. However, I wasn't giving in. Too much was on the line. It was cute, though, to watch Brooks meticulously cut out our classmates' photos. It was even endearing when he made fun of me for the little cheer buttons he kept pushing while gluing them on.

We worked for a couple of hours, until each name tag was done. Until I was very sleepy and rested my head on his shoulder. The last thing I remembered before drifting off to sleep was him kissing my head. I'd only meant to rest for a few minutes, to enjoy what could be our last moments together. My tired body had other plans. When I woke up the next morning, the summer sun was filtering in through the curtains. I was still on the floor, which explained why my butt hurt. And I was pretty sure I'd slept with my mouth open, considering how dry it felt. Suddenly, I recalled where—or on whom—I was sleeping. My head popped off Brooks's strong shoulder. I scrambled a bit, embarrassed I'd fallen asleep on him and basically nap trapped him.

I ran my fingers through my wild hair. "I'm so sorry. You should have woken me up."

He turned more toward me with this hungry look in his sleep-deprived eyes. Without warning, he pulled me to him, and his lips crashed into mine. My mouth was suddenly no longer dry but salivating for Brooks's touch. Before I could think or argue, his tongue slid across my lips, and I eagerly invited it in. He groaned and pulled me closer when I didn't hesitate to reciprocate. While his tongue tasted the inside of my mouth, the voice chanted, *YES! YES! YES!*

Minute upon minute, his mouth consumed mine while his hands deftly explored all my curves. In between kisses, he whispered my name. Moving lower, he kissed my neck, making my body explode in goose bumps. I crawled onto his lap, not wanting any distance between us. He held me gently, yet so firmly I knew he didn't want to let go. And just as unexpectedly as the best kiss of my life came, it ended with the same abruptness. Brooks gave me one last kiss before easing me off him and standing, leaving me breathless on the floor. He hovered over me and stared at me with a determination I had never seen before.

"Please don't give up on me," he pleaded.

Before I could answer, he was at the door. "Tell your dad I'll be by later to fix the trellis." And without another word he was gone.

I pulled my knees up to my chest, shaking from not only the pleasure I'd just experienced but also because I knew without a shadow of a doubt who my heart belonged to. The question was, What would he do with it?

Chapter Twenty-Seven

"I'm going to have the best-looking dates here." I wrapped an arm around each one of my best friends. They were both looking gorgeous in black, slinky dresses.

We took a moment to admire our handiwork. The event center's banquet room sparkled and gleamed in silver and navy. I swore we had strung at least a million twinkle lights. It was so worth it. It looked like a fairyland, exactly how I'd envisioned it. Except I'd thought I would be there with the man of my dreams. Not that I wasn't happy with how it had turned out, but I'd had this crazy idea to get the prom night I had always hoped for. I supposed I needed to let it go. At least this time I didn't get stood up, and . . . I looked at my wrist where the prettiest peach corsage rested. A special delivery from Brooks earlier today. It was simply lovely, with pearls strung through the flowers and greenery. It matched my coral high-low slip gown perfectly.

My friends caught me gazing at the corsage.

"You're disappointed," Colette stated.

"No way. You two better get some lip balm ready—we are totally kissing good night," I teased, making them giggle.

Lorelai swatted me. "Honey, you're pretty, but you're not that pretty."

"Oh fine. But, honestly, thank you. I couldn't have done this without you. I don't deserve friends as good as you."

"In a couple of years, I will expect payback when it's my twentieth reunion." Colette winked.

"I'm there for you."

"I wouldn't be too sure, darlin'." Lorelai wagged her brows. "You'll probably be married by then with a bun in the oven."

"That's wishful thinking." But, oh, was that my wish.

Lorelai tilted her head. "I thought Brooks was a possibility?"

That was the million-dollar question. "He's been gone most of the week, but he's called me every night." We had talked for hours about everything and nothing. He would tell me about his conference, even though he seemed hesitant to, like he was afraid his profession would turn me against him. It worried me, obviously, but I was proud of him. I'd even made him rehearse his presentation for me. He had been scheduled to present a couple of hours ago; I hoped it had gone well. It was quite informative and scary. Spouses really could be awful to each other. The way they hid or sold off assets before they filed for divorce was downright spiteful. No wonder Brooks was afraid of the M word. We hadn't talked about only him during our calls. Honestly, we'd talked more about me. He was either fascinated with my life or he was a really good actor.

Colette snapped her fingers in front of us. "No more talk of men tonight. We are going to rock this place, and if we're lucky, we'll witness Morgan trip on her self-absorption while walking in."

"Ugh," I groaned. "I really hope she doesn't show up."

"Honey, she has to prove something to you," Lorelai wisely stated. "She'll be here with bells on, I guarantee it."

Colette tapped my nose. "You keep your head high. She's jealous of you, as she should be. I mean, her own brother chose you over her."

Julian was also someone I didn't want to think about. I'd had so many flower deliveries and cards from him that had all gone in the trash. I was sorry he had grown up in such an awful family, but he knew full well that when he had asked me out, it was wrong. Still not sure what powers Morgan possessed to manipulate people the way she did, but it was frightening.

The DJ started playing some tunes like it was 1999. He started out with some "Livin' La Vida Loca" by Ricky Martin. It only reminded me of Brooks, though, since he had paid for DJ Jack in the House. His setup was incredible, and the sound was amazing. The place was thumping.

I gave the ladies another hug. "Save all the dances for me. I'm going to go check to make sure our greeters are set up. People should be arriving any minute now." It gave me some butterflies in my tummy. All our planning and the blood, sweat, and tears were about to, hopefully, pay off.

"If one of your classmates is hot and single, I'm totally ditching you." Colette applied another layer of red lipstick that looked killer with her dark pixie hair and those classic cheekbones of hers.

"I'll point them out if they exist." After twenty years, most of us were married.

"We'll check on the buffet table," Lorelai offered.

"Thank you." I sauntered over to the check-in table where all the name tags were neatly arranged in alphabetical order. Jackie and Kimmy were manning the table. We had all been on the cheerleading squad together. They were both still cute as a button and had kept their peppy attitudes. They thought later that night, for old times' sake, we should get together and do a cheer routine for the fun of it. I was down.

"Hi, ladies. Thanks so much for helping out."

Kimmy adjusted her sleeveless dress, as it was having a bit of a hard time keeping her girls covered. Perhaps we shouldn't do a cheer routine later on. "It's the least I could do."

"The place looks amazing," Jackie gushed.

"I can only take a little bit of the credit, but thank you. I'm happy you love it. It's really good to see both of you again." They had both come in from out of town. "Please let me know if you need anything. And make sure to let everyone know there is no assigned seating and there is a two-drink limit at the bar."

"Will do," Kimmy sang.

I was about to go check on Sean, a.k.a. the prom king, who had put together a slideshow highlighting our senior year, when Carly and her husband Dillon walked in looking dapper. Carly was in a red chiffon gown, and Dillon wore a dark suit and tie. They were a stately-looking couple. Both tall, with striking features. Looking at Carly had me longing for her twin to be here.

Carly was to me in no time, wrapping me in her long arms covered in poufy chiffon. "You look gorgeous. Brooks is going to be sad he missed this dress."

There he was again.

"I'm sure he's enjoying all the business suits and the stale chicken they serve at their dinners every night." He had complained about the food, especially considering how expensive the conference was for him to attend. Of course, his firm was footing the bill. Apparently it was a badge of honor to present at this conference, and it spoke highly of him and his firm. All the more reason he should be there and not here.

"I don't think so," Carly countered me. "When I talked to him last night, he seemed agitated."

"Really? He'd sounded happy—I mean, at least happy for him—when I talked to him briefly earlier today to wish him luck."

Carly flashed me a toothy smile. "You do seem to bring out the best in him."

I wasn't so sure about that. "Well, enough about him." I had to quit dwelling on him, for my own emotional well-being. It was weird how much I found myself longing for him to be here. Honestly, I'd thought I was good with just going with my girls. Evidently, I wasn't. I smiled at Carly and Dillon, who had put his arm around his wife and held her close, making me even more jealous. "You both look fabulous. Make sure to save me and my dates a seat at your table."

"Will do." Dillon did the whole finger gun thing.

Carly rolled her eyes at her husband. "See you soon." She and Dillon headed toward the check-in table to get their name tags.

I was once again on my way to check on the slideshow when none other than Morgan and her date, Olivander, appeared as if they had risen from the throes of hell. She was wearing a wine-red mermaid gown that hugged her so tight I was surprised she could walk or breathe. But, wowzers, did she look stunning. Her hair was done in an elegant twist, and the color of her dress electrified her eyes. Or maybe it was the way she glared at me with such malice. Her date, on the other hand, was a distinguished older gentleman with thick silver-fox hair. He walked in a manner befitting a royal. After what Brooks had told me about him, it was comical. I mean, hello, he was attending a small-town high school reunion. I had an urge to curtsy in front of him just for the fun of it, and to irk Morgan. Instead I decided the best thing I could do was to ignore them.

Without so much as a smirk, I turned from them and headed toward the stage, proud of myself for not rising to the occasion. Brooks had assured me he wanted nothing to do with Morgan, and if I didn't believe that, then I shouldn't be contemplating a relationship with him.

Morgan, apparently, wasn't on board with my way of thinking. How she caught up to me so quickly in her stilettos and tight dress, I had no idea. Maybe she really was half witch.

"Gracie," she spoke my name with venom. "I want you to meet someone."

Was this a joke? Why would she want to introduce me to her date? I steeled myself before turning around.

Before I could say anything, she yanked her date toward her, practically ripping his arm out of its socket. "This is Olivander Kennedy," she purred, "as in John F. Kennedy."

"Wow." I played along. "How are you related?"

Without a beat, he answered, "I hate to name-drop."

Isn't that what Morgan had just done on his behalf?

"Oh, come on. It's not every day I get to meet someone related to a president. I mean, unless you count the Bushes' nieces who have been clients of the spa I own. Such nice ladies."

Olivander cleared his throat. "You're associated with the Bush family?"

"Well, it is Texas." I smiled the smiliest of smiles.

If I wasn't mistaken, Morgan elbowed him. "Tell her about the time you visited the Kennedy Compound."

"Yes, yes. Lovely place in Washington, DC."

"Don't you mean Hyannis Port in Massachusetts?"

His face turned bright red. "Yes, I mean, no," he stuttered. "Yes, that is where the original compound is, but they kept houses in DC as well. I attended several fundraisers and mixers there." He was an awful liar, and once again, I felt a tiny bit sorry for Morgan. Why did she feel the need to live a lie?

"How nice. Excuse me."

"Where is Brooks?" She asked as if she didn't already know.

"At his conference."

She sneered at me. "Of course; his career is *everything* to him."

Okay, the tiny shred of sorry I'd felt for her went out the window. "Yes, he's very dedicated to his clients."

"You would do well to remember that."

"Thank you." I was so done with this conversation.

Unfortunately, Morgan wasn't going to let me go without another slight. "I know him better than anyone, and believe me when I say, he might have some romantic notion about being with the girl next door, but it doesn't align with his goals. *You* don't fit into his plans."

I refrained from grabbing my gut. I wasn't going to give her the satisfaction of knowing she had hit me where it hurt. That she had flooded me with insecurity. "Plans change." I turned on a dime and hightailed it away from the liars. Yet, I couldn't deny she'd hit a nerve. Perhaps she did know him better than I did. They had been lovers. Intimate in ways Brooks and I never had been.

Colette and Lorelai rushed me.

"We saw you with the hag," Colette growled.

"Sorry we couldn't get to you sooner, darlin'," Lorelai drawled. "We were having a minicrisis. The caterer forgot to set out the pigs in a blanket. No Texas buffet table can be complete without them."

"Thank you for rectifying the situation." I was struggling to hold back my tears.

Colette wrapped an arm around me. "What's wrong?"

I took some deep breaths in and out to stave off the tears. No way was I letting Morgan ruin the bang-up makeup job June had done on me. "Morgan," I hissed her name, "shoved a knife in my heart, is all. No big deal."

"Please tell me you don't believe anything coming out of her flapper." Lorelai narrowed her eyes at the prima donna parading her date around like he was a show dog now that more people were showing up. It was almost as if she had become the unofficial greeter.

I shrugged. "Unfortunately, she didn't say anything I hadn't already thought about. Brooks and I are very different."

Colette squeezed me tight. "Honey, that's where the beauty of most relationships comes from."

"I suppose. Yet I wonder how I'll know for sure that Brooks feels about me the way I've always felt about him. Or is that even a possibility?"

Lorelai opened her mouth to say something when the music suddenly ceased. My first thought was that there was a technical difficulty and a fire I would need to put out. Then I heard a heavenly voice that changed everything.

Chapter Twenty-Eight

"I apologize for interrupting."

We all whipped our heads toward the stage. There Brooks stood, tall and maybe a little nervous, looking fine in a designer suit, holding on to the mic. My heart started to violently beat out of control. Lorelai and Colette each grabbed one of my hands.

"I know I'm not part of the program, so I promise not to take too much of your time tonight," Brooks pledged. "However, I do need to thank Grace Cartwright for stepping in and taking over my responsibility in regard to the reunion. She's done an amazing job, as you can all see. I think she deserves a round of applause."

People looked my way and clapped, making me blush. Yet I stayed fixed on the man who owned my soul.

Brooks stepped toward the edge of the stage and looked out, searching for me. When he zeroed in on me, standing toward the back behind the tables that surrounded the dance floor, he flashed me a crooked grin.

I squeezed my friends' hands, not sure what he was up to but thrilled all the same.

"Hello, Grace," he crooned. "I see you now." That was full of double meaning.

My stomach fluttered.

FACIAL RECOGNITION

"I'm giving you fair warning that what I'm going to say next may embarrass you, but I promise that it comes from my heart and I have the best of intentions."

I bit my lip, nervous.

Brooks took a deep breath in and out before beginning. "Grace, twenty years ago, I stood you up on a night very much like this. Looking back, it was one the biggest mistakes I ever made, but not the worst one. Failing to recognize the way you loved me, loved everyone around you, was my biggest failure. I know if we asked everyone here tonight, they would be able to tell of a time Gracie Cartwright touched their lives for good."

Several people murmured their agreement and nodded their heads. It made my cheeks burn. This wasn't supposed to be the Gracie Cartwright tribute night. Though I was so touched by Brooks's words.

"Not only," Brooks continued, "did Grace help me get elected as student body president, but she cheered me on in anything I decided to do. She cheered us all on. She was the first person to sit by the new kid or the lonely kid. And though she suffered the tragic loss of her mother during high school, she always managed to smile through her tears."

He was making me smile through my tears now. His momma's makeup job was toast. Thankfully, she'd used waterproof mascara.

Brooks unexpectedly jumped off the stage, mic in hand, and deftly landed on his feet. His dress shoes made a loud slapping noise against the tile floor. People immediately parted, creating a pathway from him to me. He slowly sauntered my way. "I guess what I'm trying to say is, I recognize what a fool I've been. And I'm asking you to give me the chance to love you, like you've loved me. I know I don't deserve it, but, Grace, I want to prove your theory right. To show you, you were right about me."

Colette and Lorelai leaned into me and in unison said, "I think you have your answer," before pushing me toward Brooks. Picking up his pace, Brooks rushed toward me and wordlessly enveloped me in his strong arms.

I was home.

I clung to him, resting my head on his chest. His heart was beating erratically, matching my own. The crowd around us began to applaud, and Lorelai snagged the microphone from Brooks.

"Ladies and gentlemen, I think this calls for a dance," Lorelai drawled. "Mr. DJ, what do you say?"

"I already received a request for the perfect song. This one is for you, Gracie." In seconds, "Affair of the Heart" began to play.

I looked up at Brooks, who smiled at me with such adoration it made my heart sing. "How did you know this was our song?"

"Because I know you." He lightly brushed my lips. "Dance with me."

I nodded, hardly believing this was happening. It felt like a dream. The one I'd been having since I was fourteen years old. I heard the voice say, *I told you so.*

Brooks took my hand and led me past our grinning classmates to the empty dance floor. There he took me in his arms and whispered in my ear, "I don't know how to dance."

"That's okay, just hold me close and don't let go," I managed to choke out through my tears.

He pulled me to him. "I'm never letting you go again."

"Perfect. We're on the same page."

Several couples joined us on the dance floor, though I hardly noticed. I only had eyes for Brooks.

"That was some speech you gave."

He gently wiped some tears from my cheek. "I figured I needed a grand gesture to show you I was in earnest."

"There you go using fancy words again, but I like it."

"I'm happy to hear that."

"I'm sorry you had to miss your presentation, though."

"I didn't. However, I would have. I convinced them to change it to this morning, and I caught the first flight I could. The entire time I was gone, I was kicking myself for not asking you to our reunion. For not placing you first, as I should have. As I plan to do."

I rested my hand on his stubbled cheek. "I missed you, Brooks, so much."

He leaned in to kiss me as Carly and Dillon came to dance by us. "It's about time, brother," Carly interrupted, punching Brooks's arm. "Now carry on." She winked.

Brooks didn't need her to tell him twice. His lips landed on mine, and all felt right in the world for two seconds. Then Morgan reared her beautiful-yet-ugly head.

"I didn't expect to see you here," she spewed.

Brooks's lips slid off mine, and we both groaned in frustration before turning toward her and Olivander, who she held on to with an iron grip as if he might escape.

Morgan's face almost matched her wine-red gown. "How can you choose her over me?" she whined like a child. "She still lives at home, and she gives facials for a living. Not to mention she doesn't share our goals."

I might have been offended except it all sounded like sour grapes, plus I knew what a liar she was. Besides, I was proud of who I was.

Brooks smiled at me. "Thank God for all those things."

Morgan didn't appreciate his response. She dropped Olivander's hand and clenched her fists. "You're going to regret this."

Brooks narrowed his eyes at Morgan. "I regret many things in my life, mainly my relationship with you. I suggest you leave now before I make another speech about how our valedictorian isn't as perfect as she would like everyone to think. You are deceitful and manipulative, and you have no business being here."

Wow, was he sexy when he got all authoritative.

Morgan *tchted* but uttered not a word. Instead she blinked several times, as if she couldn't believe Brooks had talked to her in such a way. That someone had stood up to her. When she realized she no longer had any control over him, she melted away like the wicked witch that she was. Like all bullies, she needed to be stood up to, and once she was, her power was stripped from her.

Brooks breathed out heavily, as if he were relieved to finally be rid of the thorn in our sides, and gave me his rapt attention. "Now, where were we?" he sexily whispered.

"I think you were about to make me blush in front of all our class-mates."

"Deeply blush." His lips hovered above mine, teasing them and making me ache to touch his. "You are beautiful. Thank you for not giving up on me."

"How could I? You are *the one*," I cried.

"I was made for you, Grace." His lips crashed into mine, and, not caring who was watching, he parted my lips and followed through on his promise. I blushed deeply while his tongue swept my mouth and he pulled me flush against his body. Man, could he make me sparkle and pop. People hooted and hollered, but I paid them no attention. I was finally recognizing what I had always known to be true—Brooks was mine.

Chapter Twenty-Nine

I smiled down at the chart in my hand before I opened the door to treatment room one. I had no plans to knock. When I opened the door, I found a smug-looking Brooks sitting on the edge of the table smirking at me, though I hardly noticed, as I was distracted by his glorious bare chest. "What are you doing here?" I closed the door behind me and leaned against it. I had to hold myself back from accosting him. I internally argued with myself, We don't treat our customers like sexual objects . . . But he is technically my boyfriend . . . No. No. In this room, I swore to be a professional . . . But, oh, I want to touch him.

"You did offer me a free facial massage before I decided how to review your spa online. And I wanted to make sure I looked my best for our first date tonight."

I wouldn't consider the Rick Springfield concert our first date. Maybe it was going to be our best date so far, though that might be hard, too, considering all the make out sessions my couch had seen the last few days. And how much I loved when he would climb up the fixed trellis that could now hold his weight. Not to mention our all-night talks, listening to our favorite records. Lately, for Brooks, it was Mac Miller. He was deep and soulful, a lot like Brooks.

I stepped toward him. "Listen here, my friend, if you know what's good for you, you better give us five stars."

Brooks seized my top and pulled me closer to him. "I'm not your friend."

His sultry tone made me almost lose all reason. I had to keep the clipboard between us or I was going to be breaking all the rules soon. "What are you?"

He grabbed the clipboard and tossed it to the floor before pulling me into the danger zone. *Stay strong . . . But his lips look so inviting and the door is locked.*

He nuzzled my ear, making me shiver with delight, before whispering, "I'm your person and you're mine."

I loved that. A lot. "Good answer," I stuttered out. He was kissing my neck now and driving me wild. "Brooks, we shouldn't be doing this in here."

"Why?"

"We aren't running a brothel."

"I'm not paying you for any services."

That was true. My hands landed on his beautiful, defined chest. Oh momma, was it nice.

Brooks's lips skimmed my jaw.

"Really," I breathed out. "We shouldn't do this."

"You win," he groaned. But he stole a kiss before letting me go.

It took all I had to step away from him. "I promise we will pick up where we left off very soon." Only five more hours until Rick Springfield. I couldn't wait.

"Not soon enough."

"I know I'm irresistible," I teased, "but the more we resist, the better it will be tonight."

He ran a finger down my cheek. "You make my life better."

My eyes welled with tears. That deserved a kiss on the cheek. I let my lips linger on his warm skin, breathing in his amber scent. "For that," I whispered against his skin, "I won't use lavender or the stinging cleanser."

He chuckled.

"Now lie down, but this time you can keep the sheet off."

His brow quirked before he obeyed. "Yes, ma'am."

"You almost sounded like a Texan there. Keep hanging around me and you might be saying *momma* and *daddy* before you know it."

"We'll see." He wasn't convinced. "Speaking of my parents, though, they wanted me to invite you and your dad to dinner this weekend."

I picked up the clipboard from the floor. "Sounds great. I can bring dessert."

"Save dessert for me."

I swatted him with the clipboard. "Stop saying things like that or I'm going to have to fire myself after I accost you."

"Accosting me sounds good. I would definitely give you a five-star review for that."

"Stop it," I laughed.

He closed his eyes. "I'll behave. Maybe." He smirked.

I walked around to the head of the table. This man was going to be the death of me, though I couldn't think of a better way to go. "By the way, how are you feeling about your parents officially getting back together? We haven't really discussed that."

His eyes popped open. Turmoil swirled in them.

I ran my hand over his tousled hair. "I know it's hard, and that's okay."

He let out a deep sigh. "I can't deny that my mom is happier than she's been in a long time, and that makes me happy. Still, in my line of work, the odds aren't good for couples who remarry, especially when *infidelity* was at the root of it."

"I can't imagine how betrayed you must have felt. I won't even pretend to. Just know I'm here if you want to talk about it. I'm on your side."

"I thought you wanted me to forgive my dad."

"I do, because I know it will bring you peace and I want you to be happy."

"Grace. Thank you." He reached up and smoothed my cheek. "You make me happy."

I leaned into his hand. "I'm glad. Now close your eyes because I'm about to make you ridiculously happy."

"Mmm," he groaned. "Are you sure you don't want to join me on this table?"

"Believe me, I do, but first I'm going to earn that five-star review the right way." I ran my hand over his eyes, and they closed. I took a moment to stare at his beautiful face. I loved him. I always had.

I reached for a bottle of essential oils. I probably shouldn't have, but I chose the sandalwood oil. It was a sexy scent. As if I needed more help being turned on. However, it fit my mood, and I knew Brooks would enjoy it. I rubbed a small amount in my hand, then cupped my hands in front of Brooks's beautiful face. "Breathe in slowly and relax."

Between the scent and his warm breath tickling my hands, I almost broke all the rules. I decided to lighten the mood before I did something I would more than enjoy but probably feel bad about later. Maybe.

"You know, the last time you were here, I thought about smothering you with a towel."

His eyes peeked open, and he took my hands and kissed them. "I don't blame you. I've thought about that day a lot. Wondering why I didn't recognize you."

My hands couldn't resist, and they slid down past his shoulders and landed on his chest, where they dug in and stayed. "Any conclusions?"

He nodded. "I think deep down, I knew it was you, but I wasn't ready to recognize you. To face the truth."

"And what truth is that?"

"That I was in love with you, Grace," he said it so easily, like he had said it hundreds of times.

"What?" I faltered back toward the counter. I must have heard him wrong.

Brooks sat up, his legs dangling over the side of the table, and turned toward me.

"You said you only thought of us as friends when we were growing up."

"Grace." He reached out a hand to me.

I took it, and he tugged me toward him. I landed between his legs, gazing into his *earnest* eyes. I thought back to all our conversations and my observations. "Brooks, you told me you weren't sure if you've ever been in love with anyone. And you made love to Morgan. And," I was on roll, "she excited you. I never did."

He pulled me closer and wrapped his legs and arms around me. "Grace, I had sex with Morgan; there is a difference. And no woman has ever excited me like you do, even back in high school. Why do you think I climbed up to your room so many times?"

I shrugged. "Because I was the only person who appreciated your taste in music."

He shook his head slow, steady, and sexy. "I don't think so."

"What do you think?"

"I *know* it was because I couldn't wait until the next day to see you. To hear you laugh or see your eyes light up when you came up with the perfect cheer routine or campaign poster. Even now, I'm distracted at the office because I'm counting down the hours until I get to see you. No woman has ever had that effect on me. No woman has affected me like you. I meant what I said when I told you that you made everything better. I was just too young to understand what that meant."

I wrapped my arms around his neck, bringing us face-to-face. Tears trickled down my cheeks.

Brooks whispered against my lips, "Please forgive me for being so blind and scared."

I brushed his lips. "I forgive you."

"I love you, Grace."

My heart sang, and my soul felt whole. "I love you."

"That's good news." He let down my hair from its messy bun, and it cascaded all around us. "I think we should dispense with the facial and break the rules."

"How very unlike you, counselor. What about the review?"

"I have no doubt we will have a five-star experience."

A shiver of delight went through me. "I do aim to please my clients."

"Grace, I plan to please you for the rest of your life."

Holy crow. "I accept."

Chapter Thirty

"I think I need to get you a T-shirt that says, Brooks's Girl," Brooks spoke directly into my ear so I could hear above the crowd of people surrounding us all trying to get Rick Springfield merchandise. Brooks was in desperate need of a concert T-shirt. At least, I thought so. While he looked fantastic in his charcoal button-up and dress pants, it didn't really fit with the concert vibe.

I looked down at my Jessie's Girl shirt and grinned. "I would be up for a Brooks's Girl tee. Just make sure it has your body on it, and you're shirtless," I teased. "I'll be sure to wear it to the first company party you take me to."

Brooks's brows shot up before he figured out I was joking and his beautiful face relaxed into a smile. "Life will never be boring with you, will it?"

I stretched up onto my tiptoes and kissed his smooth cheek, taking in a whiff of his spicy aftershave. "I hope I never bore you."

He brushed my lips with his own. "That isn't possible."

"Good. And to prove the point, you're changing your clothes. So which shirt do you want? The retro raglan or the snake one?"

Brooks half grimaced. "Is this really necessary?"

"Uh, yeah, you look like you're headed to the country club for drinks. Though I give you huge props for how fantastic your butt looks in those pants."

Brooks shook his head like he had no idea what to do with me, but his smile said he was happy to take a lifetime to figure it out. "You choose."

"Ooh." I tapped my fingers together evilly. "I'm thinking snake shirt with a leather vest. If only they sold jeans here."

Brooks pulled me to him and kissed my head. "I do love you."

I reveled in his words and his touch. I almost pinched myself to remind me this was all real. Before I could, we were next in line, and I was not only getting Brooks the snake tee but a few more to add to my collection. I grabbed my credit card to pay the astronomical yet well-worth-it price, but Brooks beat me to the punch and wouldn't hear otherwise. It was weird to have someone take care of me in such a manner. I certainly didn't expect it of him, but it was sweet. Brooks was sweet. He always had been—I think he'd just forgotten it somewhere along the way.

"Thank you. You didn't have to do that."

He grabbed the receipt. "I wanted to."

I took the bag in one hand and his hand in my other. "Let's get you changed."

He looked around at the noisy venue filled with wall-to-wall people. The only bathrooms had lines out the door, for the men and women. Not to mention they probably weren't the most sanitary of places.

"How do you feel about public indecency, counselor?"

He swallowed hard.

His trepidation was adorable. "Come here." I pulled him toward one of the less populated arena entrances near the nosebleed seats. We darted into the semidark arena and found only a few people waiting for the opening acts to start while staring at their phones. I began unbuttoning Brooks's shirt.

He cleared his throat.

I stepped closer and enjoyed undoing each button. "Don't worry," I whispered. "I'll be gentle."

He leaned down and for my ears only said, "What's the fun in that?"

My brow quirked. "Ooh. I like this side of you." I undid all the buttons, and, be still my heart, his torso was a work of art. All rippled and hard, yet smooth. My mind wandered back to some of the moments we had shared earlier today in treatment room one. Holy crow. It was definitely a five-star service. Bringing myself back to the present, I took advantage of the situation and let my hands glide down all his glory. A trail of goose bumps followed my touch. He had no idea how happy I was to be able to elicit such a response from him.

Unfortunately, we had an audience. Apparently, me feeling up my boyfriend was more interesting than whatever was on their phone screens.

Brooks quickly removed his button-up, and I handed him his new T-shirt. I was sad to see his chest go, but ooh la la, did he look good in the tight tee with the snake on it. So good I wanted to rip it off, but I got ahold of my hormones, barely.

Brooks tucked in his shirt before holding out his arms. "How do I look?"

"Perfect."

That earned me a peck on the lips.

"Thank you, Brooks."

"For what?"

"Giving me this night. Giving me you. The person I fell in love with."

He rested his warm hand on my cheek. "I know I have a ways to go. Thank you for seeing me for who I can become."

"I see you for who you are. Now, let's go live out my fantasy."

"This is your fantasy?"

"One of many that you're in." I flashed him a seductive smile.

He put his arms around me and pulled me close. "I think I'm going to need a list. I don't want to miss anything."

"Oh, you won't."

He groaned. "You're going to be my undoing."

"You don't mind, do you?"

"Not at all."

With every word and touch, I knew what I had always known—we belonged together. It became more apparent when Brooks showed us to our seats. Not only were they in the front row, they were front row center. As in Rick and I would be making eye contact and he might fling some of his sweat on me.

"How did you score these tickets?"

He brought me closer and nuzzled my neck. "I can't give away all my secrets. I like that I can surprise you."

"Baby, you can surprise me like this anytime."

"Challenge accepted."

Holy crow. I was in love.

The lights onstage began to flash, and several band members from the opening act I wasn't familiar with jogged out. Soon the arena was thumping and bumping. I hardly paid attention to the unknown band. I was too busy getting lost in Brooks's eyes and enjoying everything about him, from the way he held my hand as if he were planning on it forever, to the way he tasted like the limes he loved to squeeze into his water.

Admittedly, though, when Rick came onstage with his red guitar, I set my sights on him. I was on my feet and cheering the loudest. I swore Rick and I locked eyes for half a second and he winked at me. But, honestly, it had nothing on the way I felt when Brooks wrapped his arms around me from behind and held me all night while I sang along to every song Rick belted out. I had to give the man props; he was seventy years old and still a rock god in looks and talent.

The best part of the night, though, was when Rick Springfield said, "This one goes out to Grace. You know who you are." My heart pounded wildly, wondering if it was me he was talking about. The synthesizer went wild, and Rick started singing "Affair of the Heart." I knew then that it was.

I turned around, in shock. "How?" I shouted, so Brooks could hear above our song.

Brooks wore a smug smile, so pleased with himself. He wouldn't say how he'd pulled it off. He just wrapped his arms around me and sang in my ear every word of my favorite song. He left no doubt we were having an affair of the heart.

Epilogue

Valentine's Day

"So are blindfolds going to be a new thing for us?" I reached up and touched the one Brooks had placed on me when he'd picked me up for what I thought was our Valentine's Day date.

Brooks chuckled while leading me out in the cold to who knows where. His arm was firmly placed around me so I wouldn't fall and kill myself. Which would have been a tragedy, considering I had just had the best seven months of my life. I guessed at least I would die happy.

"You didn't answer me. Now I'm worried this is the beginning of some slasher movie. Me in an evening gown, traipsing through what feels like grass, while my lover leads me on to my death. On Valentine's Day, no less."

"Was that a plotline in *General Hospital*?"

I had to think about it. "Possibly. You still didn't answer my question."

"I thought you trusted me."

"I do, which is why I'm worried. It isn't like you to dress me all up and blindfold me."

"Perhaps I'm more fun than you think."

"Oh, honey, no one would ever accuse you of being fun," I teased him.

He stopped and nuzzled my ear before whispering, "You seem to always have *fun* when we're together."

The chill of the night had nothing on the goose bumps he could produce. "I do," I stuttered.

"Plan on more tonight." Maybe he wasn't fun, but holy crow was he sexy.

We carried on. Wherever on was.

"Have you heard from your parents? Are they having a good time on their honeymoon cruise?"

"I imagine so. But we have a don't ask, don't tell policy."

I laughed. "I suppose that's for the best." I thought about how cute his parents had been as they got married last weekend in their living room. Tom's health had significantly improved. He looked like a new man with all the weight he had lost. June had been all bronzed in her spray tan glory. And she'd glowed from happiness. Brooks had given away his momma at the wedding and been his daddy's best man. His toast to them had brought me to tears. My favorite line was, "Thank you for teaching me about the power of forgiveness."

I had to admit, I was a little jealous they had beat me to the altar. But I supposed that's what I got for being in love with a divorce lawyer who was skittish about taking the plunge. He'd assured me he would get on the same page as me about it. He'd better start skimming the pages. Though, thankfully, my ovaries were still functioning.

My ears perked up. If I wasn't mistaken, and I knew I wasn't because I would know that voice anywhere, I heard "Affair of the Heart" playing in the evening breeze.

"Where are we?"

"We're almost there."

The music got louder the more we walked. It was nothing like seeing Rick in concert—especially up close from the first row, with my man holding me while Rick serenaded us—but this wasn't bad at all. In fact, this was perfect, even though I had no idea what we were doing. Anytime I was with Brooks, I was in my happy place.

Before I knew it, we stopped. Our song was playing on repeat, and I smelled something divine. Rosemary and grilled steak. I was more and more curious about where we were.

"I'm going to let you go so I can pull out your chair."

"Okay." I stood still, waiting for him to come back before he helped me to my seat.

The seat had a soft cushion, but the back felt more like metal.

Brooks kissed my cheek once I was seated. "Happy Valentine's Day, Grace." He whipped off my blindfold.

Before me was a cute white candlelit table. I looked around to see that we were seated in the city park, under a tree that had been strung with lights. Our plates were filled with steak, rosemary potatoes, and asparagus. There were flutes filled with champagne that sparkled in the flickering light. The candles were doing their best not to go out in the light breeze.

"When did you do all this?"

"Colette and Lorelai helped," he admitted.

"It's perfect." I tugged on his tie and laid a lipstick-ruining, heart-pounding, slip-of-the-tongue kind of kiss on him.

"Mmm," he groaned. "I love when we have dessert first."

"Me too. I say we just skip straight to it."

Brooks kissed my forehead and lingered there. "We'll get to dessert, but first, I have something to show you." His voice wavered as if he were nervous. So unlike him.

I leaned away from him. "You're not thinking of any public shows of indecency, are you, counselor?"

"Not exactly," he swallowed.

"Should I be worried?"

"Just look over there." He pointed out into the dark across the pond. Suddenly, a flash of light lit up the night and illuminated Pecan Orchard's water tower.

"It's the water tower." I was so confused.

Brooks knelt next to me and tilted my chin up. The most beautiful words ever came into my view, surrounded by a giant red heart. *Brooks loves Grace.*

I gasped and threw my arms around him, almost knocking him to the ground. "You broke the law for me?" It was the best gift ever.

He cleared his throat. "Well, I got a permit from the city, and I hired a contractor to do the painting."

I giggled. "That's my man."

"Grace," he spoke low. "I want to be your man forever." He reached into his pocket and pulled out a little blue box. Like Tiffany blue. My favorite blue.

Before he even opened it, the tears poured down my cheeks. I couldn't believe this was happening. After almost twenty-five years, the voice proved to be right.

He carefully opened the lid with shaky hands to reveal a stunning round brilliant diamond with a platinum band. "Grace, will you marry me?"

"Are you sure? I know how you feel about marriage."

"Grace, if there is one thing in my life I'm sure of, it's that you and I are meant to be together. Will you be my wife and the mother of my children?"

I gazed into the face I loved and recognized more than any other in the world. The answer was easy. "Yes. A million times yes."

About the Author

Jennifer Peel didn't grow up wanting to be an author—she was aiming for something more realistic, like being the first female president. When that didn't work out, she started writing just before her 40th birthday. Now, after publishing several award-winning and bestselling novels, she's addicted to typing and chocolate. When she's not glued to her laptop and a bag of Dove dark chocolates, she loves spending time with her family, making daily Target runs, reading, and pretending she can do Zumba.

To learn more about Jennifer and her books, visit her website at www.jenniferpeel.com.

If you enjoyed this book, please rate and review it on
Amazon & Goodreads

You can also connect with Jennifer on social media:
Facebook & Twitter (@jpeel_author)

Other books by Jennifer Peel:
Other Side of the Wall
The Girl in Seat 24B
Professional Boundaries
House Divided
Trouble in Loveland
More Trouble in Loveland
How to Get Over Your Ex in Ninety Days
Paige's Turn
Hit and Run Love
Sweet Regrets
Honeymoon for One in Christmas Falls
Second Chance in Paradise

The Women of Merryton Series:
Jessie Belle – Book One
Taylor Lynne – Book Two
Rachel Laine – Book Three
Cheyenne – Book Four

The Dating by Design Series:
His Personal Relationship Manager – Book One
Statistically Improbable – Book Two
Narcissistic Tendencies – Book Three

The Pianos and Promises Series:
Christopher and Jaime – Book One
Beck and Call – Book Two
Cole and Jillian – Book Three

The More Than a Wife Series:
The Sidelined Wife- Book One
The Secretive Wife- Book Two
The Dear Wife – Book Three

My Not So Wicked Series:
My Not So Wicked Stepbrother
My Not So Wicked Ex-Fiancé
My Not So Wicked Boss

Pine Fall Novels:
Return to Sender
In Name Only… Coming Soon
Silent Partner … Coming Soon

Serenity Spa Series
Facial Recognition
Couples Massage… Coming Soon
Healing Energy … Coming Soon

Made in the USA
Monee, IL
27 July 2021

74322186R20141